In a State of Opposition

Also by David Ackley

<u>Mystery</u>
The Opinion Page
The Obituary Page

<u>Magical Realism</u>
Prospero's Staff
We Write on Water

<u>Historical Fiction</u>
The Patent Clerk's Violin
The Language of Equals

In a State of Opposition

David Ackley

Rain and Breeze Books, LLC

MOSCOW, IDAHO

David Ackley/Rain and Breeze Books, LLC
1484 Sunnyside Ave.
Moscow, ID 83843
www.rainandbreeze.com

Publisher's Note: This is a work of fiction. Any references to historical events, real people, or real places are used fictitiously. Other names, characters, places, and incidents are a product of the author's imagination and any resemblance of these to actual people, living or dead, businesses, companies, events, institutions or locales is purely coincidental. Locales and public names are sometimes used for atmospheric purposes.

Book Layout © 2014 BookDesignTemplates.com
Cover photo composite: istockphoto.com/olegkalina/Allkindza/ Wavebreakmedia
Back cover composite: istockphoto.com/olegkalina/Seamartini

In a State of Opposition/ David Ackley. -- 1st ed.
Library of Congress Control Number: 2025919219
ISBN 978-1-950631-06-3 (Paperback)

ISBN 978-1-950631-07-0 (Ebook)

This book is dedicated to the American Library Association, the Public Library Association, the Idaho Library Association, and Little Free Libraries everywhere.

Never came trouble to my house in the likeness of your grace.

— Much Ado About Nothing

William Shakespeare

A Crowd

THE ROOM was filling with Green Onions. Jason was at the electric keyboard that he kept at the back of his music store. He'd had the tune stuck in his head all morning and started improvising on it at a low volume so that he could hear if anyone dropped in as he was playing. He was lost in the music when he noticed that he was having trouble hearing it over a slowly building clamor of voices. He stopped playing and realized that it wasn't a clamor—it was more like a call and response—the cadence sounded like a charismatic sermon.

Where's that coming from? he wondered as he stepped out of his back workshop and into the slightly larger sales area. His shop had display windows and a glass door on Aspen St., but also had a window facing into the central foyer in the Goodwin building which provided access to two other shops and the stairwell to the upper floors. He was surprised to see that the lobby was uncharacteristically packed with people. The windows on Aspen showed them spilling out onto the street and sidewalk. "What the hell is going on?" he wondered, this time aloud.

Not a fan of crowds, Jason hesitated, but saw that from his shop's street entrance that he could make his way outside and along the side of the building toward the center of action to see what was drawing all of these people in. No one was standing on the inner portion of the sidewalk, so a path was clear nearly all the way to the lobby. He needed to get closer to hear what was being said.

Hugging the building and nearing the foyer, the calls he could make out were faint, but the responses were loud and clear with many 'Amens' and 'Glories to God.' Nearing the crowded corner, he accidentally bumped the shoulder of a young man, causing him to jump and give Jason the oddest look.

"What are you all up to?" Jason asked, having caught the man's attention.

"We're praying for the Lord to grant us the use of this building to further his cause," he replied, as if this was a natural thing to do. He took a further step away from Jason, and turned back to join in the next response.

Jason was just thinking that the police would not be happy with those blocking traffic and access to the shops when someone shouted, "No! No!" right behind him. "You can't be here! You're trespassing!" Jason turned to see old Skip Vitus, the building's owner, trying to make himself heard above the chorus of voices. He skirted past Jason, trying to reach the lobby, but the crowd was too dense for him to make any more progress. "You stop right now, or I'm calling the police!" he yelled in a strained voice just as the entire crowd broke out into song. Seeing the futility of his efforts, Jason shouted to him and with a flick of his head guided him back down the sidewalk and into his shop.

"Why is this crowd here?" asked Jason as he pulled over a stool for Skip to have a seat. The small bird of a man accepted the perch, struggling to catch his breath. Jason hoped that he wasn't about to witness a heart attack. Skip was staring at his phone, but not punching in any numbers.

"Oh, it's all my fault," said Skip.

"What's your fault?" asked Jason.

"This whole mess," he said and visibly sagged what few muscles were left on his thin frame.

"What's all that about them wanting this building?" asked Jason.

Skip looked at him with watery eyes that seemed to be seeping regret.

"I have no choice, Jason. I'm out of options."

"For what?"

"For making it anymore. Did you hear about Edna?"

Jason nodded. Skip's wife had recently been diagnosed with pancreatic cancer and the prognosis was not good. "Yeah, I'm so sorry for her. It must be incredibly tough for you both right now."

Skip stared at the floor. "Yeah," he said. "That's why I've agreed to sell this place, pending zoning approval. We just can't afford to keep it up, and we now have so little time left."

This news came as a complete shock to Jason, and he took a moment to try and absorb it. "Sell it?" he finally asked. "To whom..." and then realized what all of the praying was about. "Not to the church, are you, Skip? Tell me it isn't to the church."

Looking even older and more haggard to Jason's eyes, Skip said, "I have no choice, Jason. You can't believe what they're offering me for this building. No one else could even come close."

Jason's expression was unsympathetic.

"Heck, I'd even sell it to the KKK if they offered me what the church is offering," the old man said in his defense.

Someone else must have called the police and the subsequent flashing lights, confusion, and bullhorn directing traffic interrupted their conversation.

Skip hoisted himself off the stool and threw Jason a look heavy with resignation as he headed outside to add his feeble voice to the commotion.

Then it dawned on Jason. *What the hell am I going to do? I'll have to move my shop?*

Jason spent the rest of the panicked afternoon on the telephone. His calls confirmed that the Goodwin building was being sold to the Holy Grace Church and that the sale was formally on the agenda of the city council during next week's meeting, so that meant he would need to attend the one tonight. He next spoke with two of the other anxious business owners who had also just learned of the sale. One had already received what amounted to an eviction notice. Jason began calling real estate companies in earnest after this news, while still hoping that since he hadn't received a notice yet that he might be exempt.

The Council Meeting

THE STREETLIGHTS popped on just when he needed them. Jason had been walking to the city council meeting and struggling to read the notes for his speech in the dusk. He was relieved that he could make them out again when suddenly something distracted him. Somehow from the clean sidewalk, a piece of gravel had wormed its way inside to the bottom of his shoe and then all he could think about was when it might move to a spot that wasn't so annoying. He considered stopping, but it was cold, and he was only a few blocks from Dunkirk City Hall, so he tried to ignore the occasionally sharp pain he felt with every other step. He wiggled his foot, but it did no good in shifting the rock to a better spot than right at his heel.

He'd chosen to testify about the Goodwin sale at this evening's council meeting rather than next week when it was formally scheduled because nothing major was on tonight's agenda and attendance would be light. The less crowded, the better for him. He had another meeting to attend in a half hour, but non-agenda items were always taken at the beginning of each session. Entering the chamber, he nodded to a few of the council members whom he recognized and then he took a seat near the front of the array of mainly empty audience chairs. Mike Lee, sitting next to the mayor, returned an angry glare from the long council bench.

As the meeting was called to order, Jason unlaced and removed his shoe, letting the surprisingly tiny bit of gravel drop to the carpet before retying.

He was familiar to many on the council because he'd lobbied heavily on an issue three years previously. Skip had wanted to modernize the exterior of the old Goodwin building with a low-cost aluminum façade. Jason, along with many other community members, had objected and advocated for a restoration of the original exterior in keeping with the building's historical designation. In a way, it was unfortunate that they had prevailed—the cost of the problematic restoration had nearly bankrupted Skip—and now his wife was seriously ill. Still, Jason sought to help stave off the landmark's sale.

He knew that his testimony would fall on more deaf ears than it had three years before. Mike, of course, would be unfavorable to anything he said, but the recent contentious election had also seen the surprising addition of two Holy Grace Church members to the city council and what he had to say would not please them. The election had been very close. There had been two ballot recounts after each side had cried that the process had been biased against them—each taking weeks. It was a shock to the community that not one, but two of the church members had gained seats on the council.

After the minutes of the previous meeting were read and approved, the mayor called for any non-agenda items. Jason raised his hand, and Mayor Larson said, "Welcome Mr. Deakins. You have three minutes to speak."

Jason rose and walked to the podium. "Thank you, Mr. Mayor, and members of the council. My name is Jason Deakins, and as most of you know, my business, Woodwinds and Brass, is located in the historic Goodwin building. Unfortunately, for me, and I think for the community at large, Mr. Vitus is in the process of selling the building to the Holy Grace Church—a major topic at your next meeting." Glancing up at the assembly confirmed to him that the two new members were already displeased. "The council cared about the historic importance of the Goodwin Building when it required the restoration of the original frontage. Now I think it needs to care about the proposed interior of the building."

He coughed to clear his throat and hide his sudden nervousness. "The Holy Grace Church has not expressly stated what its intentions are for the building, but have listed a range of possible uses—all of which evidently include kicking me and all of the other existing tenants and businesses out. Among their proposals are," and he unfolded a newspaper article from this evening's paper that he'd brought with him, "a Christian Action Center, which would, and I quote, 'provide a central place for concerned Christians to advocate for Christian values in our local, state, and national governments and schools,' unquote. They also mention opening a Christian Women's Health Center, and the possibility of a chapel. Then, they envision the upper two floors being used to house students in Ed Cutler's Academy of Christian Business which is going to relocate to somewhere downtown and this also comes as a bit of surprise to us all."

Ed Cutler, and thus his Holy Grace Church, owned a large compound on the outskirts of Dunkirk where his academy taught business practices to entrepreneurial Christians with an emphasis on real estate and acquisitions. His wife, Amanda, ran a tandem program for the spouses of the participants to teach them how to be proper Christian wives and mothers. A large housing development of upscale homes had grown around the compound, all of which were owned by Cutler's followers.

Several of the council members were looking like this was news to them when one of the new electees said, "Mr. Mayor, if I may, I can already tell that Mr. Deakins is very uninformed about this purchase and is beginning to cast an extremely negative light on a very valid project."

"Thank you, Mr. Ames," said Mayor Larson. "This is simply a statement to be added to the record. The agenda item will be brought up at our next meeting, where it will be discussed in detail. Please continue, Mr. Deakins."

Jason glanced at his notes and prepared for a bigger blowback as he continued. "I don't have time to go into all of the issues you need to and should address before this sale goes through, which include parking requirements, zoning issues—especially for a medical clinic, and the impact that the sale will have on the businesses that will need to be relocated. The entire proposal will result in a shift from a vibrant economic environment created by the diverse businesses currently in the building, to a single focus that will not be used by or benefit the community as a whole."

There was not the expected retort from Mr. Ames, but he noticed a signal from the timekeeper and said, "Lastly, I'd like to point out that if a chapel should be put in, it would require the closure of the beer and wine store located in the next building, which seems completely unfair. The regulations seem to state that liquor cannot be sold within five hundred feet of a place of worship, but not that a place of worship cannot be established within five hundred feet of a liquor establishment. This means the regulations are heavily biased toward the church. I'm urging you to consider all of the possible effects this sale will have on our community when the zoning issue comes before you at your next meeting.

"Thank you for your time," he said, and was about to return to his seat, when Councilmember Mike Lee asked him a pointed question.

"Mr. Deakins, Jason, I'm left wondering if your objections to this sale are really more about your needing to relocate rather than about the new tenants. And I'm sure that many on the council here are wondering the same thing." The two new electees were both nodding at this.

Three years ago, Councilmember Mike Lee had been happy with Jason's testimony on the Goodwin Building restoration and in his grandstanding manner had insisted on shaking hands with all the presenters after the meeting. Since taking Jason's hand, however, Mr. Lee's attitude toward him had soured considerably.

"Well, Mike," said Jason, frankly. "I'm sure the rest of the community would wonder why the council isn't more alarmed about the expansion of the Holy Grace Church, given that their leader, Ed Cutler's, stated intent is to take over our town and make it a wholly Christian community—and our recent election bears that out." He was then about to ask whether Mr. Lee, as a realtor, was involved in the building's sale when the mayor spoke.

"Thank you, Mr. Deakins, Mr. Lee," said Mayor Larson, "As I said, I'm sure that many of the items you've addressed will be brought up at our next meeting, but we don't have

time for this at the moment. Any other non-agenda items?"
Seeing none, the council began working through its schedule
as Jason put on his coat and slipped out of the chambers.

He suspected that the council, especially as it was now
constituted, would simply allow any changes or purchases to
go through without any objection. As he walked dejectedly
toward Gandalf's coffee shop and his authors' group meeting,
he had a feeling like that that rock still digging into his heel,
when in actuality his mounting concerns for Dunkirk and for
the fate of his shop were needling him even more than it had.

Betta

A FEW people were out on the sidewalks, and Jason thought that he recognized the familiar bulk of Morgan walking a block ahead and heading to the same authors' meeting as he was.

Like being in a bubble filled with ether, Jason found that the council meeting had encapsulated his sense of impotence where public matters were concerned. A few of the council members unfailingly took the heart and soul of the community into consideration, consistently backing measures that maintained the town's homey, artistic spirit. The majority, however, seemed to feel that the purpose of a town was not for it to develop in character, but for it to develop, period. New construction and expansion were their watchwords. And now the Holy Grace Church had seats at the table with their own aggressive agenda toward the town—forks set and knives out, ready to feast.

Jason cared about Dunkirk—it was certainly the town he'd felt the most comfortable in—but at the same time he knew that he would always be on the outside looking in, no matter where he was. This spot in Northern Idaho, and his current place in it, was the best he could hope for. It was not going to get any better, as was made evident again on a recent hike he'd taken with a new friend.

Jason hadn't been on a date in years, but had gotten to know Betta, his local mail carrier, through her frequent deliveries to his instrument and sheet music store. He'd wanted to become better acquainted, and the pair had agreed to go on a hike several days previously on a trail that wound up the Clearwater Mountain foothills which rose above the town. Everything had been going well until they'd hit a steep section in the tall trees, and Jason had looked back to see Betta struggling and reaching up for him to give her a hand over a large root wad. Against his better instincts and knowing what might come next, he'd extended his hand down to help.

"Whoa! What the hell was that?" Betta had asked with a shiver, rubbing her forearm and shaking her fingers after he'd released his grip and she'd regained her footing. "Was it just me, or was that weird?"

Jason hadn't needed to ask what was weird. It was a common reaction.

"Um, yeah, I have contact issues," he'd said. "Or rather, people have contact-with-me issues."

"That was so strange. It was like the pins and needles I get when my hands start to thaw out after skiing," she'd said in a wondering and not so happy manner.

He'd then tried to explain the inexplicable effect he seemed to have on others, and that it had been that way since he was born. His touch was a little like a jangly electric shock to many—in varying degrees, and nearly everyone found it to be unpleasant.

"So, you mean your whole body is the same way?" she'd asked as she'd reached out and warily laid a palm on his chest. "Oh, yeah," shaking her hand as she removed it. "The same. How strange."

Betta had asked him more about his 'effect,' as she'd called it, and they'd enjoyed the rest of the hike together, however she'd become more distant the further on they went. She'd been cordial when she'd delivered the mail the next day, but there had been no positive reply when he'd asked if she'd like to go on another hike again sometime.

He realized that he'd been lucky with Betta. Many, having had similar contact with him, would have shown true disgust and turned back down the trail. Also, luckily, despite his putting people off, the authors' group where he was headed was one place Jason felt that he was at least accepted in Dunkirk.

Jason LOVED to hear Terry speak. The entire town did. Terry Graham was the morning host for the college's classical FM station, KPAN, and his melodic basso voice made anything he read seem profound. It was just a pity that his writing wasn't pitched to the same fine timbre as the music he selected from the classical archives each morning.

The conversations in the small meeting room dropped off after Terry cleared his throat and opened his notebook to the first page. The room was finally quiet when he began. "His twin-engine Mossie fighter dropped out of the clouds into immediate gunfire. Ace pilot Smithers grinned at their feeble attempts to down him. He was sorely tempted to engage the two Messerschmitts, but he had bigger fish to fry. First, he needed to get these two off his six. He banked into a hard turn to the left and then straightened and unexpectedly pulled up on the controls to disappear into the clouds again. He immediately banked right and kept at the same altitude in the thick soup. After a minute he dropped down into the clear skies and spotted his two bewildered adversaries heading away from him two miles away. 'Now to the task at hand,' thought Smithers." Terry's deep voice thundered on like the engines powering Ace pilot Smither's vintage WWII Mosquito fighter, and Jason found he no longer paid attention to the words, letting himself be seduced by that voice alone.

Terry never took any constructive criticism seriously, and so the writers' group rarely bothered to offer helpful comments after his readings; however, he obviously felt that presenting his new drafts to the Panhandle Authors' Group was part and parcel of his being a local author. Never published in the United States, Terry had found an outlet for his writing in contributions to the UK-based *Aviator History* magazine. Apparently, his serial submissions were well received by the subscribers, and Terry had many enthusiastic letters to prove it. There were a few 'well dones' from the group but mainly a shifting in seats by the briefly hypnotized when he finished.

The final presentation of the evening was to be by Carmine DeWitt and was, as always, seen as both a blessing and a curse by the other authors. The curse was the poetry itself. The blessing was the bottle of Glenlivet that Carmine always brought to his readings, holding the belief that a relaxed mind was an open, poetic mind. Jason had found that some of Carmine's poems weren't half bad, but the leanings of the group were toward much more solid stuff.

There was a break after Terry's presentation while those who wanted to filled their small plastic shot glasses with the whiskey Carmine had uncapped. Jason waited until the others were back in their seats and there was plenty of clear space available near the bottle before approaching it.

"Here, let me get that for you, Jason," said Harry who was nearest the bottle. He poured a shot and then set the cup on the table in an open spot for Jason to easily be able to reach it, leaning away as he did so. Jason was humbled by this gesture. Harry had been one of the last in the group to accept Jason since he seemed to also be one of the most sensitive to even being in close proximity to Jason.

"Thanks, Harry," said Jason, genuinely touched, picking up the shot and returning to his seat. Harry had the face of someone who'd just eaten a sour pickle after his brief brush with Jason, but he smiled back gamely at Jason in reply.

Carmine stood and looked around the table. "The absinthe of blood in her heart..." he began dramatically, and then as quickly paused. "You see, I used the word 'absinthe,'" spelling the word out, "in reference to the drug, instead of the word absence, because she is like a non-human who can live without warm blood."

Morgan and Harry immediately tossed back their shots and rose to refill them. Jason was tempted, but merely took a sip of the warm liquor. He noticed that Charlotte, a teetotaler as far as he knew, was staring longingly at the bottle. The 'she' Carmine referenced was present in nearly every poem that the man composed, and there was no question that the pronoun always referred to the same person. She must have hurt him deeply at some point to have left such a weeping wound to his psyche. Many, in separate conversations, noted a similarity between 'her' and Edgar Allen Poe's Lenore, who represented Poe's deceased wife, but Jason thought this link was only due to Carmine's close resemblance to images of Poe with his dark eyes, brooding look, and thick black hair.

Carmine was an English major at Panhandle College, reputedly now in his fifth year of working toward a bachelor's degree. He'd never published any of his poetry, at least that anyone in the group was aware of, and his background was also obscure. However, everyone agreed that he must be well off to bring a bottle of whiskey whenever he presented.

After Carmine finished, there were a few mild claps and strained smiles of encouragement. Harry remained bent over the table and was slightly nodding, leaving Jason unsure as to whether he was asleep or unaware that the recitation had ended.

"So, any comments?" asked Carmine hopefully, looking around the circle. The only visible wince was from Charlotte, but Jason was certain that he was the only one who noticed it. Emily said that she liked the poem, much to the amazement of many in the room.

"I think that the underlying anguish was evident while remaining understated," she said. "I think your poems are really improving," causing a hint of a blush to Carmine's cheeks.

Morgan opted for a final shot, but said nothing.

Jason had his chair pulled back from the large table and resting against the wall, as was his custom to remain in some physical remove from the group. He raised his hand. "I just have one small editorial suggestion."

"Oh, good," said Carmine, grabbing his nearby pencil.

"It seems to me that 'of blood' in the first line is unnecessary."

Many in the group looked around questioningly, but Carmine lifted his finger to the top of the verse, rereading the line.

"You see," explained Jason, "if it's in the heart, is has to be blood, or some fluid, so how about 'The absinthe in her heart?'"

"Oh, yes," Carmine replied immediately. "That's much better! Thank you, Jason."

The meeting ended after they all agreed on the same Thursday in two weeks for the next gathering. Jason spoke up as they stood and pushed in their chairs, raising his voice a little above the clatter. "I just want to remind everyone that it's always good to have paper copies of the author's works available," glancing in Carmine's direction as he said it, "to give the listeners the chance to pencil in comments and not forget the points they want to bring up." This was a common suggestion that few ever bothered with.

"Oh, and legislative alert," said Morgan, just before the first to leave were at the door. "I heard from a friend in Boise that legislation has already passed out of committee that will fine librarians for allowing what they call 'objectionable materials' to be available to minors. I have a very bad feeling about this, and I think it's going to impact us all as authors. Look for an article in the paper tomorrow. It's super important to all of us, and it's moving very quickly. In fact, too quickly – to the point that I wonder if we can even stop it once it's hit the legislature."

Morgan fell into an immediate conversation with Dennis, a politically astute friend, as they left while several of the other members remained behind to help Carmine polish off the Glenlivet. Jason also headed for the exit and an early night.

The Panhandle Authors' Group had been founded by a local bookstore owner in 1970 and still carried on long after the seller had retired and moved to Portland. Initially, the writers provided entire manuscripts for the other members to review; however, that soon proved to be unworkable with the growing number of authors, so now excerpts, outlines, and query letters were expected. There were always volunteers available to beta read entire manuscripts for those who requested it, so the system worked well and allowed everyone access to help in a timely manner. They had also discovered that waiting a month between meetings caused the members to lose impetus, so they now met biweekly.

Jason was one of the least senior among them and had joined the group five years previously when he'd begun writing a biography in earnest. None of them had found the literary success necessary to quit their day jobs, but nearly all of them took their writing seriously, nonetheless. As with many local groups, their membership was aging but still represented a large-but-diminishing cross-section of Dunkirk, Idaho and the surrounding county. Significantly, there was a growing segment of the town that was not represented in the Panhandle Authors' Group - because that segment preferred not to mix with non-church members.

Art

THE MEETING had been held in one of the backrooms of Gandalf's, accessed by a narrow hall off the main café. On his way out, Jason walked along the corridor and into the central seating area of the sprawling coffee shop. Established in the '60's, the ownership had changed many times, but the hippie vibe had been infused into the building's fabric and the current owner, Willow Simonson, was happy to keep it so. A faded mural of Hobbiton endured on the wall behind the counter, and carvings of wizards and orcs adorned the support posts that dotted the middle of the central room.

Jason had carefully woven his way through the tables and sofas to reach the front door when he noticed that Art Parker was turning from the counter with a take-out cup in his hand. Melissa, who had just given Art his order, met Jason's eyes for a nanosecond and immediately turned away, displaying obvious discomfort as she did so. Jason was not her favorite customer. She had once tried to have him banned from Gandalf's after their hands had happened to brush as he'd grabbed for his cup of coffee, but Jason and his ex-wife, Ann, had known the previous owner, and Ann and Theresa had smoothed things out. Basically, Jason was allowed in the café, but discouraged from ordering anything when Melissa was behind the counter. Throughout his life Jason had unconsciously rubbed most people the wrong way, literally, and Melissa's reaction to him had, unfortunately, been of the more extreme variety.

He waited till Art reached him and then pulled the door open for the both of them to exit together.

"Hey, Art, heading home?" asked Jason.

"Yep, how about you, Jason? How are you doing?" asked Art as he stepped out first, immediately zipping his coat to the top with his free hand. It was decidedly spring during the daylight hours, but when the sun set winter still loitered in the darkness.

"Oh, man. As well as can be expected, I guess, given the recent news about the Goodwin building." said Jason, pulling his watch cap down tighter to cover his ears. "I'm still in a bit of shock."

"Yeah, I would be, too. I read online about the impending sale and the commotion in the lobby today. I sure hope that doesn't mean you need to quit your business?"

"I hope not, too, Art, but it definitely means that I need to find somewhere to relocate to—if I can. The commercial rental market is incredibly tight right now. Especially as less and less becomes available because it's all being bought up by the Entity."

"Well, here's hoping you can find a new spot to land. I'm sorry—that was such a prime location."

They walked several more steps before Art added, "What a crime that that space you were in is about to disappear. Yet another building sucked up by the Entity." He chuckled. "What a great nickname. Whoever thought it up really captured the Sci-Fi aura of that sect."

"A very well-heeled sect, too," agreed Jason. "I've heard that they're also starting two more new subdivisions in the near future. Plus, just last year they purchased the old Henderson building to house their real estate business and several other startups. I testified to the city council this evening about the upcoming sale of my building, but I know how it'll go at their next meeting. Developers just need to add buzzwords like 'improvement,' or 'affordable housing' to their project plans and they're in. And now that the Entity has two of their members on the council, it's a done deal."

Art mumbled his displeasure, and the pair headed up the shallow hill that comprised the old part of Dunkirk. Art lived in a large house built in 1906, and Jason in a much smaller one among the many relatively newer homes that surrounded the historic downtown section.

Jason heard Art sigh beside him. "Things sure have changed since Julie and I moved here in 1965," said Art. His wife, Julie, had worked at and been a part owner of Gandalf's since they'd first arrived, but she had died of kidney failure in 1984.

"In fact, the whole county is changing," lamented Art. "Back then, there was a communal feeling among everybody—even the older loggers seemed to be so much more mellow than they are today. Folks were moving into this area, but everyone tried to become one with the surrounding land. It was dark at night, and everyone loved it. Fields of stars that you could easily see, and campfires and kerosene lamps when you needed light. There were teepees, yurts, wall tents, and cabins popping up all through the woods and along the river. Downtown was a happening place with coops, art shows, and spontaneous concerts. Even the occasional protest marches.

"Now the whole me-culture is choking the area. You go out of town, and it's all clear-cut, floodlights, target practice, ranch houses, and gates." Art was huffing a little on the gentle slope, but turned with a yellow-toothed grin to Jason. "OK, I exaggerate, but that's really how it feels now. From share everything—and everyone—to cold, walled-off isolation. No wonder they need a special sect to try and get a pseudo sense of community before they go back home to guard their fortresses."

"Jeez, Art, you're really in a mood tonight."

Art thought for a while and then said, "It's cumulative, Jason. I'm doing fine and then read another bit of news that sends me over the top. The nation, Idaho, Dunkirk, it's one thing after another."

They stood at the corner of Birch and Virginia that divided their routes home. After discussing the situation in the Mideast for five minutes, Art said, "Say, if you can't find a place to relocate your business, give me a call. I have an idea that might work in a pinch."

"Oh? What is it?"

Art smiled and would have tapped the side of his nose if they were in Britain. "Purely a last resort, so no need to bring it up now. Just let me know if you become desperate."

Jason gave him a look that was a huge question mark, but said, "OK, Art, will do. Watch your step going home. Those tree roots have made the sidewalks treacherous."

"Tell me about it," said Art, having stumbled on one the previous year and broken his wrist. "See you later."

Art had taught sociology at Panhandle College before retiring and he was still one who never shied away from hot-button political or social issues. Often urged to run for office, Art always maintained that he was more effective as an activist and fundraiser, and now also declared that he was too old to become an elected official, regardless.

Jason had met Art soon after he and Ann had moved to Dunkirk. Art played clarinet in a local klezmer band and both he and Jason held seats in the Dunkirk Symphony and spots in the Rag Tag Marching Band. Despite the effect Jason had on people, the two had become friends, and Jason was always amazed at Art's tolerance of him.

Eric

JASON CLIMBED the few steps to his front porch and let himself into their house, noticing the glow coming from Eric's room as he switched on the living room light. He stowed his coat and was in the kitchen when he heard Grizzly. As he walked down the short hallway, the meows became louder, and he tapped on the bedroom door. There was no reply, as he expected, so he pushed the door part-way open, and the cat scooted out. Headphones on, Eric was glued to the computer screen, fully engaged in a game. Jason drew closer until he caught Eric's attention and gave a smile and a little wave. Eric gave an expressionless nod and was immediately back in the game.

Jason walked into the kitchen to get himself a beer. In the fridge was a sandwich Eric had already wrapped for the next day, with a bag of cored and sliced apple sitting on top—the same lunch as always. The counter was immaculate, and at the small dining room table sat Eric's open lunch sack, his work briefcase leaned against one of the chair legs, and a place was set with a cereal bowl ready for breakfast the next morning.

Grizzly was at the front door, and Jason opened it to let her out, but after sniffing at the entrance for a moment, the cat decided that she would be happier inside tonight.

Jason settled into a chair and switched on the late news with the volume on low when his thoughts turned to his son. The struggles they'd had from preschool and into Eric's teens had often revolved around the TV. His parents had been trying to make Eric fit in with school, society, and friends, and all Eric had desired during those stressful times was to watch the same movies over, and over. The VCR had gone from a reward to a necessity for the child.

Eric had been diagnosed early on with Asperger's Syndrome, a label that Jason occasionally still used out of habit, but which has been dropped as the symptoms have now been wrapped up into the broader Autism Spectrum Disorder definition. Eric was verbal, but he had required communication coaching to be aware of voice inflections and to help him read non-verbal signals in others. He'd also needed behavioral counseling to help him deal with repetitive behaviors and some anger issues. The school system had luckily provided the speech therapist, but it had taken several trials before they found a behavioral therapist to treat him in the other areas. In the end, Eric had made it through high school and college, and was now gainfully employed.

Jason had grown to appreciate some of the benefits of Eric's autism—his insistence on order and routine, and his meticulous approach to work and art. His sensitivity to physical human contact was a benefit to Jason alone, given the effect his own touch seemed to have on people. Jason was left wondering, however, how the whole no-contact thing would work for Eric, given his son's new interest in a particular woman who seemed to also be interested in Eric. Judging by a brief hand-holding between the pair that Jason had witnessed on a downtown street, it could be that a new chapter might be opening for his son. Eric had so far rejected any attempts by Jason to engage in the subject, and any advice was therefore off limits.

Drawn back into the latest local news detailing the sale of the Goodwin Building and including clips of a beaming Ed Cutler, Entity leader, Jason found that once again his anxiety about the direction the town was headed overshadowed his other concerns, like those he had for his son in his new relationship.

Dunkirk, Idaho

AFTER TOSSING and turning all night, worrying about the fate of his shop, Jason rose early and took a walk several blocks down to the St. Joe River and then followed the footpath that ran along it. A thin mist was being blown above the river's surface by a light morning breeze and fish were rising for early spring bugs. Stopping for a moment to take in the quiet scene, he finally felt his buzzing mind slow to the river's pace. He took a deep breath and looked up and down this stretch of the St. Joe. Once a runner, he had loved his morning jogs along these banks or up the trails that threaded above the town. The years leading to his divorce hadn't been the easiest of times, but the river had always helped him center.

He could make out some of the buildings of Panhandle College poking above the trees that lined the river on the opposite bank. He'd taught briefly in the angular Phillip Glass Music Building when they'd first moved here, but the view of it was now crowded by newer, boxier, structures. As the third largest campus in Idaho, new buildings continued to be added nearly every year. A hippie mecca in the sixties, the otherwise unremarkable small college had become a magnet for artists, especially those among the language and graphic arts. Ginsberg, Snyder, O'Keefe, Jahn, and others had either lectured or given shows in Dunkirk, and many of its graduates had gone on to gain national or international recognition.

The town was bisected by this lazy segment of the St. Joe River which eventually fed Lake Coeur d'Alene further to the north. On the east side, where he now walked, lay rising hills, the old town, and the Redstar Mill. In addition to Panhandle College, newer housing developments, the St. Joe Mall, and major retail stores lay on the flatter lands to the west.

As he continued downriver and rounded a bend, the Redstar lumber mill suddenly loomed to his right. From a distance, it looked no different from when he'd first seen it when he and Anne had moved to Dunkirk in 1996—a tall, gray, weathered, abandoned hulk. But, despite the exterior, the building now positively hummed with activity. A group of local artists had transformed the old mill into the vital economic enterprise that it had become. The addition of pottery kilns and a glass-blowing furnace through a cooperative venture with Panhandle College anchored the Redstar Mill as the center of Dunkirk's present-day economy. He watched as some shop owners arrived in the parking lot to get ready for their day.

Looking at his watch he realized that he needed to get back to open up his own shop, too. Leaving the river and making his way up into town, he could feel that he was also leaving behind the peaceful frame of mind he'd briefly enjoyed.

Great, he thought. *Now I need to try and run my business at the same time as looking for a new place to move to.*

Precisely the moment he entered his shop, he was followed in by a man who looked like he'd barely graduated from high school.

"Good morning, Mr. Deakins," the young man said in a cheery voice. "I'm sure you've heard that the Holy Grace Church has purchased your building, and I've been asked to hand you this eviction notice."

He was clearly attempting to seem official, because he handed Jason the envelope and cradled that receiving hand at the same time.

The reaction was immediate. The man dropped both hands away from their grasp and stood as if Jason had slapped him. After blinking for a moment, he finally caught his breath and spat out, "Fine! No need to be so rude about it!"

Jason knew that protesting would do no good and watched as the young man stormed out of the shop, slamming the door behind him.

The contents of the letter were like a slap to Jason, too. He needed to vacate his shop by the next weekend—a short timeframe he was sure wasn't even legal. He strode into the back workshop, angrily mirroring the young man's slamming of the door.

Dunkirk Realty

JASON STOPPED into Dunkirk Realty later that morning—having to close his shop to do so. He had put feelers out among friends, but it was imperative to see what the local professionals had to offer. He recognized City Council member Mike Lee who was making a point of busily ignoring him from the rear windowed office, but none of the three women and one man in the front desks were familiar to him.

The main receptionist began to reach out her hand while introducing herself, but in a practiced move, Jason dug about in his pockets for some unknown object during their greeting.

"Hi, I'm Dana, how can I help you?" she asked, letting her hand float back down.

"Hi, Dana, I'm Jason Deakins. I own Woodwinds and Brass, practically just around the corner. The thing is, I'm losing the lease on my space, and I wanted to see what options you have available for relocation. The Holy Grace Church has purchased my building, and they've said that they are terminating all existing rental agreements—almost immediately."

"Yes, Mr. Deakins, we can surely help you with that. Let me check with one of our realtors..."

"Thanks, Dana. I'm Doug Wilcox and overheard your discussion just now," said a tall man in a blue-striped suit who'd come up beside him. He swept his arm toward a walnut desk. "Why don't you join me, and we can talk about your needs and see if we can help you." Doug also tried to proffer a hand, but Jason kept his cell phone in his right hand and glanced at it to deflect the attempt.

More as a second introduction, Jason repeated his situation to Doug as they sat at his desk.

"And how many square feet are you in now?" he asked.

Jason thought about it, but was at a loss for an estimate. "Maybe 800 square feet?" he guessed.

"Oh, that spot on Aspen. Yes, that's about right. With your storeroom and entry area, I'd put the shop space at more like 600," said Doug. "Let me see what we have available."

Doug turned to his computer screen and scrolled through the commercial properties they had listed.

With an apologetic wince, he turned to him and said, "I'm sorry, Jason. All we seem to have available at the moment are either those at the very small end of the range—there are several loft spaces in the Redstar Mill that are 300 square feet each—or, at the other end of the spectrum, there are a few spaces in the St. Joe Mall that are 2,000 square feet and more. Bed Bath and Beyond just moved out, but it was huge. Nothing else is available downtown. When will you need something by?"

"Well, within a week, it looks like," said Jason.

Doug shook his head. "I'm sorry, nothing now, but as we head into summer things might open up. If you can wait until then, I might be able to find you something. Do you think one of those Redstar Mill spots could work in a pinch? They're going at a very reasonable price right now."

It was Jason's turn to shake his head. "Nope, it's not really the storefront space I need, it's the storage and work area. But 2,000 square feet, especially in the St. Joe Mall, would be way too much and out of my price range." He grimaced. "This is pretty urgent for me. Are you sure there's nothing else available? Maybe through contacts with another agency or something?"

"Let me take down your information and I'll contact you the moment something in your size requirements becomes available. I'm sure it won't be too long." Jason complied and rattled off his email address and phone number as he wrote them down. "And here is my card for you to contact me," Doug offered.

Jason reached out without thinking. He pinched the card, brushing the man's finger with his own just before Doug released it, and that was enough. Doug gave an inward shudder, and then his mouth became set, and his brow dropped.

"Deakins," said Doug. "Didn't I read something about you in the paper?"

"Nope, people always mistake me for someone else," said Jason.

Doug didn't seem convinced. "Anyway, I hope you have a good day, Mr. Deakins," said Doug dismissively.

"Thank you, and let me know if anything comes up," said Jason, ignoring his change in tone.

Doug's face had become a mask as he turned back to his screen, avoiding any formal commitment.

Jason was well beyond outwardly displaying a reaction, but inside he was uncharacteristically peeved as he shoved the door open. Glancing back in, he saw Mike Lee leave his office and walk over to speak with Doug, both turning in Jason's direction when he reached him. Jason controlled his impulse to flip them off and turned back to the street.

Now a common sight, a large pickup waving six different right-wing flags drove by, followed immediately by another with two kneeled figures in the truck bed wearing the requisite camo gear and displaying their combat-style rifles.

Miriam

Jᴀꜱᴏɴ ᴡᴀʟᴋᴇᴅ back toward his shop located three blocks away. He stopped at a light and noticed the Henderson building kitty-corner from where he stood. The far end was being reconstructed from where a popular student hangout had been, but a new business was already in the former location of Platters at the nearest end. The New Archangel Bookstore had recently opened and predictably sold Christian books, just as Platters had predictably sold LPs. The record store had needed to close several years before because the owner, Riley Kirk, had been in a horrible car accident which had crippled his left leg. Jason found himself half-glad that Riley hadn't needed to suffer the indignity of being evicted by the Entity on top of all of his other woes.

He'd barely made another block when the same pickup truck with waving flags made another pass down Main Street in the opposite direction, militia truck following close behind.

So much more division than there used to be, thought Jason. It seemed to him that the town was already splitting down the middle with people taking sides about the growth of the Entity, and now political views were being displayed on everyone's pickup truck beds and shirt sleeves.

The encounter with Doug had affected him more than it normally would have, and he knew that the recent episode with Betta was the real cause. He had rarely tried to date since his divorce, and mentally kicked himself for even attempting to, knowing how it would end. He was used to being single and only felt lonely in the aftermath of a failed attempt at a relationship, as had just happened. But at the same time, he knew that not every interpersonal relationship was doomed.

His thoughts flew back to a rainy day during his first year at the University of Washington.

The bus had pulled up, and Jason was one of several who made the dash through the downpour from the storefront overhang to the door as it hissed open. He made his way to an empty slot on the left and as he slid in next to the window, one of the other soaked boarders flopped in next to him. The man smiled at him as he pulled back the hood on his rain jacket and settled in. The bus shuttled into traffic and began its way up the hill to the Central District in Seattle. Jason's tenor sax case was tucked upright between his legs, and he rested his hands on it while watching the rain stream down the windows on the outside, blurring the slowly passing buildings.

He was beat. He'd been up late the night before, worked his temp job repadding saxophone keys at a local Seattle music store that morning, and then during happy hour attended a semi-live practice session with a quartet he'd joined at the New Orleans Creole Restaurant on Pioneer Square. He was looking forward to a quiet evening in his tiny apartment on Capitol Hill.

The bus jostled its passengers as it headed up James St., knocking his seatmate against him several times. Something made Jason twist slightly to see the young businessman flinch at the contact and jerk himself more toward the aisle. Turning the corner on 9th caused more shoulder contact which seemed to further agitate the fellow who picked up a bag he had set on the floor and began casting about the bus for a different seat. When the bus pulled to a stop at the next light, the man jumped up and headed for a free spot several rows up on the right. On the way there, he gave a glance that Jason could only describe as bewildered back at Jason as he took his new seat.

Jason was in the midst of giving a subtle shrug of his shoulders when he felt a hand gently alight on one of them. Instead of the usual feeling of a vaguely unpleasant tingling at the touch, there was a sort of warm radiance, even through his raincoat. As she removed her hand, he turned around briefly to see an older black woman with a clear plastic bonnet secured over her hair staring at him with a knowing smile. He was unsure how to react, still wondering at the unexpected contact, and so nodded at her and turned back for the remainder of the ride up to Cherry St. for his transfer spot on the number 8 bus line. He chalked up the warm sensation he'd felt to his weariness from the long day.

When they reached Martin Luther King Jr. Way, Jason followed several others getting down at this stop and pulled up his hood as the rain greeted them on the street. He was standing at the corner to cross MLK when the woman who'd been sitting behind him came up and stood at his side. He glanced down at her to find her gazing up at him and searching his face with a look of subtle wonder on her own. He was finding that he, himself, was overcome by a strange feeling of intense familiarity.

"Say, are you busy?" she asked suddenly.

Jason took a moment, not wanting to get sucked into what was probably going to be an evangelical spiel. But something made him reply, "Well, I'm catching the Number 8 for home, but I got a minute. Why?"

"I saw the way that man reacted to you on the bus, and I'm not a stranger to that kind of treatment in the slightest. Catty's Corner is right over there," she said, pointing across Cherry with a wet finger. "Want to join me for a quick cup of coffee?" Seeing Jason's hesitance, she added, "I'm not going to bite, and I'm not selling anything. My treat."

"OK, just for a bit," Jason found himself saying and followed her across Cherry at the light change and into Catty's Corner, a place new to him.

"Hey, Miriam," said a man as he was finishing bussing a nearby table.

"Hey, Charlie," greeted Miriam. "You have a free table for two? Just going to be coffee today."

"Sure, there's plenty of room," said Charlie. "How've you been?"

"I'd be better if it wasn't for the damn rain," she grinned.

"You're telling me," said Charlie as he grabbed two menus out of habit and led them to a small table by a window. "Who's your friend here?" he asked, giving Jason a questioning appraisal.

"I don't exactly know just yet. We just met on the bus."

"You play horn?" asked Charlie as they took their seats, Jason placing the sax case behind him.

Jason smiled. "Tenor sax. Just finished a little gig down at the New Orleans Creole Restaurant."

"Jazz?"

Jason nodded back.

"All right," Charlie smiled, too, "you're all right then," and went to get the coffees.

Jason turned to Miriam as he left. She was diminutive, thin, with some heavier lines dominating the many creases in her face. Jason guessed that she must be in her mid-sixties at the least. She had taken a pink hankie out of her purse, dried her glasses, and just put them back on.

"Now," she said seriously. "I keep my eyes open, and you're almost the only one I've met that's like me."

Jason mentally saw himself standing next to her. A tall, slightly pudgy at this stage, 20-year-old male, next to a tiny, older black woman. Then he suddenly realized. "You play music? You play jazz?"

She looked at him and shook her head slowly with a hint of amusement on her face.

"No," was all she said for the moment as Charlie brought their coffees and made sure that they had the cream or sugar they might need.

"I watched you board the bus, and then that gentleman sat down next to you. After a while he started getting edgy, and then when he bumped into you, he jerked away and got really agitated—so much so that he switched seats as soon as he could." She stirred her coffee, set the spoon down on a saucer and then took a sip. "Does that happen to you often?"

Jason was perplexed. Of course, that kind of thing happened all the time. It was normal.

"Yeah, so?"

"What do you mean, 'yeah, so?' Doesn't that bother you?"

"Well, I suppose it would if I let it. That's just how people are around me. I don't take it personally anymore."

"It's not normal, and believe me, I know."

Jason was suddenly uncomfortable. "Look, I don't mean to compare myself to what you must have been through in your life. I have no idea what it must have been like for you, especially earlier in the fifties and sixties. I mean, if you're that old…" realizing he might now have really stepped in it.

She suddenly smiled. "No, no, honey. This is what I mean," and she laid her hand on Jason's which was resting on the table next to the napkin holder.

It was a touch he would never forget. It was warm, calming, and the effect seemed to move up through his arm and into his entire body. He found himself smiling back at her with no urge to turn away. It was as if she had become his own beloved grandmother in a single second.

They were both silent for a minute. "So, are you one of those faith healers I've read about?" Jason eventually tried.

Miriam shook her head. "Believe me, I need this as much as you do." At his questioning look, she continued. "Sure, I've had it rough, just like most of my people. I grew up in Watts during the riots, saw my Daddy get beat up badly; saw my Momma get spit on; and I've been in jail twice just for speaking my mind. I've been given jobs with shitty pay for the same work others had and received none of the promotions they got when I did the job better. But like you say, that's just the way it is for all of us like me. My boy has it better, but not by as much as I'd like."

She took a moment for a sip of coffee with her free hand and then continued. "But on top of that, I get treated exactly like you, even by my own folks, my friends, my family. Have you noticed that people are nice until they get too close, or touch you? Then they suddenly act like you have BO, or like you pinched them on the butt without asking?"

Jason was shocked at this. That was exactly how he described himself to himself.

Miriam nodded at the expression on his face. "I could tell. To tell you the truth, I've only met one other person in my life like you and me. Too bad, she's dead now, but there was something we had that no one else ever had. And now that's the same between you and me."

Jason felt no desire to get up and flee an entanglement with a stranger who was possibly feeding him a line of absolute bullshit with some kind of hidden agenda. He knew that he'd met someone he'd cherish for the rest of his life. He felt a tear well up, and quickly used his free hand to wipe it away before she noticed.

"What is it?" he asked, now with real curiosity. "What is it with us?"

The pair was still sitting with Miriam's hand laid across Jason's. Charlie gave her a look as he poured more coffee for them, but Miriam simply smiled back at him.

"I have no idea," Miriam turned to Jason as he left. "I've thought a lot about it. At first, my Daddy made me think I had a curse of some kind or that God was punishing me—that I had the mark of the devil on me or something. It took me a long time to get over that, but then I realized that I hadn't done anything wrong, and that it was everybody else's problem and not mine. When I met Mary—she was the lady who fingerprinted me at the police station after a Black Power rally in LA by the way—when I met her, we became immediate best friends. You should have seen her when she grabbed my hand to take my prints. Whoo, boy. She told me people treated her the same way even though she was whiter than snow, and her daddy was rich. So, then I knew it wasn't my fault. She had the idea that we were wired differently. Sort of like ACs in a world of DCs. That's what she thought."

Jason was suddenly sad that he'd never had an experience like theirs. "We weren't church goers in my family, so I was never sure what was going on with me, but I knew that it had to be purely physical. Not fitting in anywhere kind of made it obvious after a while."

"I'm sorry it's been so hard for you," said Miriam, sympathetically. "And I believe, like you, that it's just a physical thing. Our bodies are somehow different. Not our minds or our souls. It's sad, too, that because of the reaction we cause, people have an awfully hard time letting us in."

She shook her head and chuckled at a memory. "Mary would break out laughing whenever she thought about her job. Why they put her on fingerprinting she had no idea. She said you should have seen the expressions on some of the riff-raff she had to touch. They were always glad to get their prints taken and get the hell on to the cells."

Recalling this first meeting with Miriam had lightened his mood considerably. He hadn't met anyone remotely like her since, and she'd died years ago. He'd become used to being like a drop of oil floating on a sea of water, but thoughts of her always made him less lonely. He was writing a draft of her interesting life in a biography, and so she was never too far away from him lately.

In a now habitual maneuver, he remained way back from the small crowd waiting to cross the street. When the light changed, he stayed on the through-traffic side of the cross-walk, walking well to the outside of his fellow pedestrians to reach the other side.

A Theory

He set his key in the lock and opened his business in the old Goodwin building for one of the last times. That memory of Miriam had stirred up another that made Jason chuckle to himself as he turned on the lights and flipped open his laptop. It was about how, by the second grade, he'd thought that he'd had everything figured out.

His mother had given him a Dr. Magnet educational set for his sixth birthday, and it was while playing with the magnets in the set that Jason had first begun to make sense of his place in the crazy world of elementary school. During group activities, there were always kids who seemed to attract others to them, and others who always seemed to be on the outs—the last picked, the ones no one wanted to join as a partner. Jason had sometimes felt that he was probably the most extreme example of this latter group. The merest contact with him seemed to repel others to the point that he had become the class pariah—a word that would have been useful to him at the time, had he known it.

The Dr. Magnet set had planted a completely erroneous idea in his head that had, nonetheless, saved him from at least a few grade school years of personal anguish and self-doubt. The concept of 'like repels like' was a brilliant flash of insight that suddenly explained his classroom dynamics. He was excluded from the groups that formed precisely because he was so much like the kids that didn't want to play with him. They were the same. It was the few popular ones who attracted everyone to them who were the oddballs with the opposite polarity. This illusory revelation had caused him to completely change his attitude toward his fellow classmates. He learned to relax and let the invisible force of relationships bounce off him—pulling and pushing, but in his case, mostly pushing him away from people he mistakenly saw as exactly like himself.

There came a time later when a nagging doubt descended over him. Why did it seem that he repelled everyone - even those attractors who should be sticking to him like the strongest magnet in his set? But aside from his brief delving into the mysteries of Dr. Magnet, his pre-adolescence was largely saved from too much introspection, as was happily the case with most kids.

Well, he thought rather wistfully, bringing up the sales app on his computer, *too bad that theory got all shot to hell.*

Spring

HE WAS in the back room of Woodwinds and Brass, worriedly beginning to pack instruments into their cases and organize his tools for the move he hoped would materialize when he heard a woman's voice try an inquisitive, "Hello?" and then a little louder, "Hello?"

"Just a sec," he shouted toward the entrance and settled a trombone into the dark blue velvet-lined case that perfectly matched its shape. He reflexively dusted off his upper pants legs and then walked to the door leading into the storefront. When he opened it, he recognized the woman standing at the small counter since she'd inquired a few weeks before about her son's French horn, but he couldn't immediately place her name.

"Oh, hello, Ms...." he tried but then jumped ahead. "You came in before about your son's French horn?"

"Kris," she said with a smile. "Kris Seever."

"Oh, right," replied Jason, unexpectedly taken by that smile. "Sorry, I forgot."

She waved it off and said, "Are you closing your business? I see from the sign that it says 'relocating,' but to where?"

"'To where?' is a good question. Nope, I'm not closing—at least, I hope not. The En..." he quickly rephrased, "the Holy Grace Church is buying this building and they're asking all of the current tenants to vacate. If I do need to close, it should only be on a temporary basis, and I'll still be doing repairs regardless—even in my own home, if I have to."

"Well, I certainly hope that it doesn't come to that, because I have something for you," said Kris. She held up a thick, squat instrument case, circular on one end to make room for the large bell inside. "I considered your estimate and decided that it was worth it to fix Kevin's horn. He's promised me he'll never drop it again," with a repeat of the smile. She was a little shorter than he was, cropped black hair peppered with some gray, slim and athletic looking, with what he took to be an air of a pixie about her—lighthearted, but somehow wary—ready to flit away in a flash.

"Great, Kris," said Jason as his phone suddenly played a John Phillips Sousa march, which meant that it was the high school concert band instructor calling. "I'd be happy to repair it for you," realizing at the same time that he wished he could get her to smile again. He stared down at his phone.

He was about to say, "I'm sorry, but I'd probably better take this," but instead let the call go to voice mail. "Mr. Perkins," he said, pointing to the display instead. "I'll get back to him in a bit."

Just then the door opened, and Betta entered with two large boxes and some mail. "Hi, Jason—just set these on the counter?"

"Hi, Betta. Yeah, that'd be great. Thanks."

Kris stepped back to give Betta plenty of room.

Betta set the packages down and gave him a convivial smile. "You're welcome, see you," as she headed out of the shop.

Jason watched her leave, glad to see that at least they were still friends. Then he turned back to Kris. "Sorry for the interruptions."

"That's all right. So, the price is still the same?" Kris asked.

"Yeah, but remember that's the maximum. If the dents come out easily and the finish isn't badly affected, it should cost somewhat or a lot less."

"OK, that sounds fair. If he does it again, it's coming out of his allowance." This was said dryly. And then more lightly, "If I still gave him one that is. The boy's a senior this year, after all. Do I need to make a deposit?"

"Nope, that's all right. These instruments are like kids themselves. We all know their parents."

As Kris set the case up on the counter next to the packages, he asked, "Do you need a loaner while this is under repair?"

She shook her head. "I don't think so. Kevin said something about Mr. Perkins having one he could use in the meantime."

"Okay, then I'll fit this into my schedule, which might be behind just a tad because of the upcoming move—if I can find a new place."

She said, "All right, no hurry," and gave a little wave. Jason had expected more of a conversation and thought desperately for something to say as the door swung closed behind her. But nothing sprang to mind. Then he came to his senses. *What on earth is wrong with you?* he wondered. *Because it's spring?* He'd been not just resigned, but happy in a bachelor's life and now two women that he'd met seemed attractive to him? He knew that this was odd because it flew in the face of reality. Nothing could come out of a relationship with either of them.

He reluctantly returned the daily call from the neurotic high school band teacher of the best of Dunkirk's musical teens.

Ames

LATER THAT afternoon, Jason was boxing up his sheet music selection near the lobby window when he noticed three or four men with tape measures and clipboards evaluating the space. One of them glanced in the window to his store and seemed to recognize him. He looked familiar to Jason, but he couldn't immediately place the face. By the time the man exited the lobby, walked along the sidewalk and then opened the door to Woodwinds and Brass, Jason finally remembered who he was—Martin Ames, the new council member from the Holy Grace Church.

"Hello, it's Mr. Deakins, isn't it?" Ames asked as he approached Jason with his hand out. Jason had the uncharacteristic urge to go ahead and offer his own hand to see the reaction, but was suddenly saved from that by a sudden urge to sneeze. He blew into his hands and then wiped them on his pants legs; Ames having dropped his own hand at the sight.

"Yeah, and you're Mr. Ames from the council. Right?"

"Yes. I saw you in here and just wanted to say I'm sorry you have to move and hope you find a new location for your store."

"I don't know that it's one-hundred percent sure yet, but I need to assume that it will be."

"Oh, it will be, unfortunately, I know, for you. The meeting's tonight and it will pass."

"I don't know that you can be so certain."

"You're right, of course. Let's just say that it's very, very likely."

"Well, that's why I'm busy packing up," said Jason, a little snippily. "I've already received an eviction notice."

"Listen," said Ames. "I know from your testimony that you're against the church buying this building, but I assure you, it's not to shove good businesses like yours out. It's that we need room for all of the projects we have going on."

Jason was blunt. "It's part of your takeover of the town. Ed Cutler has said that's his goal numerous times, and it's happening."

Ames was shaking his head. "There are two ways of looking at that. Ed is always saying that we should push people out if they won't join us, like in a battle. Then there's room grow. I see it that we're expanding and need the space to do so. Where else are we going to go with the limited land available for development around here? There are so many of our businesses that want to start or need to expand—even our Academy of Christian Business has outgrown its confines. We just have to find spaces for everything, and so we need the buildings to do so. It's nothing personal. I hope you understand."

Jason thought for a moment. "I understand that there are several ways to rationalize what the church is doing, but the outcome's the same. An unfriendly takeover."

"But we are friendly. The town's just not taking the time to get to know us."

"But your church members never take the time to join in any of the local functions, and when they do…" began Jason, then, pointedly, "Look. I don't think we want to get into this back and forth right now. I need to keep packing."

Ames nodded. "All right, but if you want, we could continue this conversation over a cup of coffee sometime."

"Thanks, Mr. Ames, I'll think about it." knowing that he never would. As Ames left, Jason found himself wondering if Ames really would ever want to have coffee with someone who disagreed with him. Hard to say, since he didn't really know the man. He just knew from past experience that similar offers were never followed up.

Jason read the newspaper the next evening with great interest. The first thing he did was jump to the classifieds to see if any new commercial properties were available to rent. The list looked exactly as it had in the previous edition, and he'd already called and crossed off every one of those as a possibility. It was starting to look like he really might need to move his entire shop into this living room if nothing opened up soon.

Flipping back to the front page he saw that Ames was right. The city council had indeed allowed finalization of the Goodwin building sale. The testimony against the sale had been by two of the present occupants and by members of the community who were concerned about the continuing expansion of the Entity. The chamber had been packed with church members and vocal opposition had erupted after each of these testimonies.

In other orders of business, the new council members had moved that any Pride Day celebrations be disallowed because of the influence such a display of immorality might have on the community. After much testimony and debate this was narrowly defeated. But, perhaps because of the close vote, a second motion to ban gay pride flags from public facilities—echoing a law recently passed by the state legislature—was passed by the council, something not thought possible before the recent election, since many other cities were simply ignoring the new state law. They had also taken the step to ban LGBTQ+ flags and posters in or near city buildings in a move that surprised him.

Jason was depressed by all he'd read and by his fruitless search for a new shop location since he needed to vacate his present spot by the coming weekend. Then he remembered Art's offer to get in touch if he should ever become desperate. He was now, very much so, so he gave his friend a call.

"Hi, Art," said Jason after his friend answered the phone. "Is this a good time to call?"

"Sure, Jason. You've just stopped me from doom scrolling through all the disasters happening in our government today. What's up?"

"Well, I don't know if you remember that you said I should call if I was desperate about finding a new place for my shop. I've looked everywhere but there doesn't seem to be a single thing available. I can always just work out of my house, but Eric and I seem to barely have enough room as it is. So... Do you have any suggestions?"

"Yes. As a matter of fact, I do. You can have my basement if you can stand it. We'd need to haul a few things out, but I got rid of most of my junk years ago. It's yours if you want it."

"Really, Art? That's amazing! Thank you—I'm sure it can't be that bad."

"Maybe not so bad as far as basements go. It has a door to the outside, and I have a separate key for the lock. When do you want to come by and check it out?"

Jason couldn't wait to see if his problem was suddenly solved. "Are you doing anything right now?"

Art had barely replied when Jason was out the door.

PAG Meeting · March 24

T̲he̲ g̲athered̲ writers in Gandalf's meeting room were all listening with rapt attention. As Samuel neared the end of the chapter he was reading, Jason and the others hoped to finally discover who the murderer was.

"Collins raised his eyebrows at me as we followed the Inspector into the victim's back bedroom. I gave him a shrug and had the same question as him. Which was—'Why were we back here at the scene?' The house had been tossed more times than a Caesar salad at Little Tony's. There couldn't possibly be any more info to be gained from yet another visit. Even so, the Inspector had insisted.

"It had been a brutal murder, and we were no closer to solving it than we had been a week ago. 'Sifting the same sand as yesterday won't reveal a new coin,' as Sgt. Emerson had so aptly put it. I had every faith in the Inspector, but this just seemed like a total waste of time to me.

"We had a suspect, but so far, all the evidence was circumstantial, even though nearly everyone on the squad was convinced that the son of the dead man was as guilty as sin. Everyone except the Inspector. He only dealt with hard facts, and the son being a sociopathic, sadistic, son-of-a-bitch wasn't a fact to him.

"Inspector Magus was standing in the middle of the small bedroom staring at the half-raised blinds, lips parted, and they seemed to be slightly moving as if he were talking to himself. Suddenly, he turned to the dresser and scanned the jumbled mess of items that had been there since we first entered the room last week. He moved closer and slowly lifted his hand to the little pile of shoelaces that lay near the dresser's left edge. He picked it up and carefully untangled the strings. There were two of them, and he let them fall as he held one end of each steady in his hands. One string was about two inches shorter than the other. He let them hover there for a minute and a smile slowly tugged at the sides of his mouth.

"'You have it, don't you, sir?' asked Collins.

"'Why yes, constable, I believe I do,' said the Inspector as he rolled up the two laces, placed them in an evidence bag, and strode out of the room. 'Gather up the suspects,' he said as we followed closely behind."

"So, what do you think?" asked Samuel when he'd finished reading.

They were all familiar with most of the story, but not yet with the ending.

"It's really come together," said Maggie, "and I can't wait to hear how he solves it."

Jason was agreeing with many of the others, when Dennis said, "Yeah, but it's not a mystery anymore. Is it?"

Maggie cocked her head back in slight disbelief. "Well, of course it is, Dennis. We don't know who did it. Do you?"

"No, but the Inspector does, and he'll soon tell his colleagues and then reveal the killer to the group of suspects whom he'll probably arrange out in front of him as he reveals all."

"That's what a mystery is, Dennis," said Luke. "We don't know who did it yet, so it's still a mystery."

"I don't agree," said Dennis. "I think it's now a suspense. The author—Samuel in this case—knows who did it, the Inspector knows, the police staff know by now, and the author is just making us wait to find out who the culprit is. The mystery is solved and now it's just a suspense novel." He took a breath. "I hate it when they do that. You're reading or watching a mystery and then everyone knows but you. I think it's kind of a cheat."

Samuel looked a little dazed, as if he was having trouble following the conversation.

"Aren't you just splitting hairs here, Dennis?" asked Jason.

"Maybe, but I think we're all being too generous to the author most of the time. No offense, Samuel." Samuel raised a finger to begin a reply, but Dennis continued. "I have two pet peeves about mystery writers. The first is when they pull up some obscure character out of the woodwork at the last minute and give us reasons that none of us were aware of for them being guilty. I mean, that's just plain fraud. And the other is when the mystery is solved, and the book goes on and on just because the reader is the only one left who isn't in on the secret. That's out and out manipulation, in my opinion."

"OK, Dennis," said Jason. "You're obviously not a mystery fan, but what about when everyone, including the reader, knows who did it except the detective?"

"Then that's honest, isn't it? It's not our story, it's the detective's story, and it's a mystery to him until he solves it. That's being consistent."

"Yeah, but in the mysteries where we're in the dark, the story is about him, but it's written for us, the readers. Just like all stories."

"Well, I don't agree. The story is the protagonist's and we're just spectators. If you string along the spectators, that's just prolonging the telling, not the real story."

The group was visibly exasperated and then as if on cue, just like in a mystery novel, they all turned as one to stare at Samuel.

"What?" he asked with the desperation of a prime suspect. He looked around the circle of accusers with pleading eyes. "I'm going to tell everyone in the next chapter. Honest. Besides, what choice do I have? I can't simply have the Inspector turn around and tell Collins and Benson who he thinks did it, can I?"

Two of the others were nodding their heads and prosecutor Dennis declared, "Yes, in fact, you could."

"But that's too abrupt," maintained Samuel as though from the stand.

"Only because a flawed formula says so," pressed Dennis.

Samuel thought for a moment and rallied himself in defiance of the court. "Well, I'm sticking to the formula."

This novel would be the fourth in Samuel's Inspector Magus mystery series. The formula clearly worked well, because Samuel had sold nearly a thousand of each of his books on Amazon. To many of those in the group, that seemed like a major success, but Samuel said that he was still waiting to 'hit the big time.' He had yet to win a meaningful book award, but submitted to multiple contests in the hopes of eventually earning one.

As this conversation finished, Morgan said, "Hey, during our break, I ran into Lisa Brooks, our county librarian. We were talking about the bill just passed by the State House that will fine librarians for making 'objectionable materials' available in the children's section and, of course, she's very concerned about it. I told her we were meeting, and she asked if she could pop in and say a few words about a rally that the library is planning. Do you all mind if I run out and see if she's still interested?"

He heard several 'yes's' and went out into the coffee shop to find her.

"I don't see what the big deal is," said Charlotte. "The fine's only $250, so the library should be able to handle that."

Dennis shook his head. "It might look like only $250, but the librarian is also on the hook for the court fees and expenses, and you know how those can stack up."

"Well, they shouldn't have objectionable materials available in the first place," said Charlotte.

"OK," replied Dennis, now sounding miffed. "First of all, who gets to define what is 'objectionable,' and secondly, why is it the librarian's responsibility to decide and oversee this? Why don't the parents monitor what their kids check out instead of blocking books for all kids? As I understand this new bill, books can be challenged, and they have to go through a review process if they are. If they're deemed 'objectionable,' they have to be moved into a restricted or adult only area."

Morgan returned with Lisa who had caught the end of Dennis's statement.

"Well, that's mostly correct," she said. "We're not going to be moving any children's books into the adult section. Our policy states that we are not going to stand in as a 'parent' for the children visiting our library. It's up to the parents to supervise their own children or be aware of and follow our policy. We also have a three-step process if a Benewah County resident feels that a book should be removed from our collection for some reason. How we'll respond if this new bill should pass depends on the final wording."

"I personally think that the library should go further and screen the books with parental feedback," said Charlotte. "Parents should be empowered to dictate what is good for their children. The library should listen to their requests if that's what it takes to protect them. No matter what, the kids should come first—anyone's politics aside."

"And we do listen," began Lisa.

Morgan couldn't help but interrupt. "The school libraries, especially, already have a request form and the ability to challenge questionable books. Why do legislation and a punitive system need to be set up, especially in the public sector? This is just book banning in another guise." he paused. "We're authors. We need to stand behind the libraries."

"We're the adults. We need to stand behind our children," countered Charlotte suddenly looking like a stern, although diminutive, matron with hands on hips.

"Well, Charlie," said Morgan, using her pet name as he smiled at her pose, "many of these challenges come from people who live outside the state and who don't even visit the library. These aren't the parents making the objections in the first place. As I said, we need to back the libraries. We're authors for god's sake. How would you like to be next on the hit list?"

"We don't accept challenges from non-county residents," clarified Lisa. Then she smiled. "I can see that this is a hot-button topic, and I'm glad that you all have your concerns about it. Come by and see me any time to talk about our policies and how we will respond to the bill if it passes. But the main reason I stopped in is to let you know that we really view this as a censorship issue, and I think that will concern all of you. We're planning a rally that should correspond to about the time we expect this bill to pass, and I think it will. We'd love your support and hope that you can attend."

"I think we can do more than attend," said Morgan. "Let us know what we can do to help organize the event and get the word out."

A few of those in the room didn't look enthusiastic about this offer, but most agreed. Morgan and Dennis volunteered to act as contacts for the effort. Lisa thanked them and had to rush off to catch her ride home.

"Can't we do anything sooner? Something to try and head the bill off before it passes?" asked Morgan.

"I think that would be chasing a speeding car," said Jason. "As I understand it, the legislation is moving quickly with full support from the Republican majority."

"OK," said Morgan. "We can protest individually. How about if I write up some template language and send it around to everyone to use to call our representatives. We can at least do that much. Do we want to put an ad in the newspaper?"

No immediate agreement could be made, and that suggestion was dropped. The topic sparked many animated discussions and as the group left the coffee shop, the members slowly dwindled away until only Morgan and Charlotte were left going at it out on the sidewalk.

Morgan Grant was good friends with Art Parker, the retired sociologist, and was a local human rights activist. He owned a printing shop in the center of downtown and donated posters and flyers extensively to local causes and the Democratic Party. His heritage was from Samoa and Kenya, and to many he looked like a heavier version of Tiger Woods. He'd earned a degree in Business Administration and was a gifted speaker. Publishing limited copies through a vanity press, Morgan's three books were nonetheless excellently researched, polished, and topical nonfiction explorations of rural conflicts.

Charlotte Adams, as her name might suggest, was extremely traditional—although not as conservative as appeared on the surface - and the author of a *'Palouse Kids'* series about early settlers in the Palouse area of Eastern Washington and northwestern Idaho. The Palouse was a fertile region of rolling hills formed from the windblown sediment of Lake Missoula, a huge, ancient, inland lake that had finally burst out of its confines to seek the ocean and carve out the Columbia River Gorge in the process. Her series was in the vein of Laura Ingalls Wilder's *Little House on the Prairie* books for pre-teens, and was illustrated by Charlotte as well. She was one of the more successful writers in the group.

It was little wonder that the two good friends rarely agreed about anything, but loved to engage in their disagreements, nonetheless.

Looking Inside

Jason was finally able to enjoy a relaxing evening at home. The last week had been hectic with him moving his instruments, tools, and filing cabinets to his new and hopefully temporary location—Art Parker's basement. Two of the other businesses in the Goodwin building had been able to find new commercial spaces and another had no choice but to quit altogether given the cost of the move and loss of prime retail exposure. Jason had felt for Joan Painter, the owner of the ironically named Devine Inspirations given that she was evicted by the church. She had struggled at first to get her chocolatier business off the ground and was finally making a go of it with a growing and devoted clientele. He'd spoken with her when they'd received the news of the buyout, and she'd been devastated knowing that she didn't have the resources to start over in a new location. He'd heard recently that the single remaining business of the five had been allowed to remain in the building—it was rumored that the proprietor was a member of the Holy Grace Church.

"Hi Annie, what's up?" asked Jason as he put his ear to the phone, muting the computer speakers that were turned on for a YouTube recipe he'd been watching.

"I just thought I'd catch up with Eric," said Ann. "By the way, how did the move go?"

"Exhausting. It took longer than I expected, but I'm getting settled in there now. It's a big change from the old shop, though, that's for sure. You're well aware of what's going on here, but it still irks me that such an exclusionary sect is literally buying up the whole town—and no one is doing a thing to stop it."

"I know, I know. Now, it can't be as bad as all that—don't let yourself get too worked up, Jason. You'll be old and gone by the time that can happen. Say, you'll have to send me some pictures of Art's house and basement so I can see what it looks like now."

"OK, I will, once I get some better lighting installed. It's darker than a well down there."

"It'll take some time to get used to the new space. I still can't believe they wouldn't renew your lease. But you'll survive, right? Is Eric around?"

"Yep, he's in his room drawing the last I saw. Just a sec, I'll get him," said Jason as he carried the phone down the hall to rap on his twenty-five-year-old son's bedroom door. Eric had a phone of his own—he'd agreed on having one in case of emergencies—he just chose to never answer it, especially when engaged in his artwork and regardless of who was calling. This had nothing to do with his autism; the young man simply hated cell phones.

Ann had left them ten years earlier. Not for another man. Nor for another woman. But for her own sake and sanity. It had finally become obvious that their family home life was toxic to her wellbeing. Happily, though, the three of them got along fine when not all together in the same room, and so there had been no lingering animosity after her departure. Ann had benefited from the separation through her improved mental health; Eric had his unique way of processing the world which was shaken when Ann had first left, but once explained the logic of it had eventually made sense; and Jason had always been amazed that Ann had been attracted to him—and had stayed for as long as she had—in the first place.

Autism can be difficult for any family, and Eric's version was not particularly severe. However, Ann was a perfectionist and had been employed in a demanding position with Panhandle College. Raising a child born with such a strong, strange will of his own had been more than she could handle.

"Annie? He'll be here in a minute. You know him—he has to finish a section of his drawing first."

"I can call back…" began Ann.

"No, I checked, and it already looks done to me, so it really won't be long. In fact, here he comes now. Say, how's the smoke from these area fires over in Cheney?"

"Much better today. The wind shifted last night and we're not getting hit by the output from that Okanagan fire."

"Oh, good. Here's Eric," as his son came up the hallway, Grizzly comfortably held like a football in his left arm.

"OK, see you Jason," said Ann as Jason handed the phone to his son. Jason found himself wondering why he continued to pay for Eric's phone on his cell plan, but knew that if ever there was an emergency, Eric would have the sense to use it, and so it was worth keeping.

Jason and Ann had moved to Dunkirk from Seattle in 1996 to escape the rain. Jason, a new University of Washington graduate, had accepted a position at Panhandle College as an assistant music professor and had lasted two years in that post. After discovering that contact avoidance was very difficult and that teaching was more challenging than he'd been prepared for, he'd quit and moved on to his second passion—

instruments of all kinds. He'd set up an instrument sales and repair business that was sorely needed by the community. Ann had secured an administrative position with the college by that time, meaning they could shoulder the costs of his new venture.

"Uh huh," said Eric after several minutes of silence. Most of the chatting came from the other end of the phone, but Eric did sketchily fill his mother in on the most recent project he had at work and summed up his artwork in two brief sentences. It was a normal conversation between the two.

"Mom says bye," said Eric as he handed Jason back his phone and headed to his room, Grizzly still tucked in his arm. The two were nearly inseparable.

Jason smiled. "Thanks," he said as the door closed behind his son. This was also a normal conversation between the two when Eric was engrossed in a project.

Eric had loved to draw from an early age and had filled pages with faithful reproductions of comic book characters, their pet dog at the time, and eventually people he knew from movies or school. His interest in art had taken a back seat to tracking what was 'in' with his friends—skateboards, cars, and girls, but was always there when he needed it for destressing.

Kindergarten through high school had been difficult for Eric, as had college for that matter, but he had stuck with it and had graduated—thanks to help from the support network the public school system provided and college councilors. Academics had mainly been a breeze for his son, but only if the subject matter was of interest to him. It was the continual encouragement needed to make it through all of the other courses that had been the issue. That and, of course, the social challenges each new class and setting provided.

Jason and Eric had been very fortunate to take advantage of a program that had eased Eric's transition from school to the real world, and being able to live with his father had helped immensely. He was now a draftsman at a local architectural firm and had held that position for the past three years. Once employed, his interest in drawing had rekindled since he now had time available that was previously taken up by studying and he worked daily with the media used in his art.

Jason finished cooking the chicken parmesan recipe he'd researched online, and he and Eric had a good discussion about Eric's new art inspiration. He was now interested in photovoltaic cells and was making diagrams of solar panels, electrical circuits, and electrons, so Jason rightly guessed that this is what their next book would be about.

Jason had been appalled when he'd leafed through a stack of pictures at the side of Eric's desk in Eric's junior year of high school. Sliced open abdomens, flayed thighs, intestines pulled aside to reveal the organs underneath—all graphic but bloodless in the sketched lines. He'd lain awake that night worrying that he had reared a serial murderer at the worst, or a very disturbed individual at the least.

A careful conversation the next morning had alleviated his fears. Eric had simply been fascinated by the layers of the human body and had spent hours watching YouTube videos of surgeries and studying medical websites. His clinical interest, as did most things, had found an outlet through his art.

Happening to come across Eric's anatomy drawings several years after the initial shock, Jason had approached his son about the two of them writing a book together using his text and Eric's illustrations. Their first book concerning surgery targeted pre-teens and young adults facing upcoming procedures and was picked up by a small publisher. The pair had then added to the '*Looking Inside…*' series with books on car engines, trains, dams, and several other oddities that had captured Eric's interest. Jason had once tried to steer Eric toward drawing a subject he himself wanted to write about, but Eric found it impossible to delve into a topic that was of no interest to him. So, in all of their books, the drawings always came first, and the words later.

Jason now knew that he'd need to spend some time getting up to speed on the vocabulary of solar energy.

Books

IT WAS late, and Jason was just thinking about going to bed when the phone rang. Caller ID said that it was Dennis Harris from the authors' group, so he swiped to answer.

"Hi Jason, hope this isn't too late to call."

"Nope, not at all. How are you, Dennis?"

"Great, thanks. I just realized that we haven't put together a list of readings for the next meeting. Do you have anything in the hopper? Do you want to present a chapter from your book about Miriam or your next '*Looking Inside*' book?"

"I don't have anything right now," replied Jason. "But I was just talking to Eric about a project he's immersed in. He's excited about solar panels, so I'm guessing that will be the next thing I write about. Of course, I need to wait for him to finish the illustrations before I start. It'll be a while. And the Miriam book is just limping along. I've had a lot on my plate what with having to relocate my business."

"Yeah, I heard about that. There's no doubt that the church, the Entity, has morphed from a house of worship into a fiefdom of business. The Christian way of life apparently encompasses every dollar they can make or control. Anyway, sorry about your move."

"It's frustrating, but luckily I can work on instruments nearly anywhere."

"That's good. OK, thanks, I just thought I'd see if you needed a slot. I know that Sharon wants to read a chapter, so we'll have that at least. Everyone I've called is interested in the next steps we should take regarding the library bans, so I expect that will take up some time anyway. Oh, and don't forget about the upcoming library rally!"

"I won't—it's so well publicized that I don't think others will either. Thanks for calling, and see you there, Dennis."

"Sure, see you there."

Instead of bed, Jason grabbed a beer and went over to sit in his favorite chair. Dennis's question about his book on Miriam got him to thinking about his progress. With the help of the Panhandle Authors' Group, he'd written his first book about his personal growth and insights gained while working as a remote fire-spotter one summer before he'd gone to college, and *Saved by Solitude* had finally been published by a vanity press. He'd then decided that he wanted to recognize Miriam and write about her interesting life, especially her experiences during the Watts riots and the Black Power movement. He'd done some outside research, but relied heavily on his recollection of her own words and those of her son, Lamar, with whom he still kept in close touch. The book was nearly complete except for some key chapters. Those covered the years that Jason had known her and the two had become friends. He had a very rough draft of this period, but so far had found it far too personal to share with the group. None of them were aware of the type of bond he'd shared with her, and revealing that would divulge too much about himself, which he wasn't sure he wanted to be made public.

Post Office

WITH NO customers to distract him, Jason was glad to have the time to catch up on his backlog of instruments. The junior high school students, particularly, had been brutal to theirs this year, and he began to wonder if each subsequent generation had less respect for physical objects given that so many commodities now were either disposable or readily available. He immediately realized that this thought was bogus, but it still felt to him like there was more than the normal wear and tear lately. Not that he was complaining business-wise.

He'd been disheartened by the switch in locations, and today was the first day that he felt that this dark basement might be a tolerable place for his shop after all. His instrument sales and repair shop had been on the busy sidewalk in central Dunkirk where drop-ins for instruments, music, or repairs had been constant. Now, it would take time, possibly too long, to rebuild his clientele on the sales end. Simply folding up shop and calling it quits, like his friend the chocolatier, had been a real possibility, and during two days of feeling despondent, he'd nearly decided to do just that. Luckily, he had contracts with both the middle and high schools to rent out and repair their band instruments, and this was the only reason he could stay afloat without needing to quit the business altogether.

His friend Art had saved him from being thrown out on the street. The older widower suffered from hearing impairment —a plus for having music played beneath him—and was only using the upper floors in his house, anyway. The basement was spacious, but seasonally damp and ill-lit. Mineral deposits streaked the walls where the water seeped through during the winter months. But still, it was cheap and could contain all of the instruments that he had in his inventory. Jason had hastily built an elevated floor along the wall opposite the basement entrance to hold the instrument cases, and he had immediately hung strings of LED lights to brighten up the space. They'd had trouble getting his workbench through the walk-in basement door that accessed the outside, but had finally managed it without too many alterations to the benchtop.

A loud rap on the door startled Jason. He set down the screwdriver and tiny screw that he'd just removed from a saxophone and went over to what was now his new shop entrance.

"Hi Jason," said Betta when he opened it.

"Oh, hi Betta," said a surprised Jason, ushering her in. "How did you know I was here? You're my first visitor."

Betta pointed to the emblem on her sleeve. "Post Office," she said. "We know everything," with a grin. And then more seriously, "You really should update your website so that people can find you, though, Jason."

"I know, I keep forgetting, but you're right. That's something I really should do today. So, you bring mail?"

"Nope, you're not on my route anymore. I took a break and thought I'd stop by and talk for a sec."

"Sure, have a seat," and he gestured to two folding chairs near his crude desk. "It's good to see you."

"It's good to see you too, Jason," said Betta as she sat on the edge of a seat, Jason taking the chair beside her. She looked him in the eyes. "I just wanted to clear the air about the day we took the hike. I felt that I was rude and wanted to try and explain."

Jason smiled and wanted to put a hand on her shoulder, but knew he couldn't. "You don't need to explain, Betta. I've had similar reactions my entire life. It's me who should apologize for not warning you ahead of time."

"Well, it certainly was a shock—in more ways than one," laughed Betta. "I've been thinking about it a lot, though, and I'm mad at myself for reacting the way I did. I realized that it's just as you said—you must have to deal with this all the time, and it must be rough." Then she gave him a puzzled look. "But then I wondered - you've been married, so is it something I can get past? Am I not giving you enough of a chance?"

Jason looked down at the floor and then back up at her. "I guess it really is a matter of chance," he said. "I've known one person in my whole life who was the same as me, the same... wiring, I guess it is, and I feel so lucky to have met her—totally by chance."

"And she was your wife?"

"Ann? No, Ann is, or was, one of those people who enjoys a certain amount of excitement or frisson, I guess, and so she stuck with me for as long as she could stand it. Honestly, you're one of the few women I've tried to date in years. We seemed to click in conversation, and I was hoping that some miracle would happen as we became closer. It's so hard to try and explain to someone what's going on with me without them actually experiencing it."

Betta winced. "And I've wondered if I could commit to being more than a friend, but I have to honestly say that I think it would be too difficult for me."

"I understand, and that's OK. Sometimes I wish this was really a superpower, and that it could do something like take down bad guys, or heal wounds, or something. But it's just a condition that I have to live with." He looked at her. "And I don't want someone else to have to struggle with it either."

"I'm sorry, Jason, and thanks for understanding," said Betta. Then she slapped her thighs and stood up. "So, friends, then?"

"Definitely," said Jason. "Don't be a stranger just because I'm not on your route."

"Oh, you'll never be a stranger." Betta opened and headed out the door. "See you, Jason."

"Bye, Betta," said Jason. He was initially happy that they'd talked, but then a feeling of melancholy settled around him now that it had been verified that they would never be more than friends—essentially a notice from a postal official that anything but regular mail from him would be returned to sender.

Abby

JASON HAD wrapped up his work for the day on another, more troublesome, saxophone and then took some time to try and improve the lighting in Art's basement. He'd bought four powerful LED lamps in decorative stands and pointed them into each of the four corners of the sterile room. That seemed to do the trick. They were programmable for different colors, and he tried several combinations before discovering that green and blue in opposite corners achieved the ambiance he was looking for.

The wind was unexpectedly warm with summer seemingly just around the corner, and he enjoyed the crocus and hyacinth blooms in yards as he made his way home. He grabbed the newspaper out of the delivery sleeve on the porch and glanced at the front page as he opened the door. There was an unexpected aroma in the house. Someone had brought in a fragrance that smelled vaguely of magnolia. That person also, apparently, wore a faux-cashmere orange sweater if what was hanging on the back of one of the dining room chairs was any indication.

Jason was now curious. It had been years since Eric had had any friends over to the house. And never a female.

He walked up to Eric's bedroom door and could hear percussive sounds emanating from a computer speaker. He was lucky that Grizzly was providing an excuse to investigate. The big orange cat was sitting patiently, waiting to be let in. He rapped lightly on the door. Eric rarely answered when immersed in a game, but he tried out of courtesy, anyway. There came an immediate "Yes?" in a female voice.

"It's Jason—and Grizzly, mind if we come in?"

"Sure, come on in," said the voice, sounding vaguely distracted as she spoke.

Jason opened the door to find two hunched figures clutching gaming consoles and staring at a battle taking place in the skies over a distant planet. The big cat leapt up on the bed right behind Eric's chair and lay down.

The young woman turned and rose from her spot to greet him. She had long, curly brown hair, dark-rimmed glasses, and tats on each arm. She extended her hand and said "Hi, I'm..."

"Nope!" barked Eric. And then in a more measured tone, "It's probably best not to get too close to my dad, Abby."

Abby stood perplexed with outstretched hand, glancing between the seated Eric and the standing Jason.

Jason broke the tension. "Hi, so it sounds like you're Abby. Eric's told me about you," he said. "He's right, I am a little 'contact challenged' as I like to say." At the questioning look from the woman, he added, "It's just best if we didn't shake hands. It can give some people a little jolt. Like one of those gimmick buzzers that a practical joker can hide in his palm?"

Abby still looked a little unsure, but smiled gamely and said, "OK, whatever. It's still nice to meet you, Mr. Deakins. Eric said it was fine if I joined him for a game?"

"Oh, yeah, by all means, it's Eric's house, too." said Jason. "And it's great to meet you, too, Abby. You're absolutely welcome anytime." He shifted back toward the door. "Don't let me interrupt—it appears that Eric's taking advantage of your absence," and he pointed at the screen.

Abby pivoted and with a laugh burst out, "Eric! No fair!" She threw Jason a quick smile and then declared, "OK, buddy, the gloves come off!" sliding smoothly back into her chair and wielding the console like a true warrior might with Eric giving a little giggle as she did so.

Jason gently shut the door and walked back to the living room, amazed at several things: his son's nonchalance at finding a friend, inviting them to their home, and her being of the opposite sex; the ease with which Abby seemed to accept Eric and his 'Ericness'; and the sense of familiarity he himself seemed to feel about the pair of them being together. He relished the unexpected sense of comfort this gave him.

He heated up some leftovers and read the newspaper while he ate. An article on the front page caught his eye. The owner of Jack's Fine Wines had previously requested that the city council disallow the establishment of a church chapel in the Goodwin Building, since it was too near his place of business. The council had agreed and had placed a temporary stay on that particular zoning of the building until the matter could be studied. The very next Sunday, the Holy Grace Church had staged a prayer meeting within the building to bless the new spot, effectively using it as a chapel. One side in the ensuing argument said that it was an illegal gathering, and the other claimed that their freedom of religious expression was being trampled on by secular laws that shouldn't apply to them.

I knew this would happen, thought Jason. *And that chapel is probably located in my old spot.*

To avoid stewing about it, he chose a new novel to read, poured himself a glass of Zinfandel, and cracked open *A Prayer for Owen Meany* as he sat in his usual living room chair.

Half an hour later, Eric and Abby emerged from his room.

"I'm heading home, Mr. Deakins," she explained. "It was nice meeting you."

"You, too, Abby," said Jason as he rose out of habit. "And, it's Jason."

"All right," she said and turned to Eric. "Thanks for having me over, Eric. I'll see you maybe tomorrow again, for coffee?"

"Yep, sure," said Eric—as usual, appearing like he had more to say, but falling short of the target.

"OK," Abby said smoothly. "Looks like we have a way to go on that game."

"We're on level two, and there are seven levels," said Eric helpfully.

"Well, then I have five more levels to beat you at!" joked Abby as she headed to the entrance, and Eric followed. She opened the door and then reached out to give his hand a squeeze as she left. As usual, Eric's facial expression showed little change, but his father noticed a reddening of the cheeks. They each said their goodbyes, and Eric closed the door. As his son headed back to his bedroom, he glanced in Jason's direction without even noticing that his father was in the room.

Hmmm, thought Jason as he picked up where he'd left off in the second chapter with Owen shouting something at John. It looked like Owen Meany shouted everything, but at least he was communicating. Something he and Eric needed to work on.

Grizzly was curled up on the sofa next to him, having escaped the noise of the video game. Jason had never touched her, and he was sure that she preferred it that way since she had never tried to jump up on his lap or even rub his leg. Eric had bonded with their dog, Percy, and was beside himself when the old lab had passed away at the age of 12. A few years later, Eric had been outside in the backyard when a neighbor dog had jumped the fence and come at him snapping and snarling. Jason had run down the deck steps to save his son when this huge orange cat had streaked out from under the deck and ballooned herself sideways, hissing between Eric and the dog. One swipe from the stray had sent the dog yelping back to where it had come from. Eric had immediately named her and had begun feeding her at the back door. Within a week Grizzly was a welcome member of the family. It was a year later, on a visit to the vet, that they discovered that Grizzly was a she, not a he, but Eric liked the name, and it had stuck.

The Library Rally

ERIC WAS the drummer for the Rag Tag Marching Band and loaded his tenor drum into the car. Jason drove the short distance to Art Parker's and retrieved the sousaphone from his shop, artfully managing the big case into the back of the Subaru. From there they drove into town, picked up Abby, and found a parking spot a block away from Library Park where people and cars were beginning to congregate. They lugged the instruments from the car to the park, with Abby and Eric chatting the whole way. He was glad to see the pair so relaxed and happy with each other and looked forward to getting to know Abby a little better.

At Jason's request, the band always played near the edge of any event, preferably near a sidewalk, so that Jason had plenty of room around him. The members of the band had long accepted that this was a requirement of Jason's participation and agreed that it was a necessary precaution given his 'nature' as they called it. He usually chose his battered baritone to help with the bottom end, but with any event expected to draw a large crowd, he brought a sousaphone, safely tucking himself into its huge metal coil.

Jason didn't do well with crowds, and crowds didn't do well with Jason. He'd joined some demonstrations in his college days but soon learned that he was more of a disruption than a help. Inevitably, someone would jostle into him and then draw back or jag to the side, then bump into the person next to them, and so on. God forbid if he was forced into a space tightly packed with people. He'd learned that if he was in the marching band, which was a group event, after all, it was best to carry an instrument that commanded some distance from those around him. The sousaphone was one of the safest bets.

Art with his clarinet and the two trumpet players were already standing under the huge, newly leafing maple that spread out over the lawn from the neighboring lot along Pine St. The remainder of the block was taken up by the small park which lay at the intersection of Pine St. and Forest St. with the library situated further up Forest.

"Hi, Art. Hey, Marcie," said Jason as the saxophone player came up beside the clarinetist at the same time as Jason, Abby, and Eric. Abby gave Eric an unexpected peck on the cheek and went off to get a place near the front of the event.

"Beautiful day for some music," said Art, while Jason set his case near the fence and extracted the sousaphone. They all began to tune up as the last players arrived.

The Rag Tags struck up the music, and the park was already beginning to fill for the rally. Jason was swinging back and forth to the first song when he was shocked to see Kris come up near him during a swing toward the crowd. He took his lips away from the mouthpiece for a moment and mouthed 'Hi' with a questioning look and then continued to play while facing her. She yelled 'Hi,' and then pointed to the other end of the park along the sidewalk where she intended to stand. He gave a little bow to acknowledge her signal, and his low bass part suddenly had some added pep.

The band had a very broad repertoire, and most of the old hands had memorized their parts so that they didn't need to deal with sheet music. Always beginning with *When the Saints Come Marching in,* they moved on to *Bill Bailey, Blowing in the Wind, Don't Worry, Be Happy,* and then *Mack the Knife.* Sharks were biting with their teeth and 'scarlet billows were starting to spread' when Lisa Brooks began her welcome and introductions.

The other members of the band set their instruments down in their cases near the neighboring fence and turned to watch the speeches. Jason normally kept his sousaphone wrapped around him like a security fence at similar events, but today he uncoiled himself from the instrument and set it in its case as well. Eric worked his way up to the front to stand next to Abby, and Jason walked to the street and then along it to search out Kris.

Mayor Larson was about to share his support for the library and its staff when part of the crowd at the intersection of Pine and Forest suddenly broke out into a very loud hymn. Jason was heading that way and spotted Kris at the edge of that group. His heart fell when he thought for a moment that she might belong to the Entity, but she saw him at the same time, gave a little wave, and began to move in his direction. The mayor was trying to yell above the raised voices, but even with the microphone he saw that he couldn't be heard by the library supporters near the choir and turned to Lisa and one or two of the council members, pointing over to where Jason guessed the police might be standing.

The Holy Grace Church often carried out 'sing-ins' at events that they disagreed with. It always followed the same pattern: the police, or in one very confrontational case, the crowd, would move in and finally herd the members away from the venue; then the Entity would later cry that this had been harassment and that they had been merely expressing their faith as they had every right to do. Why this only happened at gatherings voicing other's views, they never bothered to explain.

Searching the faces of the heavenly choir as Kris came toward him, he recognized a few of them including Will Sommers, the wealthy elder, Ed Cutler, the ringleader, and Martin Ames along with the other new council member. Kris joined Jason, and they ended up standing near the sidewalk half-way between the band and the choir.

"Hi, Jason," she said, "I thought that was you playing the tuba."

He didn't want to correct her and said, "Yeah, it's so great to see you here."

Kris nodded. "I saw it in the papers and just had to show my support." She looked around. "Even though I'm not the best in big crowds."

Jason looked at her for a moment. That was almost exactly what he would say.

"What are they doing?" asked Kris, raising her voice to be heard, rather than stepping in closer while pointing to the choir.

"Going for publicity would be my guess," Jason said loudly. "And they're likely the types who pushed for some of the books to be banned in the first place, so it's probably their way to protest the protest."

They could barely make out the mayor's voice imploring the choir to please halt their singing and let this excellent rally continue, and as if in response the ensemble moved immediately into another hymn. Two policemen and Council Member Mike Lee stepped up to Cutler, and the policemen began talking with him in an animated fashion with Lee trying his best to look authoritative. The two new council members placed themselves on either side of Cutler, leaning into the conversation. Then a member of the library staff joined the discussion with a piece of paper in her hand—obviously, the permit for the rally. Ames examined it, began to protest, but then appeared to think better of it and stepped up to have a word with Cutler. The choir sang on, and Cutler appeared to want the hymn to finish but finally, with a smirk on his face, he raised his hands toward the singers, and they fell silent. On cue, many turned and walked down Forest St. away from the library, but several others melted into the crowd.

As they did so, Jason, for the first time, noticed seven or eight men in camo gear spaced around the periphery of the event, mainly on the opposite side of the street. This made him turn to the two officers at the corner of the park. They didn't seem outwardly concerned by the presence of what was obviously some sort of militia group, but Jason found that he was. He thought it was no coincidence that just then the truck with multiple right-wing flags drove slowly past the park on Forest St., radio blaring.

"I'm sorry for the unnecessary interruption, folks," said Mayor Larson, regaining control of the microphone and the attention of the crowd. "Unfortunately, this sort of disruption is becoming more and more common lately." He then launched into his speech.

When the mayor finished, Lisa stepped up to the microphone to introduce the next speaker, but before she did so, she said, "I noticed that there are several gentlemen who appear to be together as some sort of militia. I want to let you know that we are doing fine here and don't need any of your protection. Please move on if you're not here to support our libraries." The crowd turned around to see who she was talking about, but the men with army green scarves pulled up over their mouths remained unmoved by the attention. "Next up is Benewah County Commissioner Davis," said Lisa.

Jason was impressed both by the turnout, and by the number and variety of speakers supporting the library. He said as much to Kris during a pause between presenters, enjoying standing beside her. Dennis followed Terry, the voice of KPAN, and his own deep voice sounded high and weak in comparison—but he was much more expressive. "I'm not a well published writer, but I'm a writer nonetheless, and it bothers me to see the likes of Orwell, Huxley, Vonnegut, and Bradbury kept out of anyone's hands. I've read all of their books that have made it onto the blacklist, and I have to say that they were some of the most formative books for me that I've ever read. I'm not of their caliber, but what if some potentially great author, like a future Joyce or a Hemingway, say, was denied the books that would inspire his or her love of literature, or bring him or her the realization that they could turn their ideas into great works that could benefit the rest of humanity? What if their golden words were stolen before they even formed?

"The book banners are afraid that books will have a negative impact on their children. Are any of these novels oversexed or overly violent? By today's standards, I'd say no. Not in the least. But the same parents turn on their big-screen television sets and watch utter violence. It is difficult to find a show anymore where a weapon isn't drawn, people are made fun of and belittled, and people are physically attacked. The ads in between shows promote sexuality. Yet they let their young children watch them without a thought. Every night. And movies? Now we move into extreme violence and overt sexuality. And they want to go against books? Threaten our libraries and our librarians?

"I suggest that we all take care of our own homes first before trying to control the homes of others. I would bet that many of the book banners aren't readers and haven't visited a library in their lives. Here's a challenge for you. Walk to your nearest library. Pick up a book that you can borrow for free. Sit and spend some time with the book, even if you find it difficult at first, then think about the quiet time you've spent alone with your own thoughts and imagination. If you still find the experience repugnant, fine, don't come back—after you return the book, of course—but don't stop those of us who have had a better experience than you've had with reading and literature. Thank you."

The crowd applauded, and Jason was impressed. Dennis might have been dramatic, but Jason thought that he'd raised some very good points.

Art Parker was the last to speak. As was his manner, he began by addressing First Amendment rights, but obviously couldn't help himself and moved on to the Second Amendment and the new law permitting local militias before circling back to censorship and book banning.

Worried about the effect his words would have on the men in camo, Jason turned to find that the militia had moved in closer to the edges of the crowd, with one man within ten feet of Jason and Kris. Some of the rally attendees near others of them appeared to also be concerned and stepped up to talk with them. Based on their reactions, it appeared that there was no reason to worry. Kris must have been uncomfortable, however, because she turned and walked twenty feet down the sidewalk to put more distance between herself and the man. Jason followed, assuring her that there was no need for concern.

Lisa wrapped up the event, bringing the topic back to everyone's purpose for being there. She stepped over to two tables beside the makeshift podium. Taking the mike in one hand, she pulled back a cover with the other hand to reveal stacks of books arranged across the tables. "These are books that we are either not allowed to have in sections of our library, or they are ones that are iffy enough that we don't want to take the risk with having them on the shelves, since they are on the lists of most libraries facing this same problem. Several generous donors have contributed many of the volumes as well, and we ask that you take any of them that you like. Take them home and read them. As one of the volunteers said, 'we're putting the banned back into your hands.' Thank you all for coming today and for being so supportive of your local library." She was about to put the mike back in its stand when she quickly added, "Oh, and any donations are of course greatly appreciated," with a smile.

"What did you think?" Jason asked Kris as the crowd began to disperse.

"I liked it, and I'm glad I bumped into you. I hope this kind of thing will make a difference." She looked over at the militia and said, "I don't really care for that though."

"It looks like many here don't," said Jason, noticing the large empty spaces around each of the men. And then to change the subject, "I don't know if you know it, but Terry, from KPAN, and Dennis who followed him are both part of the writers' group I'm in. Art, that last speaker, is also a good friend of mine—he's the guy I rent my shop space from now that I had to move."

"Oh, so at least you didn't need to operate out of your own home," said Kris. "That's a good thing. And I really enjoyed hearing your friends speak."

They both turned toward the crowd which was milling about the park. Many of the rally attendees moved to the tables to examine the free books. Eric and Abby stood back, waiting until the first in line had a chance to make their selections. People were reaching and reading when suddenly several among them brandished heavy-duty garbage bags and began scooping the volumes into them. It was like a shoplifting flash mob shown on the news. Eric and Abby appeared stunned, as did most others near the books. In moments, the tables were nearly bare, and several books lay strewn about on the ground around the tables where they'd missed the bags. It happened so quickly that reactions were slow, and the bag carriers were heading for the street before anyone knew what to do. Jason recognized some of their faces as being from among members of the unwelcome choir.

There was a delayed response, but shouts soon started to spread. A few in the crowd tried to stop them or pursue them down the street, but it was too late to save the books. The police were more focused on the militia and what their reaction might be and were too far away to reach them on foot. Jason did see a patrolman jump into a car and head down Forest St. after them. All the while, the militia remained unmoved. Their reason for being there a mystery, the armed men were later said to have stood at their assumed posts until the park was nearly empty.

Jason and Kris stared at each other.

"What the hell just happened? Those people stole all the books?" she asked.

"That was book banners turning into book burners, would be my guess," said Jason, still trying to process the weird turn of events.

Lisa had picked up the mike and begun to yell at the thieves to drop the bags as the last of them vanished around the corner, but she stopped as soon as they disappeared.

Then she addressed the crowd. "I don't know what that was about, but I have my guesses. It's best not to speculate, and I hope the police find who did this. I'm really sorry that this has happened at our fine event, everyone. I'm also sorry that the urge to ban books appears to be spreading beyond the confines of the library. Peace to you all."

"I've got to go," said Kris suddenly as the sidewalks began to fill with people heading home. "I hope I get to see you again soon."

"Me too," Jason said as she began to move away. He wanted to say, "I'll give you a call," but couldn't remember if he had her number. He'd felt a sudden urge to hug her goodbye and was suddenly angry that this was just another fantasy.

She gave a thumbs up and a smile as he watched her run across the street and head off on the opposite sidewalk. "Damn," he muttered as he walked over to the instruments where there were animated discussions going on about the sudden turn of events.

The Defense

THE REAL news about the rally over the next few days was mainly in letters to the editor and on the opinion page of the local newspaper. The police reported that they had been unable to apprehend any of those involved, but were pursuing leads. The Dunkirk Gazette had an article about the rally and mentioned the confiscation of books at the conclusion of the event by unknown persons, but the reporter was unwilling to journey into speculation about who the perpetrators might be. The letters the paper printed were not so cautious. Many accused the Entity directly, some going so far as to name the members who had participated in the book-grab.

Later that week, Ed Cutler wrote a letter to the editor in defense of his church. Art and Jason were having coffee in Art's kitchen while Jason took a break from his repairs. The library rally was, naturally, still a major topic of conversation. Art had the paper opened out on the table and said, "Listen to this. Cutler says, 'It is beyond my understanding why we should come under attack for our mere presence at the library rally. When we sang, we were simply expressing our joyous thanks to our Lord, and we did so away from the crowd. Those who have indicated their displeasure are at the same time admitting their willingness to take away our very right to do so. To accuse us of theft is even further beyond my belief. There was not, as many have claimed, a crime committed. It is widely known that the head librarian stated that the books were free for the taking, which someone apparently did. We are a church of law-abiding citizens and are stung by all of the false accusations which are so readily and vilely directed at us. But we will persevere. The anti-Christian movement is strong and condemning, but we are stronger and turn the other cheek. We seek a community of peace and understanding. Others in Dunkirk apparently do not.'"

Art shook his head after reading. "We were there," he said. "They were clearly within the confines of the park where the library had a permit for the anti-banning rally. I don't know the rules myself, but there is a purpose for the permit which probably is permission to hold an event in the park to the exclusion of others. And among us who were there, we could probably identify every person who took the books as being a member of the Entity, yet he doesn't come right out and admit it. It's another case of sticking their finger in someone's eye, asking why they're crying, and claiming they didn't do it."

"How could it be possible that they came armed with garbage bags to take the books in the first place? The unveiling of the table looked like it was a surprise."

"Don't forget that the Entity now has a seat on the library board. I'm sure the giveaway was discussed at their board meeting. Then that board member likely told Cutler."

Jason then asked, "What do you think they did with the books they made away with?"

"The dump or the bonfire would be my guess. If they want more publicity, I'm sure we'll find out soon enough. It will probably be on YouTube—matches, gasoline, their bombastic leader, and all."

It turned out that there was a YouTube video posted two days later, and clips from it made a spot on the evening news. However, the content was not what Art had imagined.

The video opened with a shot of the Benewah County Library and then panned to show a van pulling up to the sidewalk in front of the entrance. A beaming Ed Cutler stepped out of the passenger door; greeted an awkward looking Lisa Brooks who had been summoned to the sidewalk; and then threw open the side door of the van to reveal boxes and boxes of books.

Then came the speech. "Mrs. Brooks, I, and the Holy Grace Church are pleased to make a donation of books to your library. And you need not worry about them being banned. These 125 volumes include some of the bestselling Christian publications on the market, donations from the New Archangel Bookstore, and from several Christian presses in the Northwest. Many of these volumes have been authored by me and several other Northern Idaho church leaders. I'm sure you'll find them an excellent addition to any library collection, and my congregation is happy to make this donation."

He then faced the camera. "You see, Mrs. Brooks. We all, Christians, and non-Christians alike, love to read and we love to learn. Far from being book-burners, we cherish the words of comfort and salvation that can be found on the written page."

Then he turned back to Lisa. "I hope you will accept this gift that shows our strong support of our local library."

Ed Cutler shook her hand while again facing the camera which also captured Lisa mumbling a thank you, standing with a furrowed brow as the video ended.

THE ANTI-BOOK banning rally was also the main topic of conversation at the next meeting of the Panhandle Authors' Group. Jason had arrived a little late and excused himself to the others as he took his usual chair at the back and to the side of the table.

"And the police did absolutely nothing!" Dennis was hot. "They just stood there and watched it happen and then finally lamely followed them in a car. It was pathetic. It was almost as if they expected it to happen and didn't care."

"Exactly!" said Morgan, who was equally fired up. "And what the hell was that fucking militia doing there? Who were those guys? They seemed cozy with the police, didn't they? I'm really glad they just stood there, though. Imagine if something had set them off? What did they hope would happen?"

"We should ask for a formal investigation," said Dennis.

"But what if the response is 'nothing happened?'" asked Terry. "I've read the papers and the letters that they've allowed to be printed—I know I wrote one that I haven't seen yet—and I've listened to the news reports."

"What do you mean, 'nothing happened' then?" Morgan asked incredulously.

"If you believe Cutler and the news reports, nothing illegal did happen," Terry replied. "There was singing at the beginning of the speeches, but it's unclear if the permission of one group with a permit to gather excludes other groups from being there at the same time, especially if the main purpose of the singers was purportedly to attend the rally in the first place. Then, it was publicly stated that the books were free for the taking, so they took them. And that militia did absolutely nothing, so they were legal as well. If you look at it that way, nothing happened."

"That's ridiculous!" yelled Morgan.

"But that's probably also correct," said Dennis after taking in the points Terry had made. "Those arguments will counter everything about it that we feel was so wrong."

"That doesn't mean we can't do *anything*," said Morgan.

"Oh?" asked Terry, "Like what, exactly?"

"We can hold a demonstration in front of City Hall," said Morgan.

"To what purpose?" asked Terry.

"First of all, to protest the lack of adequate police presence and the ineffectiveness of the officers who were there. Second, to show solid support for our libraries which was diminished by the antics of the Entity. And third, and most importantly, to ask the city to formally declare opposition to the new book banning legislation."

"Isn't the last one a little late?" asked Maggie.

"Any legislation can be changed—as our Idaho Legislature is so good at pointing out to us. So, no. It's never too late, in my opinion," said Morgan.

Upon the conditions that they could get approval for the assembly, get buy-in from Lisa and the library staff, and possibly get participation by the human rights groups, a majority of the Panhandle Authors' Group voted to have Dennis and Morgan organize the demonstration.

Sharon then read her next chapter about Ladakhu finding the third stone of the Quaddari, and Jason had to admit that he might have tuned out for the larger portion of it.

"You know," said Carmine when she'd finished, "I find myself actually wondering if she'll find the fourth and final stone. Not bad, Sharon. Not bad at all."

"Agreed," said Terry. "Although I noticed that the word 'surprised' kept springing up. You might want to look for some synonyms. But I also wonder how many times a person can keep being amazed in a single day."

Jason was himself surprised by Terry's comment. The aviation author could take his own suggestion to heart, as far as he was concerned.

Sharon gave Terry a steely stare as he said this, but agreed in the end. "Yeah, I'll try and make her a little more stoic then. Like she already knew that some of it was coming or something."

Terry nodded as Sharon peered around the room for other comments.

Pressured, Jason felt like he needed to contribute. "I noticed that this is the third book in the series, and she is finding the third stone. When she's escaped the trap set by the... What were they? The Adaks? No, the Adraki, and she's wandering through the canyon, perhaps there might be some reflection on her part to bring back some of the elements of the first two books? Seems like the perfect time unless you get to that later in the story."

Sharon thought for a moment. "No, I don't get to that later, so that would probably be a good time. I don't know how I would do it, but that is a good idea."

"And she could have sex with one of the Adraki," said Luke. Everyone discretely rolled their eyes. "I mean, they seemed like hunky dudes," looking around as if that was the perfect thing to happen in that situation.

Tactfully, for her, Sharon reminded him that the Adraki were half robotic and created their offspring in the off-planet factory. There was a subtle, non-verbal show of relief around the room.

Sharon Stone was the owner and publisher of the local advertising booklet *Essentially Dunkirk* that was put out quarterly and featured spotlights on local businesses as well as discount offers and coupons. She was surly, but with a smile, and had a booth promoting her *Summoning Stones* series at any major event. Many thought that *Summoning Stones* by Sharon Stone was a bit much, but she seemed unphased. She was also unaffected by the fact that she had the opposite body type compared to the famous actress. In fact, they were so dissimilar that few even noticed the shared names.

Since Sharon was the last and only reader of the night, the conversation turned, as usual, to local gossip and politics.

"Did you hear that the Legislature has brought back the firing squad for the death penalty?" asked an incredulous Maggie.

Most of the group thought that there should be no death penalty at all, but three of them thought that if there was to be a death penalty, a firing squad might be the quickest way to go. Maggie started to describe the aftermath and the carnage that bullets caused which would need to be dealt with, and the conversation quickly shifted to another topic.

"To me, the worst news from down in Boise is that the Senate has now passed the library legislation, with the governor stating that he'll sign it once it reaches his desk." said Dennis. "As the statewide rallies have shown, the public and the libraries have all come out against it. The librarians are in a panic. The legislation is book banning and censorship pure and simple."

"We have to protect our children from offensive material, though," said Kenneth, who rarely spoke. "This whole grooming and exposing our kids to pornography has got to stop." Kenneth was the oldest member of the group and had missed the previous meeting's discussion, skipping the library rally, too.

"I totally agree with Kenneth," said Tamra, a younger member and an infrequent attendee. "I don't understand why anyone would want to write that kind of filth in the first place. It definitely should not have a spot on our public shelves."

The others seemed slightly embarrassed, having discussed this topic two weeks previously. Politics and religion were thorny areas, and they all sensed that they were tiptoeing very near the hedge. To a person, they became pointedly civil as they discussed the library bill, which came as an immense relief to Jason since he had promised himself that he wouldn't be the one to belabor the topic. He knew that Kenneth and Tamra, particularly, were highly religious and leaned heavily to the right, possibly Charlotte as well, while Maggie, Dennis, and Morgan were strong, outspoken liberals. There was a tacit agreement among them all not to devolve into political or religious arguments during the meetings. The group speculated about how the law would be enforced, what the reactions by the regional libraries would be, and the effects there might be on library staffs.

Since Jason felt passionately about the subject, he couldn't stop himself from adding, "And even if the bill doesn't make it past the governor's desk, there is still pressure on local libraries from a riled-up section of the public. Look at what happened up north in Bonners Ferry—the staff were harassed to the point that most quit—just for the books they had on their shelves which had been there for years."

There were rumblings and then Dennis shifted the conversation. "What causes a book to be banned in the first place?" he asked.

"Well, obviously pornography and gay content," Tamra immediately shot back. "These are susceptible kids we're talking about, and if the library won't protect them from this vile stuff, who will? Like I said, it shouldn't even be on the shelves."

Uh oh, thought Jason. *Here we go.*

"Who's to say what's pornographic or obscene though?" asked Maggie. "I mean the human body is everywhere in art and science books. Just because we all wear clothes, you can't hide the fact that we're all the same underneath. We all have sex. It's a healthy and natural thing. Children have to know what their bodies will become, or it will be really rough on them later in life."

"We have the concept of 'minors' for a reason, and it's a legal definition, as well," said Kenneth.

"There is the world of children, and the world of adults," Charlotte piped up. "The two should coexist, but be separate from one another. Adults should know all about children and raising them, but the children have no reason to know any-thing about the adult world."

"Are you nuts?" asked Maggie. "In this modern world, it's impossible to keep the two separate. I mean, I know that kids shouldn't be subjected to graphic porn, but their whole life is about becoming an adult. About growing up. And they need to be prepared for each stage. Girls especially need to know that a period is coming soon to their lives, and what it means if they have unprotected sex."

"They shouldn't be having sex anyway," said Tamra. "Not till they're married and start to raise a family."

Jason was the one to throw up the yellow flag. "Look, if you want to delve further into this, maybe anyone who wants should meet somewhere later. I'm not running the club. In fact, we decided that no one was, but I don't want this group to fracture because of ideology. We're here as authors."

"OK," said Dennis, "but my question is still valid. I've heard that banned books sell. You ban a book, and it's on everyone's radar, and sales go up. So, what does it take to get a book banned? We all know that many of them aren't just about sex. I notice that no books on graphic violence or psy-cho murderers are on the list, but that books about race and political views are. There are even a few that are 100 years old, like *A Brave New World,* on the list. So why those?"

Morgan nodded and then muttered, "It's no coincidence that novels about book banning and authoritative govern-ments are being banned by authoritative legislatures."

"Well, Dennis, I'd add that besides, obviously, graphic sex and porn, that homosexuality, race issues, and those attacking a religion are probably candidates, too," said Samuel. "Why do you ask?"

"My books aren't selling, and I was just thinking that if I wrote a book that got banned, it might attract some attention—both to the book and to book banning."

"Aha!" said Samuel. "I thought you might be thinking that when you mentioned sales."

"Is that so wrong?" asked Dennis.

"It sure is if you're talking about writing pornography," said Kenneth.

Luke lit up. "I would love to write a pornographic novel and see it get banned. That's a great idea!" eliciting a protracted moan from Kenneth.

"Hey, that's not a bad idea," said Morgan. "We could each take a stab at writing a banned book. It would be a way to test the waters of this censorship thing, and we could use it to take a stand for all the other authors who've been banned."

"That's the worst idea I've ever heard," said Kenneth, covering his ears to emphasize the point.

"You're joking, Morgan," chimed in Sharon. "We're a serious writers' group, and you'd be throwing your reputations away if you did that."

"What reputations?" asked Dennis, flipping up his palms. "I'm going to write a novel about an interracial marriage during the fifties, and see where it goes. I've been thinking about something like that anyway."

"And I've always wanted to write one about lesbian love," said Maggie. "Count me in."

Hearing this, Morgan decided to join the pledges. "You all know that I lean heavily toward socialism. I've already started a historical book about communism in this area of the Northwest in the 1930's and that's made me think about writing my first novel about how a version of communism from that time period slowly spreads across the globe to create a new world order. Count me in, too." He thought for a moment. "Although, I doubt I could make any kind of short deadline."

"And I've always wanted to poke holes in the arguments of those who take the Bible too literally," Robb piped up. "I might try a young adult book with pictures about that if I can talk Eric or someone into illustrating it." He turned to Jason with a questioning look.

Jason shrugged back. "I can ask him, but his focus is pretty narrow."

"Thanks," said Robb. "What about you Jason? Are you going to write anything?"

"I don't have any ideas at the moment, but I think what you're all suggesting will be a good way to make a statement."

"Making a statement that is purposefully sinful?" asked Tamra staring pointedly at Robb across the table. "I just don't get you people anymore."

Kenneth surveyed the room and shook his head. "This will be the death of this group if you go down this path," he warned. "There is no reason for us to become political or make a stand like this."

"Yeah," said Charlotte. "You can do that on your own if you want, but don't make the group part of it."

"Well, I for one, think it's critical to our future. In a way, all of what we do and bring here is being threatened," said Dennis.

"How about this?" asked Jason. "We all think about what we'd like to write, see if it really could be censored and what it would mean if it was, and also see if we think that this stand is proper for our writers' group. We can talk about it seriously at our next meeting. Don't forget that the proposed legislation is geared toward minors, so that should be your target audience if you really want to be banned in Idaho."

"And, for those of us who don't want to write a banned book, think about what the impact the rest of you would have on the more serious among us," said Sharon, clutching the draft of her fantasy to her bosom. "Remember, Aldous Huxley and Maya Angelou wrote their books and then they were banned. They didn't write their books just to have them censored. There's a big difference in intent and quality. I doubt what is written here would have a chance of being published just on the quality alone."

"That sounds like a challenge," said Dennis with a quick grin. "And I accept."

The meeting broke up, but it was difficult to tell that it had. The members continued to press their views in small clusters as they gathered their things and headed out onto the parking lot at the back, some standing next to their cars and debating for a long time afterward. Charlotte paired off against Morgan, and, unexpectedly, Maggie was deep in a conversation with Kenneth.

Settling In

While repadding a clarinet, he lapsed into thinking about the previous evening's meeting and ended up wondering whether any books had ever been written with the express purpose of being banned. He unexpectedly found himself agreeing with Sharon, and doubted that any that might emerge from the Panhandle Authors' Group would ever find a publisher—let alone attract any kind of audience if they did. Still, he could tell that the opportunity to protest the current political climate had energized most of the group. Lately, the engagement in writing by many of them needed a serious recharge, anyway.

He personally thought that the whole idea of book banning, and targeting libraries in particular, was ridiculous. Any book could easily be found in bookstores, online, in electronic format, and probably in an audio version for all he knew. The bans were focused solely on public accessibility, specifically for minors, and spoke more to the lack of interest or oversight that the banners themselves had in what their children read. The whole thing was an exercise in futility, no, in extremism. The images of people in the South burning Beatles' and rock-n-roll records in the '60's sprang to mind, and it was now obvious how ineffective that had been. He could picture the burners or their children rocking out to Lynyrd Skynyrd or Allman Brothers' records in later years—the purpose of the burnings a distant memory. Or maybe he was underestimating the enduring legacy of Pat Boone and Tennessee Ernie Ford, and they were still the popular choice?

Regardless, he couldn't see anyone in the writers' group coming up with a theme along the lines of *1984* or *Fahrenheit 451* that would address the root of banning. Despite the futility of the group's efforts, he found himself trying to think of a subject that might fit the bill. He knew that nothing he came up with would ever include his son's illustrations as the centerpiece. Eric had a very prudish streak, and if Jason suggested some topic that would be unacceptable to children, it would also be unacceptable to Eric—he would pre-ban the book.

Jason wanted to apply a finishing wax to the clarinet, but had to stop his work and his thoughts to hunt through some moving boxes to find the necessary cloths and buffing compound. He was temporarily frustrated by this, but realized that it would take some time till he could resume work at his normal pace. He was also frustrated that he couldn't join in with the other authors on their Quixotic quest atop Rocinante. They were saddling up for battle, and he was without a horse.

Ann

THAT EVENING, Abby had stopped by to pick up Eric to go out to a movie. Jason had been reading, but as they left, he closed *A Prayer for Owen Meany* and sat in the chair thinking about the pair. They seemed somehow immediately compatible, although he knew next to nothing about Abby. Their calm ease with each other had him recalling the exact opposite in his early relationship with Ann.

Jason had fallen in love with Ann the moment he'd seen her in their Economics 101 class at the University of Washington. He had intentionally walked out of the lecture hall in step with her, acting like he was heading in the same direction. They'd struck up a conversation about hating Econ but needing this requisite course, and then a friend had caught her up and she'd peeled off down the quad with her. After several 'random' encounters, Jason had found that Ann was an interesting combination of bright, imaginative, and yet seriously practical and organized.

He and Ann had had lunch together several times and Jason had been very careful not to get too close. He hadn't wanted to spoil this, but had yearned to get to know her better. After class one Friday, he'd asked if she was doing anything that evening—the Campus Film Society was showing *Doctor Zhivago* in the Physics Auditorium—and he'd wanted to know if she cared to join him. Ann had said 'Sure,' uncertainly, but he'd noticed a big smile form on her face as she'd turned away.

They'd met at the College Inn which had been a big stretch for Jason. He'd visited the bar once before and, due to the irritation Jason often brought out in others, the result had been unpleasant. Luckily, this time had been different, and he and Ann had a beer, and then walked to the auditorium, Jason purposefully maintaining an invisible buffer between them, but happily engaged in conversation the entire way. When they'd taken their seats, Jason had realized what a bad idea this had been. The auditorium chairs had been fairly narrow, and it had been difficult to avoid brushing arms or elbows on their shared armrest.

The movie had started, and Jason had kept his left arm away from Ann, letting her rest her elbow on the common armrest. But Ann had obviously desired some form of contact. During one tense moment in the film, she'd reached over and grabbed Jason's hand and immediately jerked it back, at the same time suppressing a laugh. Then had come the scene where Dr. Zhivago was riding in a frigid freight car to Yuriatin in the dead of winter. Ann had been so tense that she'd again reached out and grabbed Jason's hand, this time holding tight. She'd sputtered to hold back a quiet giggle, but had then burst out into uncontrolled laughter during the dramatic scene. She hadn't been able to stop, but wouldn't release Jason's hand either. The entire audience had seemed to turn and stare at them and no indignant usher had been necessary to tell them it was time to leave. They'd risen immediately to flee the shushes and had ducked their heads as they made their way to the aisle and run out the exit, holding hands the entire time.

Once outside, Ann had given a shiver and then embraced Jason, hugging even tighter before pulling away and staring at him with a clenched grin. "Oh my God, what just happened?" she'd asked as she whirled around like a dervish and faced him again. "I mean that was incredible, Jason! What did you do?"

Jason had been dumbstruck, mainly at having held this woman's hand for as long as he had and to not having her be repulsed by the touch. "I didn't do anything. That's just how I am."

Ann had jumped forward and kissed him quickly on the mouth, rubbing her lips briskly with the back of her hand when they pulled apart. "Wow, it feels like I either just took some uppers, or drank a gallon of yerba mate. What is it with you? Are you plugged in or something?" She hadn't waited for an answer, but had kissed him again, more tenderly this time. He'd found her bouncing off the balls of her feet when they separated.

The result of this first date had been incredible sex that night. For Jason it had been his first time, and for Ann a completely new experience.

All of Jason's previous relationships had ended after the first or second kiss. The separations had mostly been amicable, and he'd heard the spectrum of excuses as to why the pair of them could never work. He'd laid near Ann watching her as she slept and had wondered what it was about her that made him the least bit tolerable. So, he'd asked her the next morning when they'd awoken.

"Hey, Ann, this might sound funny, but how can you stand me?"

"What do you mean? You're sweet and funny—what's not to like?" She'd laid her head on her curled arm and smiled.

After a few seconds, she'd frowned. "Oh, you mean your battery?"

"Battery?" he'd asked, but he definitely knew what she meant.

"Yeah. Touching you just juices me up—I've never felt anything like it. Kind of tingly, jangly, and buzzy all combined."

"I'm sorry, I can't like turn it off."

"No, no, it's kind of fantastic, but only in small doses."

He'd reached over to stroke her arm, but she'd pulled back. "Sorry," she'd said. "I love you, but my body needs a break." Something she would come to say more and more frequently throughout their marriage.

Ann had faced a perfect storm near the end of their marriage and had nearly perished at sea. Her position at Panhandle College became increasingly stressful as she advanced up the career ladder, and the calm waters she sought at home were found only in the occasional deep troughs between Jason and Eric. Jason was able to provide some mental calm, but his physical presence had meant that she could never totally relax—even when they had decided to sleep in separate bedrooms. And then Eric had required more and more of her energy—the energy she needed just to stay afloat.

The main thing Jason had wanted to do as he saw Annie slipping away was to hug her close to him—but rather than lightening her load, it would only add to the issues taking her under. Her psychiatrist had luckily become her lifeboat and eventually floated her away to a new job and a quiet cove in Cheney, Washington.

Luke

JASON NEEDED to pick up a prescription from Patterson Drugs downtown during his lunchbreak and walked through several residential blocks before arriving at the busier side-walks in the town center. He had an arrangement with the pharmacy to have his allergy medications ready at the side of the counter so that he didn't need to stand in line with the possible disturbances this could cause. He waved thanks to Marcie, who was also the saxophone player for the Rag Tags, after picking them up and wandered through the business district to see if there were any spots that were lightly frequented for lunch today. His favorite take-out deli had a line running out the door and most other spots were busy, so Jason decided that the sandwich he'd brought to the shop would have to do.

He was nearing Luke's video store, The Rewind, when he noticed that the string of people in front of it didn't seem to be entering the door. Then he saw that they were holding small posters that said, among other things, 'Sin Shop' and 'Videos to Hell.'

Luke Thompson, a member of the author's group, had run this independent video store for years, but there were rumors that The Rewind was near closing due to the increasing popularity of online streaming services. His father had worked at the Redstar Mill, and Luke had written two historical books about the mill and logging that were published by the Dunkirk Historical Society. He was married with two children, and that left the author's group fascinated by his almost adolescent obsession with sex.

Jason was skirting the little protest when Luke noticed him through the window and came out of the store after him, stopping with Jason further down the sidewalk once they'd passed the line.

"Hi, Luke. What's going on with them?" asked Jason.

Luke seemed pleased to see Jason, despite the display in front of his store. "Well, they're obviously not fans of my business, that's for sure." He gave a wry smile. "Ever since the last election and your building going up for sale, they've been standing outside of mine. I wish I owned this spot, because they really seem like they want to buy it, and I'd have the chance to turn them down. But I just lease. Jim McBride, the owner, swears he'll never sell to the Entity, but they don't know that." Then Luke almost laughed. "The funny thing is that they also don't know that I'll be closing in a couple of weeks anyway. No one is renting videos anymore. Who knew? DVDs seemed like the space age when they came out. Now everything is available online."

"Oh, Luke, I'm sorry to hear you'll have to quit your business."

"Nah, that's OK, Jason. I've been expecting it for a few years now. I've invested, and my wife has a great job with Dunkirk General Hospital. We'll be fine."

They both stood and studied the solemn protesters. "The sad thing is, when I close, the Entity will think that it won. For the life of me, I can't think of a way to show the town that I'm folding on my own terms, but the drumbeat from the Entity is that my immoral business is next on their hitlist. I can't stand the bad optics of this, but I have to close by the end of the month no matter what happens."

The line shifted and the five smartly dressed men held their placards out for a customer so that he was able to clearly read what was on them before he entered the store.

"I hope to hell that McBride will hold out and put some other deserving business in my spot," said Luke sadly. "I've heard that despite his protests, his economic situation isn't the best right now..."

"Say," said Jason, "you don't happen to know your square footage, would you?"

"Yeah, about 1,200 square feet," answered Luke. "Why?"

"Oh, I'm still looking for another place to move my business into. But that sounds way too big for me."

Luke suddenly looked Jason in the eye. "You've just been through pretty much the same thing - the Entity swept in, ate up Vitus, and spit you out. Isn't that a pisser?"

Jason hadn't had anyone put the question to him that way, and it felt fantastic to be able to say, "Yeah. Yeah, Luke, it was an absolute pisser. I can't tell you how angry I was about getting kicked out." He took a breath. "But now it feels just deeply frustrating watching it probably happening again."

"I hear you," said Luke. "Like being herded into the slaughterhouse, one by one." He peered into the store window. "Well, a customer might be waiting." Then he paused. "Look at them. I've been watching them for the past two weeks at least. You'd think you would know everyone in our town by now, but do you recognize any of them?"

"Nope. None of them look familiar to me," said Jason.

"That's what I mean. They live here, but I have no idea who they are. It reminds me of that old movie about pod people," said Luke as he turned away and nodded to each of the protestors before reentering his shop. However, Jason had noticed that when he'd reached the last person in line, he'd adjusted the bridge of his glasses with his extended middle finger as he'd done so.

The Sign

JASON HAD taken a break from repairs and was practicing a piece for the Benewah Symphony Orchestra when he heard the basement door open and a woman's voice call out, "Hello?" and then immediately, "Jason?"

He set down the bassoon and walked around his work bench, feeling a certain lightheadedness on hearing her voice. He took note of the oddly welcome sense of anticipation on seeing Kris Seever. "Oh, hi Kris. It's good to see you again."

"Yes, wasn't that an interesting rally? Did you read about it later in the papers?"

"Yeah, it's all anyone's been talking about. And they still don't know for certain who took the books. Since that rally was pretty much ruined, my author's group is planning a demonstration to refocus the city on the library act."

"Oh, really? I'll have to make sure I go."

"Good, I'll try and let you know when and where." Jason paused. "So," he said reluctantly. "You're probably here for Kevin's instrument?"

"Oh, yes," she said. And then she smiled. There was something about the way her lips parted on her teeth, the lines around her eyes, and her eyes themselves that captured Jason.

"Well, I'm sorry to say that I'm still behind from the move and haven't gotten to it yet."

"That's OK," she said, much to Jason's relief. "I just thought I'd check while I was walking through the neighborhood. Quite the change from your old spot."

"Yeah," said Jason. "You can't believe how tight the real estate market is right now. I'm hoping that it's only temporary."

Kris commiserated. "You said this was a friend's house?"

"Yeah, a good friend of mine, Art Parker—the one who spoke last at the rally—was kind enough to rent me his basement space. I was skeptical at first, but it's slowly growing on me."

"But how do you attract customers down here?"

Jason's first thought was, *Well I'm attracted to you...* all the while knowing that the possibility was doomed. He immediately thought of Betta, and he'd been amazed that Ann had stuck with him for as long as she had.

He knew that Kris must be wondering why he was taking so long to reply, but he couldn't keep his thoughts from getting in the way of a response. *What if she's different?* he wondered. Again, Betta came to mind. He'd actually asked around town after experiencing Kris's first smile—his second meeting with her in his old shop—and found that she was a single mother, had moved to Dunkirk six years before from Indiana, was a weaver, and sold her fiber art through a space at the Redstar Mill. That was about all he knew. He'd resisted being a creep and googling more information about her. Besides, why research a failing prospect?

Jason cleared his thoughts, "Oh, sorry, I was thinking about what needed to be done on Kevin's horn. Well, the answer is that I haven't managed to attract too many walk-in customers yet. You're one of the first. Luckily, I have the school contracts to keep me plenty busy workwise, but I miss the personal interactions. Instead, now I need to go out for coffee or go shopping to chat with other people."

"Good," she said. "I hear it's healthier to stay socially involved. We can't all be hermits." Which left Jason wondering if she was including herself in that statement with the slight emphasis on the word 'all.' He was about to ask her about it when Kris turned to the door, and then back to Jason. "You know, this spot really isn't that far from the business district and a lot of people walk right by here." She stepped to the door and opened it. "Follow me."

It was when he walked out into the brilliant daylight that Jason realized what a dungeon Art's basement really was. Kris led the way out onto the sidewalk.

"If you just put up a nice sign on the street corner there," she said pointing, with Jason shading his eyes to follow her direction. "And had something to draw people to the door..." she turned back toward the shop entrance. "I don't know if you keep any instruments that are broken or lost causes, but if you do, you could put, say, a trombone with a sign on the corner, and then a... maybe a French horn hanging just above the door there... I bet people might start to come in once they noticed that you were here."

Now Jason grinned. "You know, that's a great idea, Kris. Thanks! As it happens, I do have a battered trombone, and a hopelessly destroyed coronet I could put up. It wouldn't even matter if the 'bone was stolen, it's in such sad shape. But it would be perfect for a sign." He thought for a moment. "And unique as hell."

Kris smiled back, which she shouldn't have done as far as Jason was concerned, since it made him like her all the more, despite the odds.

"You're welcome," responded Kris. She suddenly looked less comfortable and glanced at her watch.

Uh oh, she senses something, thought Jason.

"Sorry, I was out walking and just wanted to pop by and check on the progress, but I have to get to a Zoom meeting in like 5 minutes. I hate to run off, but I gotta go."

"Oh, no problem," said Jason, somewhat relieved that it was only a meeting causing her to leave.

"Do you mind giving me a call when the French horn is ready?"

"Sure, I think I have your number somewhere."

"Well, just in case, here's my card," Kris said while twisting around and reaching into her small backpack. He expected her to hand it to him, but as she reached out, it slipped from her fingers and fell to the ground. She made no move to retrieve it as Jason bent down to pick it up. He couldn't put his finger on it, but there was something oddly familiar about that tactic. It almost seemed practiced.

Even so, Jason breathed a sigh of relief that there was no danger of physical contact. "Ok," he said, tucking the card into his shirt pocket. "I'll definitely call you when it's done."

"Thanks, Jason," Kris said as she smiled again and headed down the sidewalk.

Well, at least that might not be the last time I see her, thought Jason as he pulled the card back out and studied it while heading through the sunshine to his cave entrance.

"THINGS ARE coming together for the demonstration," said Morgan. "But finding a date when we can hold it is problematic at the moment. We've narrowed it down to two different Saturdays, but are still waiting for the city's Event Planning Committee to let us know which one will work. It could be me, but they seem to be dragging their heels about this.

"By the way," he looked around the room. "Did everyone see that YouTube video of Ed Cutler donating his books to the library a few weeks back?" He then explained its contents to those who hadn't seen it.

"Lisa is livid about the donation," said Morgan. "She said that Cutler has painted her into a corner, and she thinks he knows he did it." With a conspiratorial look, Morgan continued. "She said that she has absolutely no room on the shelves for the books, most of which she says are poorly written anyway. She was going to quietly archive them, but the new library board member from the Holy Grace Church was adamant that they be included in the collection. Now Lisa is over a barrel. Adding the books will mean removing scores of other, better, books that people actually read, but if she doesn't, she'll be accused of bias by the church. She's furious that Cutler dumped the books on her. If he had created an endowment for a special collection, that would be something they could have handled by buying the necessary resources, but instead he is basically trying to fill her shelves with Christian propaganda and daring her not to put them in the stacks.

"She can't speak frankly about it to the board because of the new member, and she thinks that Cutler is banking on that. Anyway, I sympathized with her, but have no suggestions to help her out. A very canny move on Cutler's part—daring her to effectively ban the books he's given her.

"Sorry to take so much time, but I thought you'd all like to get caught up to date. I think Robb had something for tonight?"

"Yeah, Morgan," said Robb Fenton. "That sounds exactly like something Cutler would do. Coincidentally, you all know that I'm writing that book about them—the Entity, and so I wanted to share this new introductory chapter with you."

Tamra sat stone-faced. Kenneth fiddled nervously with his pencil, but he'd heard previous versions and was prepared for the reading. He wasn't a member of a church under the umbrella of the Holy Grace Church affiliates or otherwise would probably have left the room at this point. In fact, no member of the Holy Grace Church had ever been a member of the group.

"For some background," Robb continued, "I had a wonderful Thanksgiving with several friends last year, two of them Jewish, one atheist, and two protestants. Sounds like the start of a good joke, doesn't it? Anyway, the conversations were all over the map. But while we were on a tangent about how common slavery was in the Biblical era of Judaism, I started thinking about our get together compared to many similar dinners happening at that very moment all over Dunkirk. I realized that while the dinners might be similar, many of the conversations wouldn't be. There was a growing portion of the town that was not merely discussing Christian topics over their turkey dinners, but were also actively seeking to change Dunkirk into a town where every conversation, such as this one that we were having around the table, would be restricted to a single religion and its viewpoint—thrusting things back to the time of the Pilgrims, no less. For all I knew, many of them were plotting the next move in their takeover of the town at that very same moment. Remember, their stated goal is to slowly kick us out of our town. OK, so here goes."

Robb read from his laptop. "There are no artillery, Panzers, or Luftwaffe, in fact, no weapons involved at all, but like its namesake in France with the British troops on the verge of their miraculous escape from Dunkirk in World War II, the town is under siege. On one side in Idaho's Dunkirk, the conflict is a declared war, and that side is determined, purposeful, and relentless. On the other side, the conflict is largely unnoticed, and the reaction is mild whenever skirmishes break out. There is a certain angst on this besieged side, but no cohesive strategy of countermeasures or direction forward. And there is not a fleet of boats coming across the water to save them.

"In those skirmishes, the Entity is aggressively-passive, doing something provocative and then claiming that any reaction is taken out of context or overblown. To hear their side, it's the respondents who are overreacting, and they themselves are behaving normally or just joking around. Continually pushing boundaries and exerting their influence, the Entity goes against a city ordinance, say, and then backs away with hands raised saying, 'Whoa, why are you so upset? How could you think we were overstepping the line?" And, inevitably, when not getting what they want, they claim that they are being persecuted, or that they are exempt on religious grounds. It's a war of attrition, and they are slowly wearing down the rest of the community.

"With the church actively recruiting, new members arrive every year, swelling the ranks of the Entity. As we can see now, efforts by them to infiltrate the governing bodies of the Dunkirk City Council, school board, library board, or other organizations are becoming successful, and with newly developed Entity-oriented neighborhoods, the districts that include their swelling populations will eventually be overwhelmed."

As Robb continued, Jason thought about what the man had written given his history with the church. Robb Fenton was now a former Entity member with an axe to grind—much of what he wrote and spoke about seemed hyperbolic, but was nonetheless true. While a member of the church, he had been a local realtor and had been happy to find homes for those newly arrived in Dunkirk, especially those connected with or joining the church. The Entity was able to help with the vetting and securing of loans for its new members, making the process very easy for him.

All was going well until his wife, Susan, met the new, wealthy, deacon. Will Sommers came from a family of cattle barons in Texas and had settled in Montana where he increased his fortune by developing a series of ski and golf resorts there. He had then met the Holy Grace Church leader, Ed Cutler. Having retired early and with nothing but time and money on his hands, Will had moved to Dunkirk where he was welcomed into the higher echelons of the church, happy to fund the development of new church-friendly subdivisions and the acquisition of many downtown properties. He had also taken Robb's wife in the process.

The divorce between Robb and Susan had been acrimonious, and the Entity, needing to side with either Robb or Susan, had chosen Susan, and, of course, her new wealthy love, over Robb. Barely a ripple in the community, but a huge storm within the church, Robb had been driven out and was now shunned by all Entity members. His real estate company had gone under after all his church-member staff had quit and clients were steered away from him. Robb had eventually turned his life around with a new job and partner, at the same time becoming one of Dunkirk's most outspoken opponents of the Entity and its goals.

Jason tuned back into Robb's reading just as he finished. After taking comments, Robb unexpectedly jumped into another topic.

"We were talking about banned books, and I realized that one of the big push-button topics is religion. Any criticism of 'The Faith' becomes a huge target for book banners. So, taking the bait, I thought it would be nice to have a book available for kids that really makes them see how little sense it makes to take the Bible literally—as an accurate historical version of events. There are many believers who think that the earth is only 6,000 – 10,000 years old, just as God made it, and that everything written in the Good Book is fact. But if you take something like the Bible literally, then you have to accept that finding even one thing that doesn't add up, one flaw, brings the whole document into question as an accurate depiction of history or reality. Now, I'm thinking of taking the story of Noah's Ark as an example, and have laid out some impossibilities that even..."

"That's it!" Kenneth thundered, interrupting a startled Robb. "I've waited to see if you all were really going down this path, and now this is the last straw. I am not going to sit here and listen to someone attack my religion. We have enough trouble in the churches without teaching kids to turn away from the Bible." With that, Kenneth picked up his papers and coat and stalked out of the room without a look back.

"Kenneth," called Robb, and headed to the door after him. "Kenneth, wait!" he called down the hall. He shrugged and then returned to the table. "Sorry about that," he said with a sad expression on his face.

Jason had expected a few of the others to follow Kenneth out the door, but no one immediately stood up.

"See what you've done?" asked Sharon. "Somebody needs to go and apologize to Kenneth. He's a good man and a good author, and you've forced him out for no good reason. Just to make some political point? We need to all come to our senses and think about where this nonsense is taking us." She shifted agitatedly in her seat, but Jason noticed that she didn't follow her friend out. Yet.

A chair scraped and a silent Tamra stood, stared at Robb for a moment, shook her head, and followed Kenneth's lead. At the door she scowled at the group, then turned back to Robb. "You've become a bitter sinner Robb, and the church—any church—is better off without you."

The room was still for a moment after she left.

"But—so far, we're just exploring the idea, aren't we?" Dennis asked, perplexed. "I thought we'd agreed that we'd come up with book ideas, talk about them, and discuss how publishing them might affect the group. No one's even written a page yet as far as I know. Kenneth is just in a snit. And he and Tamra are very touchy about religious stuff, as we all know."

"I've seen his letters to the editor, and he is definitely a literalist, so I knew he'd be unhappy with what I thought I'd write," said Robb. "But I never imagined he'd just walk out." He looked down at some papers he'd brought. "I still think it still needs to be said, though. Even if it weren't for this censorship that's happening in Idaho, there needs to be some counter to the anti-critical thinking that's being promoted at even the youngest ages."

No one spoke immediately, so he asked, "Do you mind if I pitch my idea now, or should I wait?"

"Go for it," said Dennis, echoed by several others.

Robb took a breath. "There are so many things that you can pick apart in the Bible, even with the story of Noah. My idea is to make it simple, and I'm not going to calculate how it was possible for all of the animals to fit on the Ark, how Noah gathered them all up, or where the food was stored. Those are common questions and arguments. So, I thought I'd look at how they all survived."

He picked up a sheet of paper. "Now, this is straight from the Bible," he looked around the table for a moment and then began reading. "Noah had all of the animals loaded seven days before the flood hit. They rode the deluge out for forty days and then floated around for another 150 days before they came to rest on Mount Ararat. After two and a half months—that's 75 days—the mountains became visible. Then, forty days later, a raven goes out from the Ark. Now that makes sense—those are very brave birds and don't put up with much. Noah then sent out a dove, but it returned because of all of the water. Seven days later he sent it out again and it returned with an olive branch." He looked around. "One has to wonder where that came from. Seven days after that he sent out another dove that never returned. Then the Bible says that after another month and 27 days (57 days) the earth was dry. Nobody but those birds left the Ark during that entire time since the beginning of the flood which amounted to 7+40+150+75+40+7+7+57 = 383 days. There is another calculation, too, that adds up to within two days of the 383 days. The Bible also says that from the beginning of the flood till the waters receded till the time the dove returned with the olive branch was from February 17 till January 1 of the following year which is 317 days. So, we have 317 days, plus the 7 days when the other dove left and didn't return, plus the 57 days for the earth to dry out. Summed together this equals 381 days."

He set the paper down. "Some might concede that it was possible to have enough provisions on board for 40 days. But enough for over a year? That would be impossible by any standard. OK, then there are other questions. What would the carnivores eat during all that time? What about the animals that have a life span that is less than a year? What if many of the animals reproduced during that time period? And wouldn't the flood have wiped out most, if not all, plant life? How would the pandas get their bamboo, and the koalas get their eucalyptus? If the timeline is 6,000 years from when all of this happened till now, how did the slow-moving sloth get to South America—across oceans?" He paused. "I also wonder about the fish. The salinity would change drastically—mixing so much fresh water into the oceans and obliterating lakes and streams. How did the saltwater fish survive and end up back in the salty oceans, and *visa versa?*. I could go on and on, but you see where I'm going. With even this one story, it is impossible to take the Bible as anything more than myth and allegory. Why try and make it a literal document at all? I don't want more children falling into that trap, so I'm willing to write this book. And as befits our idea here, the religious right might see it as something worth banning from the children's shelves."

The room was silent for a moment until Dennis spoke. "Maybe it's a good thing that Kenneth left if he's a literalist. You've made some really good points, Robb, and I think it would be pretty tough for him to reason his way out of what you've laid out here. I, for one, had never thought about the duration of Noah's journey. I'm not religious, but if I was, I think I would either have to come to terms with what you're going to write or ban the book so that my kids never read it." He paused and then added. "Yes. It might be a good candidate for a censored book, if we decide to get some of our books banned."

Jason couldn't resist raising his hand, and when Robb acknowledged him, he said, "I'm wondering how you'll make this into a book for kids though. You said you want it to be illustrated?"

Robb nodded. "Yeah, and that's my stumbling block. I can see the pictures in my head and how to lay them out so that the days are easily counted and then added up at the end, but

I just don't know who could draw the pictures." He looked around the room, but his gaze predictably went back to Jason.

"I think I asked before—I don't suppose Eric would want to illustrate it, would he?"

Jason took a moment and then shook his head. "I'd say that's highly unlikely, Robb. I haven't had a chance to ask him, but I've never been able to excite him about a single one of my ideas for a book, and I'd be shocked if he went for this one."

"Should I get in touch with him? Just on the off chance that he might be interested?"

Jason shrugged his shoulders. "You never know with that guy," said Jason. "I'll try and broach the subject with him, too, but if he says no, that doesn't mean that there's no one else out there." He suddenly recalled someone local. "Don't forget that Sylvia Howe illustrates children's books, and she might also be a possibility."

"Thanks, I'd forgotten about her. I don't know her personally, but I'll try and reach out to her if Eric balks at my proposal. The more I think about it, the more I want to get the book out there and have it be read."

Then the group endured a very uncomfortable presentation by Luke about his outline for a pornographic novel. When Luke reached the next point in the plot, the entire room erupted raucous disapproval.

He'd introduced the concept of his book casually. "We'd said that if our books involved children, they were sure to be banned, so I have the idea of a middle school history teacher, Jeff, who's been secretly filming himself and a parent, Jessica, having sex in a motel room. He agrees to pick up Jessica's daughter for her after school as a favor. The kid is in his history class, so she trusts him, and he takes her to his house instead of Jessica's and gets her to..."

That's when the entire room exploded.

With Luke looking bewildered and the last shouts dying down, Dennis finally said, "Luke. In case you're not picking up on the vibe here, absolutely no one agrees that that is a good idea. Sex among consenting adults is fine for the adult section of the library. That's common in so many novels. But if you're suggesting that sex with a minor is a selling point, I think it's obvious that you'll find zero support here."

Emily had barely been able to sit through the presentation and agreed. "I'm going to be blunt here, Luke, and I hope you don't take it too personally. I'm trying not to see you as a total perv. But if you should happen to try and put this book out there, I'm afraid that that's exactly what you will be. A total degenerate creep. I'm not into it myself, but erotica is one thing, and this blatant amoral porno is something totally different." She was about to lay into him even more, but instead said, "This is a writers' group. We are all trying to be serious about what we write. Get some balls and suck it up. Erotic—OK. Kiddie porn—not happening if you want to stay in this group."

Jason and the rest were amazed at breezy, easy-going Emily's unexpectedly firm and articulate takedown.

"OK, OK!" said Luke with hands up. "I get it, I get it. I'm not necessarily into that kind of thing myself," the body language of the group as a whole showing that it wondered if this was really the case, "but I thought we were trying to get banned here."

"Oh, that will get you banned alright," said Dennis flatly. "And that is our goal. But we don't want to see you in jail and the rest of us ostracized from the community by association. You might want to think of a different angle—preferably with some redeeming social qualities in it."

Assuming that Luke was somewhat cowed by this, the group had to accept that this was not the case when at the end he said, "But the rest is good, right? Maybe I can have the daughter be just a little bit older and then seduce the history teacher?"

Emily visibly shivered at the suggestion, as the others shook their heads in unison.

Jason was a block from Gandalf's on his way home from the meeting when he heard someone shout "Hey, Jason!" He turned to see Luke come loping up to him.

"Hi, Luke," said Jason, thinking that he would want to get some feedback about his book idea.

"I gotta get to another meeting, but I thought you'd be interested in something," said Luke, panting a little. "We think we've found someone to move into my video store space after I close."

"Really? Anybody but the Entity has got to be great news."

"It sure is. I have a close friend down in Moscow who runs a women's shelter. I was talking to her about the Entity wanting to take over my space, and she said that she wants to expand to Dunkirk, anyway, and so is very interested in opening a shelter here."

"That's great! I hear we really need one."

"We do. Plus, Olivia thinks I'd be the perfect person to run it. I've talked with my wife and, if it works out, she might quit her job at the hospital, and we can run it together."

"Do you have any experience doing something like that? It might be quite the learning curve."

"Oh, heck yes. Before I opened the video store, I ran a recovery center in Bend. That's how I know Olivia. The job sort of burned me out, and that's why we moved here to do something different, but I'm refreshed now and ready to help out again. I'll let you know how things progress. See you, Jason," and Luke took off down the street, obviously late for that meeting.

Jason watched him go. After hearing his pornographic book idea, and now this announcement, he realized that Luke really was a complete enigma to him.

A Deepening Bond

ON HIS walk home, Jason found himself wondering about the fate of the authors' group. He doubted that it would fracture enough that it would no longer be viable, but Kenneth's sudden departure—followed on its heels by Tamra's—had been a wake-up call. The remainder of the meeting had been about this very topic, and a few of the members had said that they were on the verge of deciding, as Kenneth apparently had, that they might disassociate themselves from the group as well.

He hoped that it wouldn't come to that. Even though he wasn't a close friend of Kenneth's, he missed him already, and he realized that it was because this was his primary circle of friends in Dunkirk. The members of the group, Art, and some fellow musicians were the sum total of his social network. If the Panhandle Authors' Group should disband from lack of interest, or worse yet, animosity, his main social hub would disappear. He would be back to the days when he had no friends and only Ann and Miriam—but now he had neither of them. Although taken for granted lately, he realized how important his few friendships were, and this made him recall fondly the true friend he'd found in Miriam.

He and she had exchanged phone numbers at their first meeting and a few weeks later, Jason had received a call from Miriam asking if he wanted to get together for coffee again. For a moment he was unexpectedly skeptical. *How do I know she doesn't make a living conning people? Maybe she rides the buses of Seattle to find likely victims and then draws them in?*

But he immediately shook his head. *Nope, she's nothing like that. This is real, that sensation was real, and I'm going to meet her again for coffee on Thursday.*

And after the second meeting, Jason and Miriam met religiously every other Thursday at Catty's Corner. Charlie always gave them a special table, happy to see that Miriam had finally found someone she had such a close connection with.

Miriam had said that she'd known Charlie even before he'd started working at the restaurant some thirty or more years previously. He had been the best friend of her son's father. Jimmie had fallen for Miriam, but had disappeared soon after she'd discovered that she was pregnant. Miriam had suspected that it wasn't the pregnancy, but that being near her continually drove him absolutely nuts. Jimmie had shown his amorous side only when stoned drunk. Not that she had minded because no other man had even tried to get that close to her. She said that she'd heard he'd moved back to Mississippi and become a preacher. She'd tried to contact him, but never heard anything more from him, not that she was surprised.

Charlie had stepped up to the task in Jimmie's stead and had helped Miriam through the birth of Lamar and had stood in as a father figure for the boy. He and Miriam had had many discussions about her effect on people, and so when he'd seen her resting her hand on Jason's he'd known that the two were probably of the same kind—whatever that was.

"What's it feel like to you, when other people touch you?" asked Jason as he felt the warmth of Miriam's hand on his.

Miriam shrugged at this. "I don't know, just normal, I guess. Maybe some tingling or buzzing sometimes."

"For me, too. I don't know why we get such a reaction. I can't really imagine what we must feel like to everybody else."

"I know. People act like I have static electricity and zap them if they come too close."

"Yeah, maybe a slow zap. I know that's what Annie says. Makes her feel like she had a sudden jolt of caffeine, but not a sharp shock or anything."

"That's what Jimmie always told me. 'Woman, I love you, but you make me so hyped up all the time.'" She shook her head. "He did leave me the funniest note when he left though. It was a quote from *Hot Rod Lincoln*. I knew immediately what he meant by it.'"

Jason smiled at the song reference. "Sorry he left."

Miriam gave his hand a squeeze. "That's OK. Lamar and I are doing just fine without him. Maybe better than we would if he was here."

They sipped their coffees. "So do you mind if I ask what you did. You know, for a living?" Jason asked, hoping that the question wasn't too impertinent.

"Mary? The fingerprint lady?" she asked. "She gave me the idea that the police might be OK to work for if they hired somebody like her. So, when I moved to Seattle, I applied for a clerk job in their records section. I took a couple of years off when Lamar was born, but I slowly moved my way up till I was the head of records. I knew where everything went and where everything was. Then those damn computers came in, though. Once we got everything loaded into them digitally, the computer knew where everything went and where everything was, so I just spent my time twiddling my thumbs. I finally decided that my pension could carry me, so I retired. Good choice, too. I have my own time back."

Months after Jason and Miriam had first met, Miriam had invited him and Ann over for Thanksgiving dinner. He'd thought that Ann might balk at the offer, but instead she'd jumped at the chance to finally meet Miriam. Her initial skepticism on first learning of their encounter had faded, but she still wanted to check the woman out.

Carrying a bag of muffins and an apple pie that Ann had baked, they caught a bus to the Central District and walked a few blocks to find Miriam's place on 29th St. Jason had never visited her house before and he was interested to see what Miriam's homelife was like. The white-painted porch and matching columns that framed the entrance took up half of the small blue home's frontage and looked like an inviting place to hang out during summers. They climbed the three porch steps and knocked.

The door was opened immediately by a tall, thin man who appeared to be around 40 years old or so by Jason's estimation. "Hi, you must be Jason," he said with a smile. "And you must be Ann," turning to greet her as well. "I'm Lamar. Come on in." At Lamar's apparent insistence, the men shook hands, and Lamar immediately nodded. "Yep, you're just like Mama," he grinned. "You have the same buzz about you, like she told me."

"This I have to see," said Ann as she accepted his gentle hug.

They were greeted by the smell of roast turkey and Miriam turned from the kitchen with steamed glasses, quickly cleaning them and then wiping her hands on her apron to welcome her guests. "Ah, Jason and Ann, I'm glad you could make it," and she stepped in and gave Jason an unexpected hug. It was not a quick tap of arms on the back; it was an elongated embrace. He wrapped his arms around her slight frame and felt like he'd come home from a war.

Both Ann and Lamar were unphased as the two stepped apart. "You two are lucky," Lamar said to Jason. "Mama says that kind of connection is rare."

Miriam's caring embrace of her left Ann smiling and subtly bouncing on her toes. "Yep, you and Jason are exactly the same. How weird is that?"

Miriam smiled. "Or lucky, like Lamar said."

The four were sitting around the table after the meal when Ann asked Lamar, "What was it like growing up with a mom like that?" Looking around the table, she clarified, "You know, like Miriam and Jason?"

"Well, when you have kids, you'll know," laughed Miriam. This caught both Jason and Ann totally by surprise, as they'd only begun their relationship.

Ann seemed to recover more quickly than Jason and broke the awkward silence that followed. "You know, I never… I mean we have never even thought about that. But you know, that might really be why I asked in the first place."

"Well," said Lamar. "I didn't know anything different, so it was great when I was younger. Then friends started to not want to come by the house, and we learned that Mama shouldn't be going to PTA meetings and such, but Charlie would step in and take her place. There was one teacher who refused to meet with Mama at all after their first conference. And of course, there's Charlene."

At the questioning look from Ann, Lamar clarified. "My wife, Charlene. She says she loves Mama, and stops by often to say hi, but that's about as much as she can stand. Long dinners in a close room like this are out of the question, though." He thought for a moment. "Some people seem to be more sensitive to Mama than others, and we have no idea why."

"That means, if you two have kids, most of the work out in the world is going to fall on you, Ann," said Miriam. "You'd better be prepared for that."

"I can't imagine being prepared for children ever," laughed Ann. "So that's no problem at all."

Jason was so lost in the past that he was surprised to find himself suddenly in front of his own home. As he unlocked the front door, he welcomed the sense of comfort brought on by those memories that settled around him like a warm blanket on this cool night. And as time had passed, they'd found Miriam's words to have been prophetic. When they did have Eric several years later, much of the work had, in fact, fallen to Ann—doctor's visits, preschool activities, the challenges of early elementary grades, PTA—and Jason had done his best to make up for this lopsided arrangement at home, helping Eric with his homework and maintaining the house.

There had been no ignoring the fact that Eric was on the autistic spectrum. It was difficult for them to tell at first, and both Jason and Ann, as new parents, thought that Eric was merely strong willed with definite preferences. But his will and preferences came to define Eric's personality rather than being simply expressions of it. Eric was diagnosed with Asperger's in first grade, and the engagement of professionals had helped immensely. Both he and Ann had wished that they'd been more aware and taken steps earlier, but the diagnosis had explained so much and benefited them as much as Eric.

But by third grade, Ann had begun to see a therapist, and she'd had a nervous breakdown when Eric was in sixth grade. The divorce was finalized during Eric's freshman year. When Ann had left them, Jason had focused all his attention on Eric, from big-picture planning to micromanagement. And Eric had eventually, in his own way, risen beyond it. The first year of high school was difficult, if not impossible—Ann had facilitated all of their son's school, therapeutic, and interpersonal interactions. Without her there, Jason couldn't keep up with Eric's friend contacts and schedules, to say nothing of school activities and events. Eric had withdrawn and spent days holing up in his room drawing or becoming lost - binging videos or video games. However, unbeknownst to Jason, his son was internally taking the bull by the horns. A half year later found the boy more often than not ignoring his father's advice and help, and Eric was on the road to becoming a confident and independent young man—with the aid of programs that had been set up for individuals just like him.

Still, Jason blamed himself. He was convinced that the outward manifestations of his own condition, whatever the hell that was, had shaped Eric. Jason's inability to maintain healthy, constructive interpersonal relationships with the broader community seemed to be perfectly reflected in his son. Alternatively, he reasoned that Eric must have seen and internalized the reactions his father had caused in people and very few of those interactions had cast Jason in a positive light. Deep down, he knew that neither of these was the actual case and that autism had been there all along, but Jason's fatherly guilt always took over any time he thought of his son.

He had never discussed this with his Eric, but he found it very interesting that they each had different gene combinations that had led to similar outcomes, almost like a convergent evolution. They both dealt with society, and society with them, in very similar ways. He didn't know what ancestors of his own might have triggered Jason to be the way he was, but he knew that part of Eric's genetic background included some of his own. He'd always waited to have this discussion with his son until he was old enough and realized that the time may have finally arrived.

When Anne was with them, Jason had accepted that his was a supportive role—a character in the video game that was Eric and in the drama that was Anne. In truth, he and Eric were equals—to the point that their similarity—socially and with physical contact—was such that they tended to take each other for granted because their living situation now was so comfortable to the both of them. But lately Jason had found himself wishing that they were closer. He knew that Eric wouldn't be living with him forever and their current communication channel was so constricted that it might disappear if he ever left.

Thinking that now might be a good opportunity to talk with Eric about some of his thoughts, he started down the hallway to Eric's room. However, he could tell that with no sound coming from the other side of the door that Eric was either asleep or deeply engaged in an art project. Intrusion into either of these wouldn't lend itself to a heartfelt conversation since Eric needed time to transition from one event to another, so Jason mentally saved this for another day and turned back to the living room.

The Entity

HE WAS out running some errands when he drove past the Goodwin building. By chance, the traffic stopping for the red light had him positioned just across from the building's lobby where a small crowd had gathered. Jason recognized Ed Cutler, the leader of the Holy Grace Church, facing the group and obviously addressing them, so he rolled down his window to try and hear what was being said.

"… a dormitory for our expanding academy. And in this space," the man pointed to Jason's old shop, "is going to be our women's clinic."

The light changed and curiosity got the better of Jason. He took a right at the stop light and easily found a parking place on Main St. Climbing out of the car, he walked to the corner and back to a spot on the empty sidewalk across the street from the Goodwin where he could make out what was being said when no cars were passing. Public displays of militias were more common lately and Jason wondered if anyone else noticed the pairs of men in camo gear stationed at either end of the block Cutler was on.

To his surprise, Robb Fenton from the author's group had walked up to Cutler in the interim, and the pair seemed to be engaged in a tense exchange.

"Your belief is that the woman's place is in the home, and that the most important role for them is the family. Right?" asked Robb.

"As I said before, Mr. Fenton, we are here to present our vision for this building, and not to..." A car went by, then, "Will you please move on?"

"That was an easy question. A softball. Why won't you answer?"

"Because it is a waste of our time to engage with you. That's why."

"But you're being very duplicitous here, aren't you?" asked Robb.

"Duplicitous how?" asked Cutler.

"I'll tell you how. You have many publications and sermons where you state that the woman's place is in the home and that their most important duty—their duty to God—is to have and raise as large a family as possible. You want strong, large, families to serve the will of God. Isn't that so?"

Another two cars passed but Jason could see that Cutler was nodding and making a reply. Then he was listening to Robb.

"... will have male doctors examining your women in this very spot?" Robb was asking pointing to the former space of Woodwinds and Brass.

"Heavens no. We will have trained women seeing to our patients."

"Trained medically? Trained so that they know what they're doing?"

"Of course. This will be a place where women with any physical problems having children can be seen to in a safe and loving environment."

"By trained professionals? What if there are complications?"

Another damned car went by as Jason strained to hear.

Cutler answered in what appeared to be the positive, then "...safe environment with Christian values of procreation."

"How will it be possible, in a society where all of the women will be segregated and kept in a cloistered environment, for you to find these trained professionals? You have openly stated that no education for women is necessary after high school. Where will the female doctors or nurses come from?"

Cutler's face had become redder and redder as Robb spoke, but his outward demeanor appeared to be unchanged.

He stepped in close to Robb as if in confidence, placing a hand on his shoulder, and was speaking into his ear. At the end, Jason was sure that he could see "Fuck you!" mouthed by the frowning minister.

It was then that Ed Cutler noticed the camera held near them by someone who looked vaguely familiar to Jason. Cutler gazed at the ground for a moment and then transformed into the perfect image of sweetness and light. Jason was amazed that the change was so swift and complete. Even the beet red of his forehead had become pink again. Cutler leaned over and spoke to someone next to him who immediately looked over at the person taking the video.

"Now, Robb, if you don't mind, let me continue," sweeping Robb aside with a wave of his hand. And a pair of his followers ushered Robb out toward the street.

Robb was angry and shook off the pair, brushing his upper arms as they let go. He noticed Jason across the way, looked both ways to check for traffic, and then jogged across the road to stand near him.

"Robb! Good to see you," said Jason. "Looks like your little discussion is over?"

His friend seemed to ignore the question for several minutes as he took in what Cutler was saying to his followers back across the street. Then he turned to Jason and said, "God, I hate that man. Let's get out of here," and he beckoned Jason to walk with him around the corner and out of earshot of Cutler. As they left that block, Jason noticed that the nearest pair of militia men were standing as though at a post—unphased and unmoving—exactly as those at the library rally had done.

"I guess you'd call it a feud," said Robb as the pair leaned against the red brick wall across from Jason's parked Subaru. "I have a bad habit of trying to get under the man's skin any chance I get. They're very protective of him now, and he tries to appear in public at only controlled and orchestrated events, but they messed up on this one, and I was able to slip in."

His shoulders dropped, and he relaxed out of fighting posture. "For all of the good it does. We'll see what Darcy got on his camera."

"Darcy?"

"John Darcy. He's a reporter out of Boise working on blogs and podcasts about our state politics and he's also interested in the Entity. I've been helping him out as best I can—being on the outside now. The legislature has been so busy, he's mainly focused on tracking the bills as they are introduced, but he makes side trips when there are lulls. Cutler has piqued his interest."

"I think I can see why, but I hardly know anything about Cutler, even for all of the time I've been in Dunkirk. Rumors aside, that is," said Jason.

"Well, he moved here from Boise in 1990. His surname was already familiar around here because his dad had served as a state senator for several terms. He thought that he'd inherited the political mantel from his dad and had a good start by being elected the representative of our district for a single term. Then, one fateful day at a Chamber of Commerce meeting, Maggie had just finished giving a presentation about the Saturday Market when the entire room heard Cutler over a hot mike say, "All gays should be shot.""

"I seem to remember that, but I'd only just moved here and didn't take much notice."

"The rest of Benewah County sure did. The viral soundbite stuck in the minds of voters, and his re-election bid failed. Cutler then decided to embrace a group he'd been part of that would never question him or his authority again—he became a pastor in his church, aligned himself heavily with the powerful Christian nationalist movement, and he's never lost an argument since. He can deflect any criticism with Biblical quotes and circular reasoning and has become the driving force within the Holy Grace Church and even in the broader Christian nationalist movement.

"God, do I hate that man..." Jason heard the hard edge in his voice as Robb leaned sideways dramatically and spoke in a loud whisper, "He's a dickhead—the mutant cross between the guy in the American Gothic painting and an octopus." He watched Jason's face as his friend searched for the connection. "Think about it. With his shaved head, bushy eyebrows, and long face, he resembles that old guy with the pitchfork completely—sans glasses. But he's also an octopus—he can slither out of any situation and changes his colors immediately to match the scene. Did you see how red and inflamed his face became just now? And then it was suddenly pale again? He gives me the absolute creeps."

Jason nodded as he found himself in agreement. "Yeah, I see what you mean."

"But since he also resembles Stan Laurel, I see him as a clown," Robb said. "Have you witnessed his act during the holidays?"

He saw Jason's blank look. "No, of course not," continued Robb, "because it's for members only. Anyway, he has this schtick where he holds a big tee shirt cannon at waist level and fires—no, pumps—tee shirts out to the members at the other end of the church. The tees say things like 'More kids—more fun,' and 'My Man—Number One in this House.' He's almost a caricature of the macho male when he does this. Have you seen Randy Quaid in *Christmas Vacation*?"

Jason grinned, "Yeah, it's one of Eric's favorites."

"Remember? There's that scene of him on a winter's morning standing outside his RV in the driveway with a long sewer hose running from the vehicle. He's smoking a fat stogie and pumping sewage from groin level into the local storm drain with a leer on his face. They're both exactly the same. Both bombastic vaudevillians pumping it out for the money and the fame."

Knowing Robb's relationship with Cutler's church, Jason suspected there must be some exaggeration in what Robb said given that he, himself, had never met Cutler nor witnessed his holiday ritual. He asked, "But if he's such a clown, what explains his draw if it's so obvious that he's in it for himself and just acting out a part?"

"He's very charismatic. Now, don't misunderstand. It's me that sees him as a clown. He's smooth and well spoken, making sure to never come off as angry or aggressive. But that's just the public persona he's trying to project and protect. In reality, he's deadly serious. The man means business. He runs a very tight ship, controls its direction and every soul on board. He gets down to micromanaging personal—sometimes very personal—issues in his flock. Very personal."

"Oh, there you are Robb!" said a man as he ran up, camera in hand. Jason now recognized him as John Darcy.

"Yeah. Hi, John! Sorry—I just had to get away from that man once it was clear I was being escorted out. Did you get any good footage?"

"Yeah, I think so. I tried to question him after you left, but got the bum's rush before I even started."

"But you said you have an interview scheduled with him before you head back down to Boise?"

"Yep, tomorrow morning. We'll see how that goes."

Robb turned to Jason and said, "John Darcy, this is Jason Deakins, a fellow author."

"Pleased to meet you, Jason," said John, holding out his hand.

Robb was kind enough to quickly explain Jason's 'condition.'

"Really? Very interesting," said John, now studying Jason carefully. "Maybe I could talk to you some more about it sometime?"

Jason avoided an answer by saying, "Robb was just filling me in on Cutler and his background. I really don't know too much about him."

John Darcy quickly stepped in. "Did Robb say? He's actually the darling of two overlapping Christian groups. Where women are concerned, he's a Quiverfull and advocates a strong patriarchy, and where his flock is concerned, he meets across the country with leaders of Christian nationalist groups. As I've covered in a recent podcast, he's seeking dominion—a total Christian dictatorship.

"Sorry to back up—Quiverfull?"

"Oh, yeah. It's an actual Christian movement. That term comes from Psalm 127: 3-5, I think it is, where the Bible says that children are like arrows and every man should have a quiver full of them. It's a movement that thinks conception is a matter to be left up to God—and not to be interfered with. They also follow the notion that their duty is to fill the nation with as many Christians as possible."

"So, really, how much influence do you think Cutler has?"

Now Robb spoke. "Jason. Just look at our town. They have a seat on the library board and now two council members. He wants to take over the town, and it's happening before our eyes. I think that it's no coincidence that the state legislature is in lock step with what Cutler wants. They're making all of these laws that are slowly stripping women of any rights at all. They've made abortion illegal and are even talking about trying to control the ability of a woman to move across state lines to have one. They want to limit contraceptives and the morning after pill. They want to take away women's right to vote and have the man be the voice for the household. Make gay marriage illegal again? That's being pushed by them so that they can destroy families of same sex couples. And now they've adopted a Family Values Month where the glories of traditional families are put on a pedestal. They want women married, barefoot, and pregnant."

Robb took a deep breath. "I'm sorry, Jason. I try and not get too emotional about this, but to me it's serious stuff."

"That's OK, Robb. I was aware of the problem, but not its extent—and I think we all need to know."

"Well, it's bad," said John. "And on top of your local issues, Christian nationalism is on the rise nationwide, and none of these sect leaders live in isolation—they're all part of a greater movement that appears to be underground to us. Do you know the new term Cutler has come up with?"

Jason shook his head and John continued. "Gospelpocalypse. Can you believe it? He says that the word of the Gospel is going to come down on us like a hammer. He says that when the downtrodden evangelists become the majority and gain more power, the law of God is going to become the law of the land and that no one will be exempt from its terrible reach. It will be exactly like Sharia law that the Republicans are so terrified of.

"There is a very militant vocabulary being used now by Cutler and the Christian nationalists. They describe themselves as being in a war and that they are the soldiers of Christ, promoting dominionism and taking umbrage at secular law. But I'm afraid that it might be even more sinister than that. The senator from southern Idaho who introduced the militia bill in the first place is a devout follower of a Christian nationalist church down there. I can't prove it yet, but I've heard that the hidden agenda behind the legalization of militias in this state is to pave the way for a Christian army that will be ready to help enforce Christian law when dominion is achieved. I'm working at getting the evidence and want to create a dedicated podcast about it."

"Oh, jeeze," said Jason, glancing over to the street corner where the two militia men had just been standing. "What you've said is so damn alarming. What can we do to stop it? Call our legislators?"

John shrugged. "With the recently enacted school voucher bill that diverts funds for public schools to religious schools, attempts to require Bible reading in public schools, and other legislation like it, it verifies to me that the foxes of the Entity are already in the legislative chicken coop."

They looked at each other and each could sense the foreboding in the other's eyes. "The feathers are flying," said Robb bleakly to break the spell. "Say, John, I need to talk to you about your next podcast," and they said goodbye to Jason as they walked up the street. Jason felt that he should do something but had no idea what that could be as he opened his car door, wishing for an answer.

Clearwater

Jason knew that he'd extended his sax solo much longer than necessary, but it felt so good just to let it all out that it was hard to stop. He finally dropped back to some scattered clapping, and the eager guitarist bent a note into his own take on Selkirk Jump, a surprisingly popular number with a Latin flair that had been composed by their own keyboardist, Scott. Jason let his neck strap take the weight of the tenor saxophone and waited for the melody to come around before he could join in again. The crowd was amped up, and most in it were dancing to the livelier numbers. The band, the Clearwater, was playing at a wedding reception for a prominent local businessman's daughter in the Moose Lodge. It always made him feel complete to play for a lively celebration like this—part of the crowd and contributing to the energized scene, but at the same time apart from it on the stage.

Jason was sure that the dancers could sense a little of what was behind the solo he'd just played, but they probably didn't know that he was expressing his frustration and disappointment with recent events—Becca, the move, censorship, his recent conversation with Robb—all of it was adding up. And it didn't matter to him if they couldn't tell because it helped him heal, nonetheless. Music had always been his safe haven.

He had become increasingly isolated in middle school and would have been completely lost in high school, but for a transformative refuge—band. Rather than dreading practice time or daily band sessions, as did many of his peers, he found immersion in music to be his comfort zone. He would hide out in the instrument room during breaks and try out various instruments—eventually he was able to play nearly all of them.

The only problem with performing in bands or orchestras was that it required mixing with the people playing the other instruments. No one wanted to sit near him. When he had tried out for clarinet and was awarded the second chair assignment during his freshman year in high school—beating out juniors and seniors for the spot—the displeasure of his bandmates became readily apparent. He was sabotaged. More times than he could count, he would find that he had a broken reed or something disgusting had been stuffed into the bell of his instrument. Once, just before a concert, someone had removed the tiny screws from several of the instrument's keys, rendering it unplayable.

The concert band conductor had personal issues with Jason which were never articulated, but obvious, nonetheless. Mr. Merton was, however, struck by Jason's talent. The final solution for the remainder of Jason's time in the high school concert band was for him to play the bassoon. No one sat next to the bassoonist, he had his own musical parts, and he shone whenever the score featured a bassoon solo, which was rare. In pep band, he played one of the big tubas at the back of the stands, and in jazz band, he played the vibraphone—standing apart from his seated bandmates. So, for him, high school meant surviving classes and then devoting the rest of his time to practicing his various instruments. The vibraphone was special to him, since he was allowed to play it by himself after school in the big concert hall where he became lost in jazz improv for hours at a time.

Jason was brought back to the Moose Hall as the guitar player gave the cue, and they all hit the main melody of Selkirk Jump to end out the song.

They took a break when the tune finished, and the band wove their way through the tables on the left to the bar for some of the gratis refreshments. Jason noticed that the end of the counter near the wall to the left was free of customers, and so he headed there and had plenty of space around him, with the wall as a sure buffer on one side. He finally caught the bartender's attention and ordered a pint of an IPA. He'd just taken a few sips and was turning to the side to check out the crowd when three guys, who had obviously been partying since the beginning of the reception, came up to claim the space between him and the next person down the bar.

Jason quickly set down his glass and was taking a step back from the bar but couldn't avoid being squeezed into the small space between them and the wall. The man next to him who was doing the squeezing suddenly turned on him.

"Hey! What was that for, fucker?"

Before Jason could react, the man squared up, grabbed Jason by the collar, and with both hands slammed him into the wall. Letting go of Jason's shirt, he was pulling back his fist to strike when the alert barman and two of Jason's bandmates intercepted the arm's trajectory and turned the three rowdies away. Two of the drunk trio were asking their partner what the hell that was all about as they were ushered to a different section of the bar. The third man looked both angry and confused and was obviously having a hard time expressing why he'd wanted to beat up a member of the band.

A shaken Jason thanked his friends and the barman, unwound his own fingers from a fist, grabbed his beer glass, and disappeared to the small alcove behind the stage. *God damn it!* he swore to himself, slamming his glass down on the top of a spare amp and quickly picking it up again to suck up the resulting foam. He sat on a folding chair and tried to recompose himself. An altercation like this hadn't happened to him in quite some time because he always took pains to avoid any situation that might cause it. But now it had, and some old, shrapnel feelings tore themselves to the surface.

His first solo in the next and final set was terrible—filled with only anger and those past memories. He deferred anything but playing backup for the next three numbers and then bowed out for the rest of the set with a wave of apology to the keyboardist as he headed for backstage and his instrument case.

Once in his car, he didn't start it, but pounded the steering wheel before gripping it tightly and staring out at the jammed parking lot and the tall dark trees beyond. Not only was he pissed off at being shoved into a wall, but he was also angry with himself. He'd been ready to fight. That was something he hadn't done in ages, although he'd been close a couple of times—like tonight. Memories of his scrappy past came flooding back as he waited to calm down.

Socially, the senior year of high school and the one that followed graduation were the worst for Jason. Tired of being in the 'out' crowd, and basically friendless, he'd spent those two years trying to force his way into acceptance. He crashed parties, showed up at dances, and leaned heavily on substances to help him navigate.

Starting off with the best of intentions at parties, simple banter would become an argument, and congenial pats on the back would become a shoving match. At heart a peaceable young man, he got into more fights than he could count during that period. The alcohol was, naturally, counterproductive, and always inflamed the situation.

In the end, there were two or three of the local guys who would actively seek him out for a fight, and he was soon made unwelcome everywhere. Finding a job in any downtown business was, of course, out of the question given his reputation.

He eventually came to realize that his gap year had been a huge mistake. Or at least what he had chosen to do with it had been—which was to try and fight his way into inclusion. Luckily, at the nadir of that bleak period, his father had steered him into two decisions that changed his life: a summer job with the Forest Service, and application and acceptance into the University of Washington in Seattle's music program.

With these memories of his dad's intervention and advice, Jason's fingers had eased up on the steering wheel, and he listened to the thump of the bass and drums of Clearwater as he drove out of the parking lot at a practiced, measured pace.

Fishing

J ASON FOUND Art just where he expected him to be—standing on a short, tilting wooden pier on the edge of the St. Joe River, a short walk downstream from town. He watched as Art took in line with his left hand and began to whip increasing lengths of it out over the water until he let the entire stretch of line settle out over the stream. Art seldom caught anything worth keeping and knew that the better fishing lay further upriver, but he said that this was his meditation.

"Catch anything?" asked Jason as he came up beside his friend.

"I'm fishing, not catching at the moment," smiled Art.

"Not the right time of year for trout, anyway, is it?" asked Jason.

Art shook his head. "It was fun to be able to play music outside again," he said to change the subject. The Rag Tag Marching Band performed for any worthy cause or demonstration in town—rain or shine, and on Saturday for the Pride march, it had been shine.

And then, with a laugh, "And Trent didn't end up with a bloody lip this year."

"I know. I'm so glad that the neo-Nazis didn't show up as expected," said Jason.

Last year, the march to Riverside Park had been met by eight uniformed neo-Nazi militia at the entrance. These red-shirts had held their flags and banners in such a manner that Trent, the Rag Tag's trombonist and leader, would need to walk through them to reach the park. Trent, apparently feeling that some pushback was necessary, had begun playing his horn straight into the faces of each of the men, swinging the bell and slide of the trombone around with each beat of the Dixieland song they were playing. His motions had set the flags to waving back and forth. One of the last presumed Nazis in line had taken exception to this and had grabbed the slide of Trent's horn as it swung toward him and had yanked it free from the instrument. Unfortunately, during the process, he had shoved Trent's mouthpiece against the trombonist's mouth, causing his lips to begin bleeding, and the Nazi had fallen over backwards as the slide left the horn.

A huge uproar had erupted from the crowd in the park, and a silent signal among the Nazis had them suddenly running along the edge of the park to jump into a waiting black van. The police, slow to read the situation and slower still to pursue, had been left watching helplessly as the neo-Nazis had sped out of sight on the road along the river.

This year, the town had expected a huge militia turn-out and the media had assembled in anticipation. However, the opposite had occurred. The supportive crowd had more than tripled in size over the previous year's, and the militias were a complete no-show—probably due to the huge media presence and much to everyone's great relief.

"But they might have come," said Art, watching the fishing line float slowly downstream. "You know, the Deep South was always the stereotypical seat of racism and bigotry. Remember Neil Young's song, *Alabama* in the '70's?" Art asked, turning his head to Jason. "Or maybe you're too young—no pun intended. Well anyway, I think things may be getting better down there in the South, at least I hope so. However, the Shallow Inland Northwest is quickly becoming what the Deep South was with the same racism and bigotry, but unfortunately lacking the long and deep-seated history and culture."

"Well, I'm flattered that you see me as young," laughed Jason. "The Shallow Inland Northwest—I love it!"

Jason knew that the Inland Northwest was becoming more and more conservative and that white supremacists had a record, with varying degrees of success, of establishing themselves in the northern part of the Idaho panhandle. A call to make the area a redoubt for Christian nationalists was being heard, and religious right-leaning wealthy transplants, especially Californians, were buying up properties throughout the region, especially since the COVID pandemic had freed many of them from their offices and desk jobs. The Idaho Republican party was embracing the Make America Great Again movement and had a stranglehold on the state's politics. The values embraced by Idaho's right wing even extended beyond the state. Several counties in Oregon had voted to remove themselves from Oregon and join a Greater Idaho, should it be formed, and the sentiments of many Eastern Washington residents ran along the same vein.

"We don't actually see much racism here in Dunkirk," Art continued, "but only because there are so few people of color here anyway." He began to pull in the line. "But that thing up in Coeur d'Alene really ticks me off."

"What thing?" asked Jason.

"Just a sec." Art finished taking in the line and then began the beautiful looping casts that finally settled the fly at the end far out into midstream.

"You hadn't heard, Jason? NCAA tournament basketball games were held in Spokane, but the hotels were too full to hold all the teams. A Utah women's team had to stay across the Washington/Idaho border in Coeur d'Alene and bus the half-hour trip over the state line to Spokane for the games. They ended up only spending one night in Idaho, though. They'd walked over to a restaurant for dinner and were harassed by a truck waving a Confederate flag with the driver yelling racial slurs at them as they did so. On the way back to the hotel, more racists showed up and harassed the ladies with their roaring trucks.

"To make things even worse, when they went down to the bus the next morning, a militia had gathered near the entrance. Their leader later said that they had heard about the incident and had assembled to assure the safety of the basketball team. The team's coach said that based on their demeanor and aggressive stances, he had the impression that the militia was there to marshal them out of town. They felt very threatened by the whole situation. That day, the NCAA found the team rooms in Spokane where they felt safer."

"I hadn't heard—it was on the news?"

"The national news, now. You know what? I've had it. I've been thinking about this for a long time, but I'm finally going to put an advertisement in the paper that asks why on earth any company or family that isn't a white nationalist would even want to consider moving to this state. Especially if any of their members are non-white or of different gender identities or sexual orientations. This kind of thing is costing the state potentially valuable members of society and economic growth, and I can only see us going downhill from here.

"The state legislators..." There was a tug on the line, and Art reeled it in without much effort. He'd caught a small brown trout that he carefully removed from the fly and let slip back into the river. Then he recast out into the same spot.

"Where was I?" asked Art.

"You were saying that you were going to place an ad," reminded Jason.

"Oh, yeah. The state legislators—mostly Republican, the party supposedly of no governmental interference in our lives —are passing legislation that manages down to the cellular level now and they see no consequences for their actions. I think it should be made abundantly clear that if you are different in any way from straight white male, you will suffer here. You will become an unwelcome commodity rather than a valuable person with freedom and rights.

"It's bad enough that that team had to move to Washington, but no one has talked about the costs. The hotel they were in lost revenue, the restaurants and shops lost money because the team didn't feel welcome. Then there are plenty of sports fans who would now think twice about ever visiting Coeur d'Alene, to say nothing of other tourists that might have been thinking about checking out the town and northern Idaho and will now go somewhere else."

"You know you're preaching to the choir here, Art," said Jason. "I sometimes wonder if it's worth staying in the area myself. Luckily, Dunkirk, and I guess Moscow, are still little islands of sanity, but the tide's rising."

"I wish the fish were," said Art as he began the casting process over again. Jason could appreciate how Art saw this as meditative, without all of the conversation, of course.

"I had lunch with Maggie the other day," continued Art, "and she said that she knew of two same-sex couples who were selling and moving to a more friendly state. The legislature has been enacting all sorts of legislation that is controlling and suppressive, but hasn't faced the consequences of its actions yet. The economy is still doing good, but society isn't. I want the economic implications to start sinking in. So, given the fiasco in Coeur d'Alene, instead of saying, 'Please come to Idaho, we didn't mean it,' I'm going to give them all of the reasons that they should stay away."

"I can't wait to read it," said Jason, quickly looking at his watch. "I have to go pick up an order at Morgan's before he closes. Are you going home soon? I can walk you back up."

"Nah, I think I'll keep trying my luck for a while. Have a nice evening, Jason. And say hey to Morgan for me."

"Will do, Art," said Jason as he stepped carefully off the pier and began the walk into town. He turned for a moment to watch Art make another cast, the long shadows from the trees on the opposite bank nearly reaching the old man now and wrinkling when the line hit the water.

Morgan

JASON WALKED up Main St. to Quality Printing and Copies owned by Morgan Grant and stopped in to pick up an order of business cards he'd requested due to his forced change of address.

"Hi Jason!" greeted Morgan, looking up when the door chimed. He set down a stack of lime-colored paper and hit some buttons on a copier. "Your cards are ready—just a sec and I'll get them." Morgan was a big man but moved easily and was at the sales counter in a moment. He pulled out the sample card from the top of the order and, being accustomed to Jason's preference for no contact, set it on the center of the counter for Jason to examine. "How are you doing?" he asked.

"Fine, Morgan. And you?" Jason replied as he looked the card over. "These look great."

After settling the bill and some small talk, Jason asked, "Have you thought more about your book on communism for possible banning?"

"I have. In fact, I've been grabbing free moments here at work to jot down some ideas, and they're different from what I was originally thinking about. Can I ask your opinion about one that I had?"

"Sure, I'd love to hear it."

Jason was certain that the big Samoan was looking somewhat bashful.

"It's a little embarrassing since I haven't run this by any-one yet, but here's what I've come up with. You're familiar with Chairman Mao's little red book?"

"Yeah, but I've never read it."

"I was thinking of something similar to it, like 'Morgan's Better Red Book.' It would be geared for young adults, or an easy read for adults. Following the structure of Mao's book, it would lay out snippets of ways society could operate, and people's place in the society, if things were fashioned in a more communistic—no, socialistic structure. It wouldn't hit anyone over the head, but would be more, 'Hey, what if we did X instead of Y' kind of a thing. What do you think?"

Jason pondered the idea for a minute. "I guess I would need to see some examples first, but if it's in an easy-going format so that it wasn't rejected out of hand, it might be some-thing that would work. You should mock it up and see what the group thinks."

Morgan smiled. "Thanks, I think I will. I just need to find the time to do it!"

"I know what you mean. Hey, thanks for the cards, Morgan."

"Anytime, Jason."

As Jason pulled the package off the counter, Morgan asked, "By the way, have you heard the latest about the Redstar Mill?"

"No, what about it?"

"Well, two things have happened nearly simultaneously. A few days ago, our legislature declared that there was a budget shortfall in education and decided that there needed to be cuts to the university system—including Panhandle College. They specifically targeted the Mill and said that money was being wasted by having off-campus facilities—the pottery kiln, glass blowing furnace, and the woodworking shop located in the Redstar Mill were all highlighted. They said these operating costs were beyond what the budget could absorb. They are going to close everything on the ground floor of the Mill by the beginning of next semester. End of discussion."

"I can't believe it. That will be a huge blow to the Mill. I hear that it's struggling somewhat anyhow."

"It is. It only has like a seventy or eighty percent occupancy rate right now, and the co-op is having a hard time keeping it up. But you haven't heard the worst."

"Uh-oh. What could be worse than that?"

"Now, this is very suspicious if you ask me, but yesterday, Will Sommers—that deacon or elder or whatever he is with the Holy Grace Church—he has made a very generous offer to buy the building."

"What in the world does he need another building for? Especially the Redstar Mill—that's one of the main economic anchors of Dunkirk."

"Get this. To expand Cutler's 'Academy of Christian Business.' There was a press release this morning, and he's outlined the zoning application, the business plan, the academic structure, and the upgrades that he'll make to the Mill once it's acquired."

"Oh, surely the co-op will turn him down," said Jason. "They'd be the first to say, 'fuck no' to the expansion of the Entity."

"You would think," said Morgan. "But I talked with Julia Reems, the head of the co-op board, this morning, and she said that without the payments from the college coming in, there is no way in hell they can afford to keep it open. It was pure luck that the college put the facilities in there in the first place, but without them, the rents paid by the current occupants won't even pay for insurance. She basically said that they were screwed by the legislature."

"There just has to be a connection between the two announcements," muttered Jason. "Don't you think? I mean, Dunkirk has always been hit from both sides—the Republican right wing and the Entity. But to think of the two working together…"

"Yeah," said Morgan, now hanging his head a little. "My fear exactly."

Jason was at the door. "Not to mention the kick in the gut to the college's ceramic arts program," he added as he was stepping outside.

He watched Morgan, standing behind the counter, dramatically sink his head onto his hands as the door closed.

The Ad

JASON OPENED the paper the next evening, read the depressing article about the Redstar Mill, and then halfway down the next page saw that Art had carried out his threat to publish a half-page ad in every newspaper in the state.

Welcome to Idaho!

You're thinking of moving your family or business here?

You are indeed welcome, but please be aware that The Idaho Way may not be for everyone. This state is not the Gem proclaimed in its nickname.

If you are a business, you will receive great tax benefits, but remember that means the money must come from somewhere, and that is from cuts to important programs and from support by the rest of the taxpayers, including you as a new resident.

If you have a wife, daughters, or female employees, remember that 35% of OB/GYN doctors and nurses have already left the state, meaning some towns have no prenatal care because any pregnancy complications may lead to criminal consequences if they occur in this state. Abortion is illegal here, and leaving the state to find one may soon be, too.

If you have children, your schooling choices may be complicated. The state has passed a tax credit to allow public funds to go to private and religious schools, severely impacting the public school system. It may push you to private schools, vastly increasing your personal costs should you choose to send your children there. These schools would have little or no governmental oversight.

Also, if you have children and want them to be well-read and informed citizens, realize that local librarians can now be fined and face court expenses for providing you with the materials you may prefer your children to be exposed to—all the way through high school.

Both open and concealed carry of weapons are permitted in this state without a permit for those over 18 years of age, so that may either comfort or deeply concern you as you hike, walk around town, or attend crowded events in our fair state.

Similarly, the state has now acknowledged the formation of private militias, so that the attendance of any event that opposes their worldview may become dangerous, and they may 'strut their stuff' for no other reason than to make themselves visible. If there is an emergency, I would recommend that you trust only trained, licensed response personnel.

If you, members of your family, or of your business are persons of color, LGBTQ+, or transgender, you or they may find yourselves unwelcome by many who live here. Your collective level of discomfort may affect your desire to stay. If those members are transgender, they will have difficulty with their choice of restroom, and transgender care may be severely limited or impacted by recent decisions.

Finally, there are cities in Idaho that have religious leaders who make no bones about their desire for their sect to take over towns, and they are actively pursuing that goal. Establish your business with the knowledge that there may be efforts to push you out unless you are a sect member.

Otherwise - Welcome to Idaho!

PAG Meeting - May 5

THE NEXT Panhandle Authors' Group meeting had an odd beginning. As the writers arrived, they noticed several unfamiliar people holding to-go coffee cups and standing next to the entrance to the group's reserved room in Gandalf's, simply staring at each member as they walked in. One of the last to arrive was Dennis, and he stopped at the entrance, looking first into the room and then back at the strangers. "We're having our authors' group meeting here. Can we help you?" he asked one of them. There was no reply. They all averted their eyes, but stayed where they were.

Dennis shrugged and pushed the door closed behind him. "What's with them?" he asked the group while throwing a thumb toward the door. Several said they had no idea, but Robb said, "I recognize a couple of them from the Entity."

"But why are they..." began Dennis, and after a pause, "Maybe Kenneth said something?"

Robb shook his head, "He's not one of them. They do this. They target someone or a group and just start following them around as if to say, 'I'm watching you.'" He turned to Tamra who apparently had decided to still attend the meetings. "Do you have any idea, Tamra?"

She looked surprised at the question. "No. Why would I know?"

"Creepy," said Maggie, and the meeting began.

Robb updated them on his progress and difficulties in finding an illustrator, and both Terry and Sharon read chapters from their non-book banning books.

During a quick break, Robb walked over to Jason and said, "Hey, Jason, I thought you'd be interested to hear that John Darcy is being sued by the Entity."

Jason thought for a moment, *Darcy?* "Oh! The blogger who was interested in Ed Cutler at the Goodwin building ceremony?"

"Yeah, him. I heard from him and found out that this is the second time he's been sued by Cutler."

"Sued for what?"

"This time, it's for allegedly recording him illegally at the ceremony."

"But it was a public event. Or at least it was outdoors and available to anyone who walked by."

"That's exactly right. It seems that the Entity will sue at the drop of a hat. Luckily, John said his lawyer isn't worried in the slightest, and this will be another suit that comes to nothing."

"That's good to hear. It makes me think that you need to keep your head down a little, though."

Robb grinned. "If they sue me for anything, they'll find out how much I have to say in court."

Jason began to see that there was more spunk to Robb than he had thought.

Returning from the break, those who went to the restroom reported that the lurkers in the hall were gone. Moving on to group issues, Morgan spoke up. "Well, it's starting to happen. The public library in Donnelly, Idaho has declared itself an 'adults only' library. Apparently, they were too small to be able to segregate the minor patrons from the adult ones and, because of the newly enacted *Children's School and Library Protection Act* signed into law by our governor, the library decided to exclude minors—which would include many high school seniors, by the way—because of their inability to properly section off portions of the library. The ambiguity of the law and potential for lawsuits have all the librarians in the state on edge."

"Yeah, just think about it," mused Dennis. "Most high school seniors about to go off to college can't enter their city's main public library section on their own. It's just gone too far."

"Wait till you hear this," said Morgan. "I also saw a social media posting of a sign in an Idaho Falls library that read something like 'STOP—you must be at least 18 years old to enter this main section of the library unless accompanied by a legal guardian,'" said Morgan. "And did you see today's news? A mother with her young daughter and a new baby tied in a sling went into the same library. The mom and her daughter both had library cards and so thought that everything was OK. The daughter was with her mother who, naturally, was her guardian, and she held the required library card. The librarians were extremely apologetic, but pointed out that since the infant the mother was carrying was a minor and had no library card, they couldn't let her into the adult section—which was in fact most of the library—because they were afraid of the library's liability under the new law. The infant couldn't even talk yet, let alone read. We're sliding down a very slippery slope."

Harry, who wrote westerns and hailed from southern Idaho, chimed in. "Yeah. The population of Donnelly is only something like 250 people so I can understand their decision. The library must be tiny. But the population of Idaho Falls is like 60,000 and has a much bigger library. It's sad that they feel the need to protect themselves from being sued by roping off the majority of their holdings."

Morgan was irate. "I can't wait for the demonstration to be approved so that we can do something more effective than sending in our individual letters and phone calls. Our voices need to let the governor and the damn legislature know that we're livid about this fucking new law. We're authors for Christ's sakes. The whole reason we write and create is to get our ideas and visions out into the hands of the public. Book banning aside, this is censorship, and something like that could become a monster that eats up our histories, philosophies, and even religions that aren't in the mainstream."

"We won't have to wait much longer for the demonstration," Dennis reassured the group. "We had some trouble with permits, but it's now moving ahead."

"It's going to be a big event, I'm sure we'll all be there to show our support," said Maggie.

"You're just assuming that we're all in on this," said Sharon a little sternly, as was her style. Surveying the faces around the now quiet room, she realized that they nearly all were.

"Well, I'm certainly not," spoke up Tamra, siding with Sharon.

They were nearing the end of the meeting and expecting Carmine's presentation when, to everyone's utter surprise,

Charlotte made an announcement. "I've thought long and hard about this, but I feel it's the right thing to do. At first, I thought you were all raving mad for going down the book banning route, but now I agree with you. Who's to say that someday someone will find *Little House on the Prairie, Anne of Green Gables,* or *Little Women* objectionable for some reason? I suddenly came to see that no one is really safe once certain extreme viewpoints take over. If you don't like a book or its author—just don't read it, I say. So, I'm also going to try my hand at a book that might be banned but is about something that needs to be said."

"What's it going to be about?" asked a fascinated Emily.

"I think that the recent discovery of 215 children's graves near that Catholic school in Kamloops was one of the worst things I'd heard about in a long time. I'm going to have the children in my *Palouse Kids* series travel up to British Columbia with their mom in 1910 to visit their mom's sister there. I'll somehow work in that some of the sister's children had indigenous friends who suddenly just disappeared. And I'm going to really go after the Catholic Church and its ability to cover something like this up for all this time. Plus that this happened to only indigenous kids will be the central point. At least that's as far as I've gotten for a draft.

"Now, you all know that I'm a devout evangelical Christian, and you might suspect I'm using this as an excuse to go on an anti-Catholic rampage. But that's not the case. The disappearance of thousands of indigenous children across Canada caused by anyone is a tragedy that needs to be spoken of. Those kid's stories need to be told." She took a moment and then looked around the room. "I'm as surprised as anyone here by my change of heart, but I wouldn't have had the courage to write something like this until you all started testing the boundaries of what's supposed to be acceptable literature for children."

"Thank you, Charlotte," said Dennis. "I'm so impressed that you want to write about something that you feel so deeply about, and yet something that might get pushback from readers. I hope you write it, and I actually hope it doesn't get banned but gets read."

The mood had become sober when Carmine was next on the agenda to present another selection of poetry. As was his custom, he set out the plastic cups and the bottle of Glenlivet. He nervously shuffled his papers as those who wanted poured themselves some of the whiskey. Not more than two words of the first poem had passed Carmine's lips when his fingers holding the pages trembled, and he stopped.

"This is weird," he said, and stared for a long time at the words before him.

The room was silent, but for plastic rubbing on wood as cups were picked up or set back down.

Looking up, Carmine said, "Uhm. Yeah. For the first time, I don't really feel like the poems I was going to read match the occasion."

Harry of all people, who was mainly silent at meetings and obviously hated poetry, couldn't help but say, "But this isn't a special occasion—it's our regular meeting where you always read your poems."

"Yeah, but this meeting changed," said Carmine. Struggling for the right words, he continued. "I mean, our meetings are just meetings. You know. Somebody reads something, and we all say what we think and then get on with our lives. But now it's something different. I mean," looking suddenly at Charlotte, "even Charlotte is moved to write something that makes a difference—something that might even get banned."

Seeing that everyone was seeking clarification, he cleared his throat and said, "I write the same thing every time. I know I do. I thought that poetry came from someone hurting someone. I thought that was the inspiration. But now it just seems to really be saying nothing about nothing."

"Now, Carmine," said Jason. "Your poems aren't about nothing. They're nothing of the kind. They're insights into your feelings and emotions—very valuable sources for poetic inspiration, I'd say."

"Then why does it all of a sudden seem so shallow?" Carmine wondered aloud.

Setting his pages down on the table, he smiled and raised his splash of whiskey. "Drink up lads and lasses!" and tossed the Glenlivet back, his black curls bouncing as he did it. Reaching for the bottle and a refill he muttered, "I can do better." And then louder, with a grin, "We can all do better! There are things that matter out there. Here's to those things!" Holding up his cup in a toast, many suddenly rose to join him and he tossed back another drink.

For a change, it was Harry and Morgan who were struggling to keep up.

As had been reported during the break, the strangers at the door were gone when Jason left, and he found himself wondering who they would be following home. It would have been difficult for them. An early May sleet hit him as he headed out the café door.

Fireside Chat

ART HAD told Jason that he hadn't always been a liberal. He had been what he called a 'quiet conservative,' following the ideology of William F. Buckley when he'd gone to school and then begun teaching sociology. His wife, Julie, had been a bra-burning early feminist, but Art claimed that she hadn't been the cause of his conversion. It had been the slow morphing of what it meant to be a conservative—the arguments that he read in his student's papers over time and the spinning of the Vietnam and Iraq wars by those in power. It all had left him no choice but to become a 'liberated liberal,' in his own words.

They were sitting in Art's living room in front of a fire after a rehearsal with the Benewah Symphony Orchestra, and Art was settled into a comfortable antique chair sipping scotch. He reminded Jason of an Oxford don relaxing after a lecture. He also reminded him of an older man who was having trouble keeping warm lately, especially since the temperatures had dipped.

"I saw your ad in the newspaper," said Jason. "You really got to the point."

"Yeah, it'll be interesting to see if I get any blow-back from it. If this doesn't get their attention, I have some other surprises up my sleeve."

"One thing I was wondering, though, is if you think that many who read it will see it as a real 'Welcome to Idaho' sign.

There are plenty of people who will look down that list and think, 'Yeah! I'm moving there!'"

"Oh, definitely," said Art. "I thought about that, but realized that the word is already out among the people who are seeking a strict Christian nation. I want to reach the ones who aren't in the know and might consider moving here while uninformed."

"Well, it should do both." Jason admitted. "Have you heard the latest about the Redstar Mill?"

"Yeah, it's in the news and all over several chat groups I'm on. Morgan and I talked for quite a while this morning, and it's unfortunate that there's really not much we can do to stop the sale."

"Given the timing of the two announcements, do you think there's a connection between the legislature and the Entity?"

"There are a lot of Christian Republicans down there in Boise, and I'd be surprised if there wasn't some form of communication between the two. Whether they would work together to orchestrate something like this is another matter, though."

Art stared into the fire. "That damn church just keeps pushing and pushing, and they always seem to get their way. Without the college's financial support, I know that the co-op won't be able to keep the Mill open unless the public steps up, which is a big if. So, if the co-op needs to sell, the only thing stopping the Mill from turning into a religious academy would be the city council. Well, them and zoning. The problem with our Planning and Zoning Commission is that they are really just the Zoning Commission. There's never any foresight or real planning, and so what a purchase like this would do to the community in the future blows right by them. Looking at all of the developments that they've allowed around here, my guess is that any required zoning changes will be a slam dunk for the church. At this point, I honestly don't know what could save the Mill."

"And the Entity gains another step in taking over the town," said Jason.

He was discouraged by Art's take on this, and it was evident that Art was feeling down today, too.

The phone rang, and Art rose to answer it. He listened for a minute and then swiped it off. Jason had a hard time reading his expression, but he guessed that 'bemused' fit it the best.

"My first threat," said Art.

"Your first what? A threat? What did they say?" asked Jason.

"They said, 'That ad just put you in our crosshairs. And we know where you live.'"

Mr. Perkins

IT WAS late at night, and Jason was surprised by a phone call from Mr. Perkins, the high school band teacher. After a few words, it was evident to Jason that the man had had a few before making the call.

"Hi Jason. This is Jeff... This is Mr. Perkins? From the high school?"

"Oh, hi, Mr. Perkins," said Jason. "Everything OK? You don't usually call so late..."

"Oh, yes, yes, everything's fine." There was a long pause. "No emergency."

Another long pause. "Anything I can help you with?" asked Jason.

Yet another dead phone connection, until Mr. Perkins half-mumbled, "Um, I've had some... I myself have had some late-night phone calls, Jason."

"Oh?"

"Yes, and they have all been about you."

"Are you joking? Who was it and what did they say?"

Jason was now accustomed to Perkin's pauses, but becoming increasingly frustrated by them.

"I've had about eight of them, in fact, and they mostly claim you're corrupting my students."

"What?!" Jason erupted. "Are you serious? What contact do I have with any of your students?"

"I think it's more your influence that they're worried about, based on what they've said, anyway. What the callers have said."

Jason had quickly gained control of his temper. "And what do you think that influence would be, Mr. Perkins?"

"They all say that you and Art Parker are anti-Republican, anti-Christian and leading their children away from... well, either the Constitution or Christ, depending on who called."

"Wait a minute," said Jason. "They *all* say this? They all say those same things?"

Mr. Perkins sounded like this peculiarity was finally dawning on him. "Um, yes. To a person." Another pause. "That is a little bit odd, isn't it?"

"Yes, decidedly so," agreed Jason. "Where would they possibly get that idea from?" Then he remembered Art's notice in the newspaper. "Oh," he said to himself and into the phone line.

"But still, so many calls," continued Mr. Perkins. "So many angry calls. I'm afraid that..."

Jason had several ideas about what Mr. Perkins was afraid of. But he waited.

"Jason, they say that they're going to pull their kids out of band if you don't stop your extremist ways and your collusion with Mr. Parker."

Now Jason was dumb for several seconds. "And what kind of collusion would that be? Art is a friend of mine, but I had no input or part in the ad he placed in the paper."

"But you are his friend and live in the same house."

"I don't live in his house, I've had to move my business into his basement because it was the only available space I could find, but that's it."

"Anyway," said Mr. Perkins. "There's a clamor for me to disassociate with you. I'm afraid..."

That again, thought Jason.

"I'm afraid that, that... I won't be able to continue doing business with you until this is all settled," said Mr. Perkins.

Jason was somehow unsurprised. "So, Art wrote something in the newspaper, I rent from him, and you have contracted me for your instruments, and they're threatening you? Isn't that a bit of a stretch... Jeff? Are you keeping a list of those names? Who the parents are?"

"Oh, um. None of them have mentioned their names, but they were very adamant."

"So, they might not even really have students in your classes?"

"I'm sure they... Look, I just can't take the chance, Jason. We have a concert coming up, and they sound very serious."

"OK. What about all of the instruments I have that are currently being worked on?"

"Oh, well, those of course, we will need, but I mean any future business."

Jason had heard enough. "I think we need to speak to the schoolboard. Don't you? Goodnight, Mr. Perkins," and clicked off the conversation.

Jesus, some kid's parents.

He thought the call hadn't affected him much, but the harder it was to fall asleep the angrier he became. *God damn it!* he thought. *How could Perkins drop a bomb like that on me just before bed? Am I really going to lose my contract over a stupid misunderstanding? On his part? Of course not!* But the way his mind ran through all of the possible fallout to come, his conviction dimmed and glowed radioactively until the early hours.

Riley and Mona

RILEY KIRK, a good acquaintance of Jason's and former owner of the Platters record store in the old Henderson building, had ordered two new harmonicas from Jason and had asked him to drop them by the park when he had a chance. Riley still played with a local blues band, and the highlight of his musical career had been when Paul Butterfield had walked into the bar where Riley was playing and joined him up on the stage for a jam.

As Jason neared the strip-park leading down from City Hall to Riverside Park, he remembered that Riley had recently lamented that the park was being increasingly taken over by Entity members, especially after the Christian high school got out for the day. He'd said that many of his pals were avoiding the area because the church members would hog all of the benches, break out into song sessions, and have large circular prayer events in the middle of the grassy slope. Riley had mentioned that when he did have a seat at a bench, it was not unusual for someone to come up to him and want to talk about his salvation. Occasionally, some would even try and lay hands on his crippled left leg in an attempt to heal him.

Riley had said that he wanted to be nice, but that the laying on of hands was a bit much. It did something for them, but absolutely nothing for him.

Jason easily found Riley who was sitting on his usual bench and speaking with another savior who was hovering a hand just above his leg. From his tone of voice, the man appeared to be adamant that this would help him. Jason walked up, wondering if Riley was OK with this.

"Hi, Riley. How's it going? Your harmonicas came in today," said Jason, handing him the small package.

"Oh, thanks, Jason," said Riley, taking his eye momentarily off of the hand. "I'm pretty good. OK if I drop a check off tomorrow for these?"

"No problem." Then Jason turned to the earnest young man next to Riley. "And you are?"

The man looked up from his concentration on Riley's leg and said, "Seth," returning immediately to the task at hand.

Jason knew that Riley was easygoing and ever polite, and so he tried to be delicate.

"So, Riley. Do you know Seth?"

"No, not really."

"Are you needing any help with your leg today?"

"No, actually, I'm not. I never do."

"Then, Seth, I think we can agree that your attempts here aren't necessary, or even welcome for that matter. Don't you? You're not being sensitive to his wishes. I think Riley would like you to leave."

Seth looked up and said, "I can feel the energy. It will only be a little longer."

"You're not listening," said Jason. "It's time to move on." And, knowing it would make the man uncomfortable, he reached out to gently remove the man's hand from hovering over Riley's leg. They made contact.

"Don't you touch me!" yelped a transformed Seth who jumped up from his crouch and moved in so that his face was inches away from Jason's. The close proximity didn't help. "This is assault, and I'm calling the police!"

Seth himself looked ready to assault, balanced on the balls of his feet and leaning forward aggressively. Fortunately, a small crowd of his friends immediately gathered, and in their presence, he remembered his devout demeanor. With Riley rising with some difficulty and telling Seth and those present that he really didn't appreciate having his personal space invaded, the crowd moved off, but with reluctance on Seth's part. After talking with Riley for a spell, Jason moved on, too.

Seeing Riley struggle to stand had once again made Jason appreciate that he had made it through life so far without a major physical impairment. However, calming down now from the encounter with Seth made him wonder what it would have been like to have lived another life, unhindered by his... He had never thought of this before, but it suddenly came to him that he might have what would be considered a disability. Nothing on the scale of Riley's, but one that kept him from living a 'normal' mode of life. That had definitely been the case when he was growing up.

Jason thought back to a conversation he'd had with his mother, Mona, one afternoon when he'd stopped by to see her for a few days at his parents' small home in Kent, WA. His father was still teaching shop at the local high school even though he'd been able to retire anytime during the previous six years. On the second day of Jason's visit from college in Seattle, his father was at work and Jason had been sitting with his mother in his parents' dining room after lunch when he'd broached the subject.

"Mom, as I recall, we seemed to fight half the time when I was growing up. So, what was it like to raise me? Was I an absolute terror?"

Mona stared out the window and then looked back at him with a barely perceptible smile. She stubbed out her cigarette and coughed before answering, which was something she had been doing more frequently lately. They discovered her lung cancer a year after this visit.

"It's funny you should say 'half the time,'" she replied. "Did you know that I was aware of you the very second that you were conceived?"

Jason raised his eyebrows in amazement.

"Yep. I felt a little buzz in my gut the moment it happened. And that little buzzing never went away—it only got stronger the bigger you got. By the time you were ready to be born, I almost couldn't take it anymore. Sometimes it was a comforting sort of glowing warmth, but other times it felt like my stomach was being electrocuted. Hard to describe."

"Sorry, Mom, but no news to me. Pretty much everyone reacts that same way. My new girlfriend, Annie, says that sometimes when we kiss, it's like she's touched a 9-volt battery to her tongue."

This brought a bigger smile to Mona. "She's lucky she doesn't need to breast feed you."

Jason spontaneously laughed at the image.

"You weren't so hard to raise—half the time." She shook another cigarette out of the pack that lay on the red Formica tabletop, tapped an end against a Zippo lighter, put that end in her mouth and lit the other. Her inhale made the cigarette fire blister red, then smoke preceded the next words from her mouth. "You were lucky though, you know? Glenn and I each couldn't stand you, but only when the other could."

Jason thought this sounded just like Mona. Instead of saying 'Glenn and I both loved you, but only when the other didn't,' she chose the negative. Still, he knew her so well that he suspected she loved him some, too.

"Yeah, but I don't really remember fighting so much with Dad, though."

"That's because he was always the 'buddy.' Always your pal. It was me who had to lay down the law even when I wasn't fed up with you. When he reached his limit, he just handed you to me and went fishing or to the bar."

"Sorry I was such a handful, Mom."

Mona idly flicked ashes as she again stared out the window. Then she slowly shook her head and turned to face him again.

"You weren't really a bad kid, Jason. You never fussed more than a normal kid, and mostly did what we told you to. You didn't like to do the wrong thing or get in trouble. You were a good boy."

Jason was gratified to hear this and amazed to find her already lighting another cigarette.

"There was just something about you. Like I say, sometimes it was like you were shining out a kind of warmth. Or at least that's what I felt. But other times it was like... like... like I'd been stuck in a carnival funhouse for too long. You agitated me to the point where I had to either explode or go get a drink, and I didn't want to drink when I was with you, so I just let it out, I guess by yelling."

She set the cigarette in the ashtray, put her two palms together, and then pressed her forefingers against her lips. The white slowly rebounded to red when she took them away.

"I'm sorry. Looking back now, I see I wasn't a very good mom. Your childhood could have been a whole lot better, couldn't it?"

Jason would have reached across the table and held her hand, but that wasn't something they did in this family.

"It's funny, but that's not how I recall it. Sure, I remember us fighting, but that's just how it was, there were never really any hard feelings. Like you say, when you were off, Dad was on, and when he was off, you were there. We did a lot of fun things, and I don't remember it being totally miserable."

They looked at each other. "Except for Cub Scouts, 4-H, and other kid's birthday parties, that is," he added, and they both burst out laughing, Mona's morphing into a cough.

Class time had been bad enough, but the structure and teachers had made elementary school navigable for him. Any other group activity, however, seemed to end in disaster. On a camping trip in Cub Scouts, the other boys had sewn his tent closed while he was sleeping and left on a hike, and on one field trip, they had locked him in a bathroom at a rest stop and the bus had taken off without him until one of the den mothers had discovered him missing a half hour into the return trip. It was similar in 4-H where his rabbit had mysteriously disappeared during a show, never to be found, and at birthday parties where he was always the last picked for any game, when he was invited at all, that is. By fifth grade, his mother had put her foot down, and any kind of extra-curricular activity was off limits for his own safety and wellbeing. So, she was a good mother.

"Mom, you really should quit smoking; you're starting to cough a lot," said Jason as he was saying goodbye.

"I know, I know, but I think it's just a cold."

Mona had been lucky—it had turned out to be just a cold on that day. And, she had, even more luckily, survived her subsequent battle with lung cancer for several years beyond expectations.

With his parents now gone and Ann in Cheney, WA, Jason only had Eric left with whom he had any history. Given his circumstance, he would have expected to be completely alone, but luckily here in Dunkirk he had found a few close friends.

And without them, I'm sure I'd feel like I never left that lonely watchtower on Lookout Mountain. Good thing I loved it up there.

That pivotal summer before college had changed Jason. Always alone when among people throughout his life, he'd grown to be hypersensitive to their presence and opinions of him. He never expected that physical isolation would be a way he could learn to deal with others in the world. Over his season at the watchtower, he had become comfortable enough in his own skin that the reactions he caused in others flowed off him like water on an otter's back. He became confident about his place on the planet, and about his own musical abilities, so that he was completely prepared to enter his freshman year at the U of W that fall.

Saved by Solitude was the result of his experiences that summer and the lessons he'd learned about self-containment and self-image—living by himself after several unhappy years post-high school marked by drinking and fights.

Just a Job

Jason HAD carried a pile of laundry into Eric's room and set it on the end of his bed, and Grizzly had immediately jumped up and started making biscuits on top of it. He'd broached the idea of illustrating Robb's book on Noah's Ark to Eric, and his son had seemed disinterested. So, Jason was floored when he turned and saw some sketches of what was obviously an Ark on Eric's drawing board.

First a girlfriend, and now this? Jason wondered while he blurted out, "What?!"

Eric had heard him from the kitchen and padded into the room holding a plate with a peanut butter and banana sandwich neatly cut into sections. Jason, almost accusingly, pointed at the sketches. "How can you pick up Robb's idea just like that, Eric?" he followed, sounding a little hurt. "I've asked you about illustrating books that I've had in mind for years, and you always say no. What makes this so special?" He paused, looked at his son, and then described his emotion. "This makes me a little sad."

"I'm sorry," was Eric's immediate response, although Jason could tell that his son wasn't sure why this would make someone feel sad. Eric thought for a moment. "But your ideas aren't really that interesting, are they, Dad?" Leaving Jason speechless. Eric continued, "I could just see Robb's idea immediately in my head. I could draw the Ark in cross-sections, and then later have side views of the water levels showing the mountains under the oceans and then gradually showing more in the air. I think it would be kind of fun."

"But you don't know anything about the Bible at all. Do you even know the story of Noah?"

"No, not entirely, but I can learn, just like I learned about dams and car engines. I already found some pictures online, and Robb told me what he has in mind."

"And you know that this is a religious subject and you've never even been to church."

"I know, but it's just a job."

That was the end of the conversation. Jason knew that once Eric made up his mind on something, especially something that grabbed his interest, there was no dissuading him.

That evening, Jason tried to watch the news, but his mind was on both Mr. Perkins and on Eric. *How could Perkins be swayed by what was obviously a smear campaign started by someone? Who could possibly be behind it since it seemed to be a coordinated effort? What did they have against him or Woodwinds and Brass? How was he going to approach Perkins and the school district to keep his business afloat?*

And he'd always thought of himself and Eric as a team working on their books, but now Eric was pulling away. *Accepting the idea Robb had lobbed at him? A steady girlfriend, of all things? But isn't all of this exactly what he should want for his son? Shouldn't he be more supportive?*

The questions kept coming long into the night as Jason tried to fall asleep.

Essentially Dunkirk

EVEN WITHOUT any signs up yet, customers had begun to find his shop in its new location, and several were browsing through his sheet music collection while he sold some alto saxophone reeds to the high school's standout player.

"Thanks for coming by, Mikah. I look forward to seeing you in the next concert. When is that again?"

"May 13th, Mr. Deakins. Thanks, a lot."

"Any time. Say hi to your dad for me."

"Will do."

Mikah had just left when the door opened again, and Jason was surprised to see Sharon Stone stride in.

"Hello, Jason," she said as she approached the small counter he had set up for sales. She got right down to business.

"Since you've moved, I'm expecting that you will need to advertise your new location and let the world know where you are. I know I had a hard time finding it. The next edition of *Essentially Dunkirk* will be coming out in a few weeks, and I wanted to make sure you had the opportunity to place an ad."

"I hadn't thought about it, Sharon, but that's probably a good idea. Didn't I have a quarter page slot last time?"

"I believe so," she said as she thumbed through her copy of the most recent edition. "Yes, here it is," and she held out the spread to show him.

"OK, sure. Let's make it the same as the last issue with the change of address. I'm not certain how long I'll be here, but it will be worth it for at least this quarter's publication." He paused. "The way this town is being bought up by church interests, it's getting harder to find a place to rent unless you're one of them."

Sharon's face was skeptical. "Now, I'm not sure that's the case. There are plenty of new shops going into the Henderson building that the church just purchased, and I doubt they are all members of the Holy Grace Church. But even if they are, every one of them is enthusiastic and wants their business to succeed. I spoke to Mr. Sommers who just bought that one and the Goodwin building, and he's excited about the new ventures that will be opening in both of those places soon. He put me in touch with several of the business owners, and they're already buying ads."

"All I know is that there were perfectly good businesses in the building before we were evicted, and none of us were church members." Jason wanted to point out that Dunkirk was slowly reverting to the closed-shop town that it had been back in the days when the Redstar Mill owned the town and every business in it. But he held his tongue, not wanting this to turn into an argument.

"There are so many people just like you against the church," replied Sharon, "and I can't for the life of me see why. Those Christians are all committed to success and are fiscally responsible. Perhaps even more so than many of the old established shops that have, frankly, become lazy and shoddy."

This was quite the insult, but Jason, again, held back a response. Normally, he would happily engage her, but with customers nearby, he didn't want to take the time and effort.

Instead, he deflected. "Well, we each see this town a little differently."

Sharon nodded back. "And that's becoming more and more apparent in our authors' group, too, isn't it? I still can't believe the negative direction you're all headed in. We should be looking up toward the future and success rather than trying to tear others down or stir up a hornet's nest."

She folded her copy of *Essentially Dunkirk* and stuffed it into her bag. "Thank you, Jason, and I'll send you the bill," she said curtly and headed for the door.

Jason was left wondering whether real estate was going to be the avenue that Cutler and Sommers used to finally take over Dunkirk. Except for zoning practices, the city council had no avenues to halt purchases by the Entity, and the acquisitions by the church seemed to be slow but inexorable. The things that had stopped company towns in the past had been revolt against the limited job opportunities and the trapping of those living and working in town by debt and obligation. If Dunkirk should become an Entity town, would it be possible for any kind of backlash by its members given that they were all happy to have their lives totally controlled by the church? He doubted that much could cause the town to revert to a diverse community if a total takeover should happen.

The Delivery

JASON HAD hoped that it wouldn't be awkward, but it was. He had loaded his Subaru with seven instrument cases and was making a delivery to Dunkirk High School's music department. His lawyer had assured him that there was no problem with him meeting briefly with Mr. Perkins and that he was making progress in settling the dispute.

Jason was emotionally prepared for their meeting, but Mr. Perkins apparently wasn't. The band teacher greeted Jason warmly, but couldn't keep his mouth from gaping and his long fingers from twitching as if he was playing the piano. Mr. Perkins was tall and thin with a prominent forehead and Adam's apple. With his thick straw-like hair being whipped by the wind, he reminded Jason of a scarecrow. He was, it seemed, the stereotypical high school band teacher, at least in Jason's experience.

"Hello, Jason. Thank you so much for returning these instruments," said Mr. Perkins in a tone that Jason thought sounded like he had expected that it might not happen. "Can I help unload?" he asked but stayed well back from both Jason and the rear of the car as he said it.

"No, that's OK, I've got them," said Jason, as he began schlepping the instruments. "How are you today?"

This seemed like a momentous question in the way that Mr. Perkins considered it, but he finally said. "Good... And you?"

"I'm doing fine, thanks." He carried cases two at a time from the parking lot into the open door of the music room. "Remember, the new corks on the two saxophone necks might make it a little tough to put the mouthpieces on at first, and it might take a bit to tune them, but otherwise all of the others should play exactly as before."

"Ah," said Mr. Perkins.

There was an awkward silence. Jason was wondering whether Mr. Perkins had come to his senses after the late-night phone call, but wasn't sure how to ask.

"Are there any more you have that need work?" he asked instead.

"Um, yes," said Mr. Perkins. And then a moment later, "Er, well, actually they are no rush. We can wait till after…"

Jason put the last case down and faced him. "OK, Jeff. I'm not sure how things will work out with our contract, but I'm a little angry—no, confused—about why you made those assumptions about me. Right now, I'm just dropping the instruments off. Let's leave it at that."

Mr. Perkins seemed surprised by this sudden frankness. "Jason, I'm sorry you think that I maybe jumped to conclusions, but I have to believe the callers. The main concert of the year is coming up, and if I lose even one player, the whole sound of the concert band will change. I hope, like you do, that those callers were liars, but how can I be sure?"

"Well, that's not for me to say, but it sounds coordinated. Anyway, have a good day, Jeff," said Jason as he opened his driver's door to leave before he lost his temper.

"Oh, you, too, Jason," said Mr. Perkins, a little too perkily.

Mr. Perkins, thought Jason as he watched the tall, thin band teacher return to the music room through the rearview mirror. *Like a reed blown by the wind.*

He began to feel sorry for the man, but then was suddenly overcome with worries about the outcome of their contract.

The Memorial

THE HOUSE was quiet and dark when he unlocked the door. There was no note from Eric, but his son never left one if he was out. Jason felt cold from the recent turn in the weather, and so instead of grabbing a beer from the fridge, he put on the kettle and made himself a hot cup of tea. While the brew steeped, he lifted his backpack and extracted his laptop, opening it up on the dining room table. Grizzly had heard him, jumped up on to the chair next to him, and curled up to go back to sleep.

He'd let his book about Miriam languish for too long and felt inspired to try and work on the ending after hearing about the effort the other authors were putting into their own novels. He'd written the book as if she were dictating her story to her son, Lamar, with him asking questions for clarification along the way. Jason had worked through her family moving from Chicago to LA during the Great Migration in the early '50s when she was six, her growing up in Watts, and the increasing troubles there, which had taken quite a bit of independent research on his part. He had then written about her becoming politically active, losing a friend to gunfire, becoming disillusioned with the violence, and then teaching at one of the first Liberation Schools in Oakland. Lamar had helped fill in gaps on her moving north to Seattle, meeting her husband, and having and raising her son while working for civil rights and the police department. Jason had the story of her life drafted up until the time that she'd met him.

He'd tried several times, but had never been able to capture the moment of their meeting. This was due to both writer's block and to the difficulty in revealing something that was like a sacred trust or a forbidden secret that could not be stated aloud. Ann, of course, knew about his special relationship with her, but he'd never revealed details about it to another soul—at least beyond Catty's Corner.

He thought back to that long ago bus ride and their meeting at the little restaurant, and then began to try again. The first sentence flowed, but then the keystrokes slowed to a stop. With a feeling of regret, he closed the laptop once more without saving his work.

He and Miriam had stayed in telephone contact with each other on a weekly basis when he and Ann had moved to Dunkirk, and the news of the sudden death of the friend who could warm him with a touch of her hand had devastated him. The importance of Miriam to him was beyond words, even as he sought now to put them on the page. The ache and longing that came with memories of her only made him feel more keenly the isolation he'd lived in without her. And how to express all of this personal anguish to a reader? Was it something he should try to do? Once again, he found himself at a loss as to how this inner narrative could become part of the book.

He wanted to include some of the events that happened after her death, some elements of his own life without her. How to do this and have the story remain internally consistent? He recalled his trip to Seattle after her death, something he wished he could include.

He and Ann had driven from Dunkirk in their old Datsun with infant Eric asleep in the backseat. They had been invited by Lamar to Miriam's old house on a late August Saturday a week after she had passed away, but were unsure of whether or not there was going to be a formal memorial service. As he parked the car, Jason recognized a much older-looking Charlie and a few of the regulars from Catty's Corner standing on the lawn outside of her house still painted blue. It was an overcast day, but not raining, and most of the memorial guests were in shirtsleeves or light sweaters. A cooler of beer and an array of snacks were laid out on the front porch. Jason couldn't see Lamar in the crowd.

Charlie noticed them approaching up the sidewalk and broke off a conversation to walk slowly over, now with a limp, to greet them. "Hey, Jason. This must be Ann and... now, don't tell me, um, Eric?"

"Yeah, Charlie, how did you know that?"

"Well, you know Miriam. She kept me well informed about you after you moved."

"That was her, alright," said Jason. "I'm so sorry for your loss, Charlie."

"Oh, yeah. She was my rock. But you know, life goes on. I think it's going to be you rather than me that ends up missing her more."

Jason was taken aback by this but then nodded in agreement.

"Ann, this is Charlie. You two finally have a chance to meet."

"Hi Charlie," said Ann as she handed Eric to Jason and shook Charlie's hand. The infant squirmed uncomfortably for a moment, but then settled into the cradle of Jason's arm.

Charlie smiled. "I knew not to shake Jason's hand, but I wasn't sure about you. Nice to meet you, Ann. How's things in Dunkirk now that y'all are settled in there?"

Just then, Jason caught sight of Lamar emerging from the front door to replenish a tray of sandwiches. Excusing himself, he left Ann and Charlie to their chat and wound his way around several folks to reach the front steps.

"Hey, Jason!" smiled a thinner and much grayer Lamar. "Glad you could make it! And I finally get to meet Eric!" He stepped up and scooped the infant from Jason's grasp, cuddling him and giving him a loving peck on the forehead. He then held the baby at arm's length, looked him up and down, and said, "You and Annie did good," with a grin. Then, "Hey Betty," to the nearest woman to the pair of them. As she turned to look at Lamar, he said, "This is Jason, a dear friend of Mama's and mine, and this is his new son Eric. Could you do me a favor and hold him for a sec?"

"Be my pleasure," Betty replied, "and nice to meet you Jason. I heard nice things about you."

After Lamar relinquished Eric to her, he turned and gave Jason a long hug. Jason knew it made him physically uncomfortable, but it was a loving embrace for both of them.

"Ahh," said Lamar when he finally released Jason. "That felt just like hugging Mama." Tears suddenly filled his eyes. "I could do it all day. Thanks for that, Jason."

Jason was also beginning to well up. "Oh, that was good for me, too, Lamar. But I'm so sorry that Miriam's no longer with us to give us her hugs."

Lamar grabbed a napkin and dabbed his eyes. "Well, we're here to feel better about it. It happened so quick."

"You told me a little about it over the phone, but do they know what caused the heart attack?"

Lamar shrugged. "The doctor said her heart just gave out. She'd started having a real bad cough and was about to go in and see him about it when the attack occurred. The doctor said that it looked like she had walking pneumonia and the strain on her heart was just too much."

"I hate to ask, but did they do an autopsy to be sure of the cause?"

"Yeah. I heard about it after I talked to you on the phone. It was kinda weird."

"What do you mean?"

"Apparently, the doctor was suspicious that early signs of pneumonia would trigger a heart attack like that, so he ordered an autopsy. Come to find out, it was a heart attack, and pneumonia was the cause. He said that she had a buildup of plaque in her arteries, and the lung infection helped loosen that up and brought on the attack. But that's not the weird bit."

Jason gave all of the signs of asking a question without verbalization.

Lamar leaned in closer. "The weird bit is that her heart was in a mirror position from normal – facing the right, instead of the left."

"Huh?" asked Jason.

"Yeah, I know. A right-handed heart."

"What do you mean right-handed? How is that possible?"

"Well, it looks like a small number of us are born with our hearts as mirror images. It's called, I can't recall exactly... Oh yeah, something like dextrocardia." He pulled a piece of paper from his pocket. "Yep, dextrocardia. He said that the heart performs perfectly normal, but that it's like a mirror image."

"Honestly? That's common?"

"Not common, but not rare either—I asked him that. He said that people can go their entire lives without knowing that they have it. Just like Mama."

"So strange. I wonder if it had anything to do with her—vibrations—like I have?" Jason immediately put his hand up to his heart to see if he could feel it beating from the other side, dropping his hand again when he convinced himself that it wasn't.

The two let the moment hang for a bit, and then Jason said, "I wish I had a chance to say goodbye. Your mom was more than special to me."

"I know she was, but the great thing is that that's what they all say," said Lamar, sweeping his hand to take in the gathering. "Hey, where's Eric?"

They surveyed the yard and found Betty and two women unfamiliar to Jason surrounding Ann and the baby.

"Let me buy you a beer," said Lamar. The two popped open their cans and then made their way over to join Ann, Charlie, and Betty.

There were no speeches, but everyone eventually met each other and, through long and heartfelt conversations, learned much more about the heart and soul of Miriam than they had known before.

Taking a sip of his cooling tea, Jason was again left wondering how he could capture this scene properly for the book. Perhaps he could have Lamar's narration continue after his mother had passed away. Or maybe it wasn't important for the reader to know these details at all. He was well aware that he would never be able to include the story from his perspective. He knew deep down that that side plot would be a self-indulgence—this after all was Miriam's story.

Denied

JASON STOOD between the awards display and a support post near the door in a spot protected from the crowd. Like the post, he was there to provide support, too—specifically of the moral kind—for Morgan and Dennis. Their application for a parade and demonstration near City Hall had been denied and the pair, along with Lisa Brooks from the library and many others, were at the Dunkirk City Council meeting to question the denial.

Martin Ames, one of the new council members, was explaining. "At our Event Planning Committee meeting, we decided to deny the application for two main reasons, and I can read the minutes if you like, but I'll summarize. First of all, since the stated purpose of the demonstration is to protest the new *Children's School and Library Protection Act*, it is expected that, despite your best intentions, there are likely to be several gay pride and pro-LGBTQ+ banners on display within the immediate vicinity of this hall—a display that is now expressly prohibited." Much more than a loud murmur arose, and Ames held up his hand to quiet the crowd. "Many of the banned books have been about this subject, this LGBTQ+ fad, and since the parade is requested because many feel strongly about the ban, they are likely to display their displeasure in the form of posters." More protesting voices were heard, and Ames waited patiently for them to die down.

"The second and most important reason for the denial is a major safety concern we all had. The vitriol and accusations aimed at the Holy Grace Church after the previous library rally has us worried about not only a repeat, but an escalation in anti-church sentiment. There was the feeling that, rather than the stated purpose, the real reason for the demonstration is to amplify the false accusations against the church. The proposed demonstration has the potential to overwhelm our city police force's ability to control the crowd. By the tone and attitudes on display here tonight, I would say that our concerns are well justified."

"Mr. Mayor, if I may," said Cheryl Small the moment he had finished. "I would just like to point out that it was a bare majority committee vote to disallow the application for the reasons Mr. Ames has just stated, and that I and several other of our committee members voting in the minority feel the concerns are hugely overblown."

"Thank you, Ms. Small," said the mayor. "Mr. Ames, anything else?"

"Yes. I have heard anecdotally that threats have been made against the church and some of its members. I believe that this demonstration will only serve to fan the flames against a very peaceful group."

Public testimony was soon permitted, and Morgan stepped up in turn to state his opinion.

"Mr. Mayor, members of the Council. My name is Morgan Grant, and I am one of the cosigners of the request for this demonstration, the purpose of which is to ask the State of Idaho to rescind the *Children's School and Library Protection Act*. I have to say that I'm actually in awe of the way the processing of this application has unfolded.

"We are asking for permission to hold an event that is similar to countless events this city has allowed over the years, and none of the previous events have ever been questioned. All, including two recent rallies by militias, have been rubber-stamped by this city council. It is the deflection that is amazing to me. This discussion is no longer about the purpose of our demonstration. The conjecture that there *might* be LGBTQ+ banners and that there *might* be demonizing of the church are completely manufactured. Why would a rally to support our libraries carry those banners or cause a disturbance? Where is any proof of threats against the church? The denial of our permit is based solely on reasons that are not even based in reality. I hate to say it, but I sort of demand that we be issued the permit, or lawyers might be needed to help decide if the denial is within the history of precedents that have been set before us."

Jason saw the council perk up at the mention of lawyers. After much more testimony and discussion, it was agreed that the mayor, a member of the council, Lisa from the library, and a representative of the church would meet in a timely manner to come up with a solution that would allow the permit to be issued and allay any safety concerns.

Jason ducked out before anyone moved toward the door, but he was very happy with Morgan's testimony, and the now more likely issuance of the permit—barring legal intervention.

Willow

A FEW days after the meeting of the Panhandle Authors' Group, Jason had stopped into Gandalf's for both a cup of coffee and with an ulterior motive. Luckily, Melissa wasn't behind the counter, and he could easily order a latte to go. He was glad to see that Willow was stocking pastries into slots behind the glassed-in section of counter down at the other end because he had really come to see her. Willow Simonson was the "new" owner even though she'd purchased Gandalf's eleven years previously. When Jason picked up his order, he walked over to where Willow was just finishing up.

"Hi Will," as everyone called her.

"Oh, hi, Jason," said Willow. "How are you doing this morning?"

"Great—just like the weather."

She smiled. "Hard not to be, isn't it?"

Jason agreed and then asked, "Hey, do you have a minute for a chat?"

"Sure, I could use a break. Let me get my coffee, and I'll meet you over there," she said pointing to a small table at the other end of the counter.

The pair arrived at the table at about the same time.

"What's up?" asked Willow as she got settled.

"Well, we had a strange thing happen at our last meeting. You know—the Panhandle Authors' Group."

"Oh, what was that?"

"There were three men standing at the entrance of the meeting room as we all walked in. Dennis asked if he could help them and the only reply was an avoidance of eye contact. They were gone when the meeting ended."

"What do you think that was about?" asked Willow.

"We have no idea. A few of us are talking about writing books that could be banned in order to draw attention to the book censorship that's spreading across Idaho and the rest of the US, so we suspect it might have something to do with that."

"Hmm," she thought for a moment. "Writing books to be banned is certainly a different approach. Do you think it'll do any good?"

"I think some in the group hope so, but if you want to know the truth, I have my doubts."

Willow had to ask, "So, what's the problem?"

"Well, I was wondering, if something like that trio showing up uninvited happens again, is there anything you can do?"

"I don't know. Do you know who they are?"

"Well, one of us recognized two of them as being from the Entity, um, the Holy Grace Church."

"Oh, them." Willow was shaking her head when she said, "Nope, there's really nothing I can do. They weren't causing a disturbance, were they?"

"Um, no. Not really."

"Truthfully? Unless they do something criminal, my hands are tied. They have every right to be here, even though they never are. I'm actually surprised that they set foot in my place if they are from that church."

"That's OK, I just thought I'd ask."

Jason was about to thank her and stand when she said, "You know, it's funny. There's a local group who've posted a Facebook page that lists all of the Entity-related businesses in town, and folks who care about it actively avoid those businesses."

"Yeah, I myself pay attention to where I shop," said Jason.

"Me, too," she whispered. Jason knew that as a businesswoman she didn't want to openly take sides. "But the funny part is, members of the Holy Grace Church write in letters to the editor saying it isn't fair to boycott them just because they are part of the church and that they're only trying to make a living. But then they do exactly the same thing. They don't call it boycotting—they probably call it shunning or say that they're supporting their own businesses, but it's the same thing. It's boycotting. I never see them in here."

"So, do you think things should be more equitable? We should shop at their places?"

Willow quickly looked around and leaned forward. "Hell no. Not only are you helping their businesses then, but they tithe their earnings into the Entity, and that only makes it stronger. No. Don't feed them. They'll just underwrite more businesses and feedback into themselves, growing all the time."

The barista called from behind the counter, and Willow stood. "Sorry, Jason, I gotta go. Sorry I can't be of more help."

"That's fine. Just thought I'd ask," and Willow was gone to lend a hand with the long line that had formed while they'd talked.

Bosworth

THAT AFTERNOON, Jason was playing a trumpet to check the new valve he'd installed when his cell phone rang. It was Eric, who never used his phone. Jason was immediately primed for an emergency, but calmed as soon as he heard Eric's explanation for the call.

"Hi Dad, I'm calling because Abby said that I needed your advice."

Eric also rarely asked for advice, so Jason was intrigued. "Sure, son. My advice about what?"

"I had a couple of phone calls that I thought were spam, but then Abby made me check my voicemail, and it sounded legitimate to me. Abby thought so, too."

He and Abby are certainly getting tight, thought Jason. "What was it about?" he asked.

"Here, I'll forward it to you. Call me back and tell me what you think," and Eric ended the call.

A few moments later, the message arrived.

"Hello, Mr. Deakins. I'm Patty Nolan, an aide to your district representative, Peter Bosworth. Representative Bosworth is interested in learning more about the publishing industry. You are among many authors in his district who he would like to gain knowledge from. If you could call me back, I would greatly appreciate it. I just have a few simple questions that will help Representative Bosworth better understand the writing and publishing business. Thank you for your time."

Jason called Eric back. "Hey, son. Yeah, the call seems legit to me, too. I think it's OK for you to call her back. I'm sure that they're mainly interested in taxes, like publishing through Amazon. Let me know what you find out."

Eric told him about the call that evening after dinner. "We had her on speaker phone. Abby said that she sounded very nice," he said. "She mainly asked about how we and other authors published our books and a lot about where the actual publishing occurs. I told her I didn't know for most, but that our publisher is in Des Moines."

"Hmm," said Jason. "Interesting that she got in touch with you. I wonder how many others will get the same call?"

"I guess we need to wait to find out," replied Eric, moving on to other things as he made himself busy washing up the dishes and preparing lunch for the next day.

Jason found himself becoming worried as he put away the leftovers and went into the living room to think. *How did they get Eric's number?* he wondered. *He never uses his cell phone, and I don't think it's listed anywhere. And why call him? He's an illustrator – a coauthor. Why not call me? What is Bosworth angling for? What does he really want?*

Jason received his call from Patty Nolan the next morning, asking the same questions that Eric had described. He asked Ms. Nolan why the representative was gathering the information she sought and specifically wondered why he and Eric were being contacted. Were they being singled out? Ms. Nolan was evasive in her answers, which left Jason feeling even more paranoid.

Patriarchy

THE ONLY local store for commercial signage was in the St. Joe Mall, and Jason stopped in to get a bid on a display for his new location. Kris had had a great idea about hanging real instruments as part of the signs, and he worked with the owner of Dunkirk Displays to come up with a design that would compliment the trombone he had in mind. They agreed on the appropriate size and on a few possible approaches, and the owner said he would email Jason some mock-ups.

Jason was leaving the decorative store front and walking along the long interior of the mall when Robb emerged from the entrance to Ross.

"Hi, Jason," he called, holding up a plastic bag as he approached. "New set of socks. It was about time."

"Hey, Robb. How's it going?" as Robb caught up and the two walked toward the far entrance to the mall.

"I'm OK, Jason. Say, you didn't happen to get a phone call from Representative Bosworth's office, did you?"

"Yeah, and Eric did, too. What do you think that was all about?"

"I don't know, but what struck me as odd is that none of us are what you'd call big-time authors or experts on publishing. How did he even know to call us?"

"I was wondering the same thing," said Jason. "I assume that the state is trying to find yet another way to tax us and is reaching out to anyone who's even tangentially involved."

"Oh, probably so."

The pair chatted about Eric and the weather for a bit before Robb motioned to a nearby bench and asked, "Do you have a sec, Jason? There's something I need your advice on."

Jason and Robb had known each other for some time, but Jason was somewhat surprised that Robb had sought him out lately to vent or ask for advice. Not exactly a close friend, Jason wasn't sure why Robb had chosen him for feedback, but perhaps he asked the same of everyone he was familiar with.

"Sure, Robb. What's up?" as the two sat at opposite ends of the short bench.

"It's about my ex-wife, Susan," said Robb, sounding a little distressed.

Jason's immediate reaction was that he should tell Robb that he really wasn't any good at relationship advice, but he held his tongue until he heard more.

"She came to my apartment the other night, which is something she'd never done before. I didn't even know that she knew where I lived now."

Jason stopped him right there. "Look, Robb. My own marriage didn't work out at all, so I don't know if I'm the best one to ask for advice on this."

Robb hesitated for a moment and then said. "Oh. No. That's not the kind of advice I'm looking for, Jason. Just hear me out."

Jason gave him a nod, and he continued. "It was awkward at first, of course—us suddenly being face-to-face after all this time. I have a new partner now, Stacey, so I told Susan she wasn't welcome and nearly closed the door on her. But Susan pleaded for me to hear what she had to say and once she started talking, she couldn't stop until it all came out. Even in front of Stacey."

Jason noticed that Robb was very aware of his surroundings and that he would drop his voice to a whisper when people passed by, as a pair did at the end of his last sentence.

When the old couple moved on, Robb began again, and concern was back in his voice. "She's in a bad way, as you'll see, Jason. You remember she married Will Sommers? All that money and good looks? Well, now she feels trapped and doesn't know what to do. Apparently, things started off fine between the two of them, and Susan felt like she'd struck gold, literally. But it sounds like Sommers is more like iron pyrite than real gold. Once he settled into his position in the Holy Grace Church, things began to go great for him, but terrible for her. She isn't sure if it was his true nature all along, but he started with verbal abuse, and now is down to some physical abuse, although, I saw no signs of that myself."

Robb took a deep breath and looked up and down the mall before he continued. "Susan said that while we were together, she of course knew about the church's patriarchy and that women were to mind their place since it was in every one of Cutler's sermons. But, since I never practiced anything like that in the house, she thought that it was all really just lip service. Then she married Sommers, who apparently takes his position in the church very seriously, as do all the elders. She feels now like all her rights have been stripped away. She is to have no opinion at all—in fact, during the last election, she said that Sommers insisted that she not vote—that he was the voice and authority of their family. And now we know that is one of the stances that the Entity is trying to export, even through proposed legislation at the state level. They want a single household vote. Anyway, she is only allowed to socialize with other women in the church, and Sommers uses force to keep her in line. She feared for her safety in even seeking me out.

"She claims that she doesn't have it the worst, either. Talking to the other women, there are whisperings of rape and abuse—even of minors. Not to mention a total lack of financial independence. She had no idea of the extent to which her sex was being subjugated until she hooked up with Sommers and started to share her story with the other women."

"Wow, Robb," whispered Jason as another couple strolled past. "I'd heard rumors, but had no idea..."

"I know," said Robb in a low voice. "I'm so glad I got out, and I'm actually glad that I got away from Susan, too, to tell you the truth, but this is terrible. To think that it is so widespread. I had no idea that this was happening even while I was in the church. I got kicked out, so it was easy for me to leave. For someone who wants out on their own, though, it's an entirely different matter."

They sat for a moment, and then Robb said, "So the advice I want isn't about my failed marriage. There's no way I want to get together with Susan again. But what can we do to stop this treatment of women, or to publicize it? I don't feel that I can say anything because they'll claim I'm out for revenge. But I feel like I have to do something. The women who are trying to leave will be shunned by the entire church community— even their friends and former support network. They'll need any kind of help they can get. I know from experience that it's hard to break into new social circles once you're on the outside. You not only have to find a new path, but they try and put up roadblocks while you're trying to do it. Those women are like runaways who have lost everything once they're free.

Jason shook his head. "I have no idea what to do for them, Robb." He thought for a moment. "I'm sure you looked, but is there any kind of existing organization that can help them?"

Now Robb shook his head, too. "Not that I've found, but I might not have the contacts that would know about one if it did. I think some of the other local churches would be supportive if the outcasts wanted to join them. They might know."

"Yeah," said Jason. "Oh, I just remembered. Luke is opening a women's shelter soon, and he might already be up on the situation. If not, what if you, or someone you knew, maybe those other churches, set up a sort of lookout group? A small network that could watch for the escapees and help them get back on their feet?"

"That's not a bad idea, Jason. Thanks. The women who leave the church can't just sit in isolation. I don't think. I need to find out more about those who've made it out. Maybe they do have some connections."

Robb looked at his watch. "Man, I didn't realize we'd been talking for so long. I'd better get back to work." He stood up, and Jason rose with him.

Robb reached out his hand, but seeing Jason take a half-step back, he remembered and dropped it. "Sorry, I forgot. I can't thank you enough for this, Jason. See you at the next meeting."

As Robb headed for the exit, Jason was thinking that he hadn't really done anything but sit there and listen. He also thought that he might need to do more than sit if the allegations against the Entity should ever become more than just whispers and suspicions. He knew something about being an outcast and was disheartened that a church would be built and held together on the threat of hate and retribution to make people stay in it.

Protesters

JASON TOOK a shortcut between the house and some privet bushes, up the front steps, and knocked on Art's door. There was no response. Jason knew his friend was home because he'd heard him walking around upstairs in his kitchen only moments before. He knocked again and called Art's name. The door opened a crack, and then Art threw it wide when he saw Jason.

"Why the cloak and dagger?" asked Jason as he was about to enter.

Art's answer was to walk out onto his porch and point in the direction of the street. Jason glanced over his shoulder and saw several men and one woman standing on the opposite side of the road that he hadn't noticed because of the route he'd taken. One held a hand-lettered sign that said 'Libtards' in a circle with a slash through it.

Art cupped his hands and yelled, "Go home, you idiots!"

Their reply was a few shouted slurs, and Art gave an exaggerated shrug with both hands before turning back into the house.

"First their ilk, and then a few reporters," said Art as they walked back to the kitchen. "I don't mind the reporters, but being lectured at my own front doorstep by those wackos is something else. That's why I don't open the door to just anyone."

"Yeah, I totally get that," said Jason. He hadn't yet told Art about the phone call from Mr. Perkins and this visit to his friend was to let him know about it.

He relayed the gist of the late-night call, and then said, "I've tried to contact the school district, but keep getting a runaround. They say they need time to review the contract and have a discussion with Mr. Perkins. They also need to talk to the police about the phone calls to him and said that that would take time."

Art shook his head. "In this day and age, who knows if the calls were really from one person, or if they even came from someone in this state. If any rants about my ad went into the dark web, they can come out anywhere. I get emails from hate groups all the time, and they go straight to the trash bin. Some irate conspiracy theorist in Sheboygan could be the source. I doubt that the police could ever track down those calls to Perkins after the fact." He thought for a moment. "Although, the link from me to you and then from you to Perkins is pretty damn telling. Isn't it? It actually could be someone local which is maybe even worse. More like a smear campaign."

"You know, my contract shouldn't be threatened based on hearsay, and in fact I've called a lawyer and he's finding out what my rights are in this case."

"That's a very good idea," said Art. "I asked the police to do something about what may become a daily vigil in front of my house. They said that they had no power to remove people from a public sidewalk unless they were obstructing traffic. The few signs and placards the protesters carry give no clue as to what organization might be behind them, so there's no ob-vious point of contact for me to lodge a complaint. I've asked them in person about who's behind it," pointing out toward the street, "but they aren't saying anything. The police said that they are likewise stymied. I'd get a lawyer if I knew who to go after, too."

Jason later learned that the small, but constant presence, occasional signs, and scattered shouts had at first deeply disturbed Art Parker, but he had evidently soon become philosophical about it and had written a letter to the editor of the Dunkirk Gazette.

A change of norms has occurred in our country, and it is difficult to predict if things will ever go back to where they were.

It was once the case where a slur was met with a slur or a more civilized word; a letter to the editor was met with a contrasting letter in kind; a demonstration was met with a counter demonstration; or a political viewpoint was met with an opposing view. The slurs met face to face, the letters sparred in the newspapers, the demonstrations took place on the streets, and the political views were voiced in the halls of government.

But now the boundaries are disappearing. The walls of privacy and respect have eroded.

There is now this sense that "taking it to the man" by getting in one's face is OK. If someone works in an abortion clinic, it is acceptable to confront them not at work, but in front of their home. The same goes if you are a judge in a courtroom, an election official, a librarian, or someone with any political views at all—you can be confronted at your home.

This is the bully mentality that hopes to sway your employment, judgement, or opinions by personal attacks outside of the arenas where the judgements or opinions occur. I say "bully" because instead of countering an idea or position with an opposing idea or position, the bullies try and counter the person who represents those positions by their sheer personal presence and meanness.

Yelling louder than the other person doesn't win an argument. Talking over a person trying to make a point doesn't prove a point. Threatening someone over the phone doesn't change opinion. These are all just bully tactics and intimidation—the dwelling place of the cowardly and uninformed.

It's a shame that our society has let the animals out of the cage, and I fear that there is no way of bringing some of them back. Once you've felt that false sense of power, of superiority, it is nearly impossible to rein you back in. Please realize that bad behavior doesn't become good behavior simply by your saying that it is so. Being a bully only reflects on you— not the person you are attacking.

Art would later tell Jason that after he wrote that letter and it was published, he could calmly walk past a thousand protesters and not have a qualm.

Cutler's Letter

A FEW days later, Jason opened the paper to find Art's letter. After reading it, another letter to the editor caught his eye. It was written by Ed Cutler, the antagonistic pastor of the Holy Grace Church.

There are those who sin despite their best intentions, fully repentant for their transgressions as they make their way through this world made up of constant tests by our Lord to be overcome.

Then there are those who knowingly sin, and worse yet, are unrepentant when they do so. Yes, unfortunately the world has murderers, rapists, thieves, and blasphemers. Every one of them, even if they escape our earthly laws, will find ultimate judgement one day.

If there is a crime against God about to be committed, however, we would be remiss in not trying to stop it in its tracks. You would attempt to halt an assault, try and save a woman from a robbery, or stop a murder if you knew it was going to happen.

I am trying to halt a crime against God with this letter. There is a group of writers in our area who are committed to writing books that will be immediate candidates for being banned. They are planning to write smut, communist propaganda, and openly gay literature for the sole purpose of having it be confiscated or burned.

Why would they do this? It is not for me to say. Why they would want to pollute young minds is beyond my imagining. I am, with this letter, simply imploring them to use their craft for good rather than for evil. I'm asking them to step closer to our Lord rather than farther away. In the words of Thumper in Bambi, *'If you can't say something nice, don't say nothin' at all.'*

Ed Cutler

Jason was floored, as were, he expected, many of the rest in the authors' group who read this.

How did he hear about our idea? wondered Jason. *And what business is it of his, anyway? This is censorship—before the fact! We're not allowed to write what we want to write?*

He was just picking up the phone when it vibrated. Dennis was calling. He got right to the point.

"Hey, Jason, did you see the letter that Cutler wrote to the editor today?"

"Yeah, Dennis. I just finished reading it when you called."

"What do you think? He's trying to ban us before we even get started! This just proves our point, and it really pisses me off."

"I was just thinking the same thing," said Jason. "I know we have an open group, but as far as I know, none of us belong to the Entity. So, how the hell did he hear about our idea? It's not like it's a secret or anything, but it makes me think of spies and moles."

"I'm guessing Sharon, Tamra, or Kenneth. But it really doesn't matter. Here we are, an interest group—really non-political—flying under the radar, and he suddenly points his guns at us. Now there will be scrutiny from one side and great expectations from the other. I really don't want attention for something we haven't even done yet. What's he playing at?"

"Man, I don't think I'm the one to guess at that. Have you talked to Morgan? He'd be more on top of this. I was just going to call him."

"Yeah, I tried him twice, too, but got no answer. I thought I'd call you while I waited for him to ring back."

"I'd be interested to…" there was a sudden beeping in the background.

"Oops, sorry Jason. There he is now. I gotta take this."

"OK, but real quick. Did you get a call from Representative Bosworth's office?"

"No, what about?"

"I'll tell you later."

Dennis rang off, and Jason set his phone down feeling somehow violated, as if his home had been broken into, and at the same time wondering if this was going to be much ado about nothing or grow into something much bigger.

The Redstar Mill

IT WAS a Saturday morning, but Jason found he was too anxious to sleep in and rose to take advantage of the day. He had awakened only to find himself stewing about Ed Cutler's letter, but decided that he would try and not let it ruin his weekend. He quietly made coffee and breakfast so as not to disturb Eric. When he sat down at the dining table to eat, he noticed a sweatshirt of Abby's lying on the chair next to him. He wasn't sure if she'd left it there before going home, or if she'd ended up staying the night. He also wasn't sure how he would feel about it if she had stayed. His son was an adult now and, with his salary, could easily be living on his own. It was mainly due to habit and convenience that he still lived with Jason. But that his son was now a complete person—a totally independent, functioning adult—was hard to accept in the protective-parenting mode that still resided within Jason.

He washed up the dishes and intentionally watched while the rinse water ran down the drain, carrying all those worries away with it. Feeling better, he stepped out into a warming morning. The Saturday Market wasn't far away, but he drove the car because he had other errands to run as well. Parking a block from Riverside Road, he walked down to the street that bordered the St. Joe River, now sectioned off for the Market. Since it was still early in the season, not many fresh vegetables were available, but some of the stalls had fresh greens, which he bought for salad, and he was surprised to find zucchini. Other vendors offered crafts, honey, wine, hot sauces, and food. Most of the Panhandle College students weren't out and about yet, so the crowds were still thin, which was exactly how Jason had planned it.

After the market, he drove to WINCO and did his weekly grocery shopping, again timing it so that there were few shoppers in the store. He appreciated that following the COVID pandemic, customers still tended to stay a reasonable distance from one another. He was always careful to use his debit card, not cash, and to refuse a receipt when the cashier asked. Without any physical contact over the several years that he'd shopped there, the checkers knew him and were always friendly. When he came out into the parking lot, the truck now with seven flags waving from its bed was making its routine, slow pass up and down the rows of cars. A new banner was plastered along one side that read: I'm With the Militias!

Art's birthday was coming up in a few weeks, and Jason thought he'd look through some of the shops in the Redstar Mill when they first opened in the morning for some ideas. He drove the short distance downriver to the three-story timber building sided with gray-weathered planks. The parking lot, bright display signs, and gaily decorated windows belied the image from a distance of a derelict mill from a forgotten era.

Once inside, the drab, historical building came alive. The ground floor was an open plan currently occupied by the college's woodworking and pottery sections. The public was welcome to walk along roped-off areas and watch the craftspeople at work, with the louder machinery enclosed and visible through windows. The center of the building was open all the way to the ceiling, and the upper two floors had shops along the outer walls with access and views fronting the inner courtyard. It broke Jason's heart to think that by next fall the potters, the glassblowers, and all the cubbies of craftsmanship would likely be gone.

Jason remembered that Sharon Stone had said she had a shop on the second floor. While browsing, he found the darkened room between two empty storefronts and, peering in the glass door, he could make out two interior sections. On the right was a bright banner promoting *Essentially Dunkirk*, the town's marketing magazine, with stacks of recent publications and 'Support Dunkirk' pins. On the other side, a royal blue background with gold lettering proclaimed '*Summoning Stones*' in medieval script. Posters of her book covers were on prominent display, as were stacks of her books. It looked like she also sold crystals that matched those on the book covers. The sign on the door said that she would be back at 1:00, so he guessed that she was at the Saturday Market even though he didn't remember seeing her there. He had never heard how her book sales were going and was surprised that she could afford a shop space based on sales alone.

He wandered around the remainder of the second floor, but nothing struck his eye. He had just passed an open shop on the third floor when he stopped. It was a room filled with weavings, which was something he wouldn't consider getting for Art, but he had seen Kris Seever working at a loom.

Somehow nervous, he stepped in to say hello.

"Hi Kris," he said as she turned to the door. "Nice shop you have here."

"Oh, hi Jason," she greeted him with that smile. "Thanks. You haven't been up here before, have you?"

"Nope, I haven't been in the Mill for ages. If your store was here then, I never noticed it." He scanned the displays. She had ornate wall hangings, woven bags, table runners, napkins, and more, all made of fabrics ranging from linens to wool, some with unexpected additions like twigs, shells, and baubles woven into them. He was amazed at the range and quality. "Hey, this is something. I had no idea of the types of weavings you made."

"Thanks, it's fun to try out new things. Like this old Dutch pattern I'm working on," and she leaned back so that he could view the delft blue-and-white work in progress on the loom.

"Oh, hello. Welcome," she said as a customer came in behind Jason, startling him. She gave him a just-a-minute look and helped an older woman pick out a matching table runner and mat set.

He examined her works more closely while she was busy. They really were beautiful, and the quality of the weavings was professional. What else did he expect of a successful businesswoman?

When the customer left, Kris said. "Hey, I need a break and to get my morning coffee. Do you want to join me at the little café downstairs?"

Jason was surprised. "But who will mind the store?"

"Oh, no one. We're very casual here. I'll just hang up my 'Back in Ten Minutes' sign and we're good to go."

"OK, if you're sure it won't hurt your sales."

"It's always slow when the Market is open anyway, so no worries. Follow me."

They walked downstairs to The Mill Café which was tucked into a corner on the ground floor just past the glass-blowing furnace. Kris made a quick run to the restroom while Jason ordered their coffees. He was worried that he would need to hand her her cup, but managed to set them down on a table just as she returned.

After some small-talk, Jason asked, "So, where are you from, Kris?"

"The mid-West, really. My dad was in the navy in New Zealand and met my mom who's Māori. We moved to the States when I was two. Dad became a sales rep for IBM, and we lived in Minneapolis for a while, then Dubuque, and finally Indianapolis. I graduated from high school there, and then earned a degree in fabric arts. How about you?"

"Washington. My dad was a high school shop teacher, first in Auburn and then in Kent. I went to U-dub for a degree in music, and my wife... ex-wife and I moved here in '96. I tried teaching, but it wasn't a good fit for me and then I started my repair business. Oh, and Kevin's horn isn't finished yet, by the way—but soon. I have the dent pounded out, but still need to make a tiny solder at the rim. And then the lacquer." He was about to take a sip of the still-hot coffee, but just had to ask, "And, what does your husband do?"

Kris shook her head. "Nope. No longer married. In fact, it might have been the shortest marriage in history. We had the ceremony when I was four months pregnant, and he left us when Kevin was one week old."

"Oh, that's too bad," said Jason, but finding himself secretly happy that at least she was now single. "Sorry to hear it."

"Oh well, I think we both knew that we weren't suited, and it was better not to try and prolong the inevitable. How about your marriage?"

"I guess it was the same. We held it together probably much longer than we should have, but it took two of us to help Eric."

"Oh? Was there a problem?"

"Eric's on the autistic spectrum. He has what used to be known as Asperger's. At first, we wondered how in the world he would make it when he grew up, but he's doing great and is a draftsman at a local architectural firm. That, and he illustrates books."

"Really? What kind?"

"We have a little series called '*Looking Inside:*' for children or young adults where we examine the details inside the body, dams, engines, things like that."

"So, you're an author, too?"

"I'd say that I'm at least a writer. I have a little book out about a pivotal summer for me, and I provide the wording for Eric's drawings. He's really the creative one of the team on our '*Looking Inside*' books."

"I'll have to keep my eye out for them. I'd love to see what you two have published."

"I can give you a copy of at least one of them," and they arranged the details while verifying phone numbers.

"Say, Kris," said Jason when they'd finished. "I've heard a rumor that the Mill has a possibility of being sold. Have you heard anything about that?"

"Oh, heck, yes. It was in the papers yesterday, and I received an email that the co-op board is planning a meeting to discuss it this Friday."

"So, what are you going to do if it closes?"

"I don't know yet. The email said not to panic about the newspaper article, and that all leases would be honored at least till the fall. It said that they were going to start recruiting for other investors immediately. Beyond that, we'll see."

"But all of these businesses? I know I was one of five tenants in the building where I was located, but this is a big place. Where will you all go?"

"Some have been here forever, so I really feel for them. My shop is pretty mobile – weavings can be packed into suitcases - so I can relocate to a trailer if I have to. We'll just need to wait and see."

Jason was impressed by her adaptability and hoped it would last if the possibly imminent sale became a reality.

Kris suddenly looked at her watch when it buzzed. "Oops, I better go. Sorry, Jason. This was fun."

"It was," said Jason. "Maybe we could do it again some time."

"Yes! That would be great."

She stood while Jason gathered the cups and placed them in the bussing tub. He walked her back to the stairs leading up to her shop.

"That second demonstration to support our library is hopefully going to be next week. The permits aren't guaranteed yet, but we're acting as if they will be. I'll be playing in the band at the beginning. Maybe see you there? It's going to be in the strip-park in front of City Hall."

"Sure, I'll look for an announcement in the newspaper for details and try and make it. See you, Jason."

And she was off.

Jason left the Mill thinking how nice it was to know a little more about her. *And not married,* he thought, wistfully.

Self-Discovery

WOW, DO I *like her*, thought Jason. But what are the chances that it could work?

He wandered back to his car and found himself wondering if his marriage to Ann had been worth it. Of course it had, because they had Eric—but it had nearly cost Ann her sanity. Did he really want to put someone like Kris through that? What was he thinking, wanting to see her again at the demonstration?

God damn it, sometimes I really hate my body and the disasters it causes!

When they'd moved to Dunkirk, and thanks to personal computers in an ever-widening world-wide web, Jason had spent hours searching for any information he could find about his 'condition.' He'd found that the most closely related medical information concerned galvanic skin response—the change in electrical charge on the skin when an emotional event occurred, such as when someone was telling a lie. The only thing was, this response was induced by immediate stress, and the duration of the change in charge was only on the order of seconds or minutes rather than over an entire lifetime, as it was for him. It also meant that he would need to be sweating continually for the response to be ever-present—which he knew wasn't the case. So, he discounted this as a possible source for the reaction he caused in others.

He'd also discovered that the cells in the human body do generate a magnet field, but it is normally so weak that it is effectively undetectable by other humans. Magnetic fields weaken greatly with small distances from the magnet, and since there were people who could become uncomfortable by just being in his proximity, he also ruled this out as a possibility.

And then there was the holistic, metaphysical realm which talked about biofields and the stimulation of the magnetic field through meditation and other techniques. He'd actually gone through a phase where he'd tried to use meditation to reduce his own field, if that's what it was, to no avail.

The doctors he'd seen had said that they had no clue what was going on with Jason's body. Since it wasn't a threatening medical condition, he couldn't afford the tests or investigations it might take to uncover the underlying cause. One doctor had tried an EEG on him, but for some reason the readings had come out as normal.

Jason was also in the habit of scouring the internet several times a year to see if he could find others with the same symptoms. There were common reports of people whose electromagnetic fields seemed to cause electronic devices to malfunction, but these never seemed to carry over into the area of personal relationships. This was where Jason's problems lay, and not in wonky TV remotes and cell phone touchscreens. He'd thought of posting on a forum or chat site, but feared what the responses might be. It often occurred to him that others with the same strange indicators might be thinking the same thing, but he wasn't going to be the first to chance public exposure.

When he returned home, he spent some time on the web, going down several rabbit holes—beginning with the search 'electricity between two people' and devolving from there. He realized that this was a hopeless distraction and closed the browser. He then brought up his email. Near the top was one from Morgan who was ever vigilant about events coming out of Boise, so Jason opened it.

Hi fellow PAGers,

I received notice of the following framework legislation that was just passed out of committee in our State House. How they hope that this can ever become a bill, or be enforceable if it does, is beyond me. They obviously have no clue about free speech and how the publishing world works, but to even have this pass out of committee shows the leanings of our legislature.

I wonder why this is coming up now. Maybe some retaliation against those who support libraries? See below:

Bill Framework: First Strike for Children Act.

This legislation is conceived to help take the burden off our libraries and librarians in deciding what books might be acceptable to parents. The world is awash in books, and so many can have a negative influence on our children. With the ease of publishing on Amazon and of self-publishing, our librarians are swamped with too many choices. Without enough information, libraries can purchase books, only to find them to be objectionable. Money and time are wasted on many substandard books that appear on the surface to be acceptable, are considered for inclusion in the library stacks, and are then rejected through no fault of the librarian.

This proposed legislation consists of the establishment of two committees to help screen materials and ease the decisions made by librarians.

The first committee, composed of two librarians from two counties, four legislators, and three Idaho residents, would pre-screen all children's books. Those books which are approved by committee would then be available for selection by state librarians.

The second committee, with a similar composition, would require that any book manuscript originating in Idaho or published with an Idaho address on the copyright page be subject to similar screening. This would be considered as a First Strike for Children and prevent objectionable materials from being disseminated from our Great State of Idaho.

Jason was at first flabbergasted and then depressed, as Morgan must have been, that this sort of language was even under consideration. This was definitely state-sanctioned censorship and boded dark times if it actually entered the legislative process. He couldn't imagine the lawsuits that would spring from this bill if it passed.

Jason shut down his computer and headed straight for the fridge and a beer. As he thought about what this bill would mean to authors everywhere, he found himself realizing that Representative Bosworth's telephone call was no surprise at all. He hadn't checked the crafters of the framework, but he was certain that Bosworth's name was at the top.

"FUCK THE legislature," said Morgan. They'd just spent the past twenty minutes discussing the ill-conceived *First Strike for Children Act* that would potentially require the screening of their works prior to publication. Jason and Robb had described their conversations with Representative Bosworth's aide, and after lengthy debate most agreed that the bill would most certainly be DOA. "Even if it does pass, the lawsuits would bury it after considerable cost to the state. This is just grandstanding to make the actual *Children's School and Library Protection Act* seem like reasonable legislation."

"But what sparked it in the first place?" asked Dennis. "Do you think it was because of Ed Cutler's letter to the editor about us?"

"No idea, but it does seem like the two are really closely related, doesn't it?" asked Morgan. "Anyway, I'll keep tabs on it and let you all know if it starts to go anywhere. But, once again, we'll need to start writing letters or calling in our objections. I'm sure there will be some speeches about it at our demonstration, and Dennis will say more about that later.

"Now, any book presentations for this meeting?"

Before anyone could answer, Robb asked. "Has anyone else been getting hate emails about our books?"

It seemed that no one had, and he said, "Well, I have. They are all about my book on Noah's Ark which I've barely started, saying that I'm going to hell if it ever becomes public. A few even hint at how they're going to help me get to hell in the process. I've been used to getting harsh emails from the Entity, but nothing like this. No one else has?"

No one said they'd received any, and Dennis asked, "Is this room being bugged?" looking up at the ceiling. "How does the Entity know so much about what happens in our little group?"

They looked around at each other, and Morgan said, "Well, I don't know, but I sure don't want us to start an Inquisition. We trust each other as authors, and so it must be something like overheard conversations somewhere."

"Is there anything we can do to help, Robb?" asked Dennis.

"No, I don't think the threats are serious enough to bring to the police," said Robb. "But given that it's just me and that they're of the same tone as what I've received before, I'd say they're all from the Entity, and I can deal with it."

"You should keep all copies in case they might come in useful later on," said Morgan. "And let us know if they get worse, OK?"

"I will."

"And now to the books," said Morgan.

"I have a good start on my interracial marriage book for the book banning project," said Dennis, "and want to get some feedback from you all."

"I do, too!" added Maggie. "I'm nearly ready to have someone review my draft young adult book about a first love between two lesbians."

These announcements took some of the others by surprise, as several who had talked about writing a candidate for banning hadn't even begun outlines yet.

Dennis went first. "As it stands right now, I actually doubt if my book would be banned by anyone. Interracial marriages were rare in the '50's but so common now that that aspect of the book will hardly raise an eyebrow. I've thought about an angle to add that's a little edgier, but I'm unsure about it right now. At first, I thought of going down Luke's path of adding in some quote, objectionable, unquote sex, but just couldn't bring myself to do it. Instead, what I've done is wrapped that love story into a… a social statement, I guess. Here's my idea.

"I see so many parallels between populists like Trump and Vance along with their authoritarian, racist goals and someone like George Wallace in the '60's, that I've created a fictional southern governor who is eerily similar to Trump and is the father of the protagonist. The governor publicly slanders the wife-to-be's father who is a prominent black man in town to the point that his business fails, and he commits suicide. Or is it suicide? Signs point to a political hit-job. Then the father turns on the son and his new wife after they secretly wed."

He looked around the room. "Well, what do you think? A good direction to head in?"

"Sounds more like a thriller with political bite," said Morgan. "I like it." There was much discussion around the table, and they all ended up agreeing with Morgan's summary in the end.

"What I'm hearing from everyone, and I agree," said Morgan, "is that if you lean even more heavily into the portrayal of the white, privileged, and powerful governor as someone immediately recognizable as your average populist right-wing politician of today and bring out the sins that white society has committed on people of color, you have a great candidate for a book that they would want to ban. Especially if you focus on the white guilt for systematic repression—and those who deny it."

"Do you think I could go too far?" asked Dennis. "I mean, I don't want to get hate emails like Robb, or a knock on the door in the middle of the night or anything."

There wasn't the immediate response of "No, no," that he was expecting which worried Dennis.

"Ten years ago, I would have said you had nothing to worry about, but now…" said Morgan, letting the sentence hang for a second. "Since it doesn't portray anyone too local to our area, I think you should be safe, though."

"And that's how it might be with any banned book nowadays," said Harry. "I wonder how much hate mail living authors who have been banned get. But that could be similar to anyone just expressing their opinion about anything. Just look at Art Parker. I hear that there was quite the vigil outside his house for putting that ad in the paper."

"That's cooled down lately," said Jason. "But it sure surprised me that responses are getting to be so personal and in-your-face now."

"So, you're saying that we might actually be attacked for publishing something that someone doesn't agree with?" asked Dennis.

"Oh, I'd say definitely if you put it online and the attacker can remain anonymous. Them coming to your doorstep? I really doubt it," said Morgan.

Dennis didn't look overly reassured, but said that he should have a reviewable draft available by the next meeting and asked for volunteers. Several hands went up, and Dennis took note and thanked them.

Dennis Harris was actually Eric's boss, an indicator of just how small the community of Dunkirk really was. He'd started his architectural firm in the '00's and now had a staff of 12 architects, engineers, and draftsmen. He was well respected, and his business came from all around the Northwest. He resembled Jimmy Stewart, sounded like Walter Cronkite, and had the design skills of Frank Lloyd Wright. His was one of the most successful businesses in town, and he was extremely philanthropic, supporting many worthy causes statewide. Somewhat out of character, he had written and still wrote a fictional series about generations of a family as it grew and became powerful along with the city of Seattle.

Dennis had also been a godsend to Eric. With an eye out for talent, he gave annual tours of his business to high school sophomores and had taken notice of the boy. He'd arranged a meeting with Eric and Jason and had shown a sensitivity to neurodivergent learning styles. Helping Eric see that taking the courses that he wasn't interested in at the time would help him get an architectural job in the future had made all the difference in Eric's attitude towards school. Dennis would even meet with Eric when his interest in a course started to wane and show him how what he was learning would eventually apply to architecture, providing some real-world examples to help him refocus. Jason was eternally grateful to him for taking Eric under his wing.

"Maggie, you had a book to discuss, too?" asked Dennis.

"Um, yeah. I hadn't thought of these repercussions, though," said Maggie. She appeared to be hesitant to introduce her book, but then said, "What the heck. I'm used to ruffled feathers for being who I am." Maggie ran the local Saturday Market and was one of the most outspoken and popular women in town. She had been married to her wife, Bethany, for eight years, and the pair had adopted a two-year old girl from Columbia four years earlier.

"OK, I also had the problem that just writing a book about LGBTQ+ romance was unlikely to get banned, since that happens to be a hugely popular topic right now in the US market. I know that the Christian right, especially, is targeting children's books for banning, and so mine is about three girls who are good friends and what happens to that friendship when they come of age and one of them realizes she is in love with a new girl in town. It's written for the young adult market and, of course, takes a very sympathetic view of a girl coming to terms with, and being very comfortable with, her newfound orientation and sexuality."

"It seems like something that should be published, regardless, but I have to admit that I know next to nothing about that genre," said Jason to some agreement around the room. "We'll have to rely on your expertise to know if it could be a candidate for banning. I assume that it's introducing the subject to such a young audience that would be the trigger?"

"That's exactly right," said Maggie. "I'm showing it to be a comfortable and normal thing for that age group, although the initial reactions and conflicts with her two friends keep it as a real and believable story."

"OK, I'll be a volunteer to read a copy," said Jason and several others also raised their hands. "You make it sound like an uplifting read."

"Yeah, I actually had fun with it. And writing for young adults took me back to when I was that age, although I wasn't brave enough to recognize my natural self until I was in college," said Maggie. "Attitudes have changed since then, although there's still a section of society not willing to accept it."

Dennis had an announcement to wrap up the meeting. "Morgan and I are beyond frustrated at the pace of getting our demonstration permit approved. The Event Planning Committee, chaired by Ames, is dragging its heels and delayed the special meeting among the principal parties that they stipulated at the last council meeting. Lisa Brooks has gone to the mayor directly and asked him to shake things loose. We just heard that they are going to finally meet tomorrow night. We'll have the demonstration as soon as we can after the permit is approved. That's all I have for now, but stay tuned."

The View

THE NEXT Sunday morning, Jason felt that he had to get out of town for a while to clear his head. He'd asked Betta if she wanted to join him, but she'd said that she already had a golf tee time scheduled with some friends. He drove to a trailhead a short distance from town, parked the car, and headed up a path that would eventually lead to several scenic views and small lakes. The going was easy at first, but then the trail became steeper and began to switchback as it etched its way up through the trees.

His legs were burning at times, and he recalled how easy it had been for him to make similar climbs when he'd worked as a forest fire lookout. A pain started to develop in his right knee that he'd never noticed before, and he slowed his pace, hoping it would work its way out. Taking his time on the steeper sections helped, but he knew that he would make it nowhere near as high as he'd initially hoped today. Another unwelcome reminder that he was starting to get old.

He came to a side-trail that he'd explored before which led to an outcrop with a wonderful view and decided that this would be a good spot to stop for lunch. After a rest, he would see how he felt about a further climb.

He'd barely met a soul on the trail, and this lookout was deserted. He took off his backpack, set it on a nearby rock, and stood looking out over the vista, letting some of the sweat evaporate off his back.

Facing south and west from here, he could make out most of downtown Dunkirk below, Panhandle College across the St. Joe River, the highway as it emerged from the lower hills into town, and the flats to the west beyond which he knew lay Lake Coeur d'Alene. There was some haze in the air, but not enough to hamper the distant view.

He chose a spot where he could lean against a rock, dangle his legs, eat, and enjoy the scenery. While he unbagged his sandwich, his gaze fell on the downtown area, and he happily felt far removed from all of its problems and politics. Inclined against the warm, solid granite at such a remove, he suddenly felt omniscient, and his thoughts became more philosophical.

What is our sleepy Dunkirk going to look like in the future? he wondered. If it had normal growth, development on the opposite side of the river would certainly expand and, when the population grew, more big-box stores would very likely finally move in. Traffic would be worse downtown—or would it, if the Redstar Mill was no longer the town's main attraction?

Then his thoughts became more dystopian. What if the militias become more organized? What if they should all rally around a single person or purpose at odds with the citizenry? In his mind, he could see armed patrols roaming the streets like Belfast in the '70's. And what if they should start to disagree among themselves? Those imagined patrols became street gangs fighting over territory.

Sweeping those images aside, he laid out another scenario for his town. Or, he thought, what if Dunkirk was an entirely Christian community under the dominion of the Holy Grace Church? What would that look like? And then many questions came to mind. Since the church was mainly tax exempt, how would taxes and businesses be affected? Would there be more or fewer tourists? What would happen to Panhandle College if the new religious academy was established? What laws would the city council enact and enforce by what kind of police? Would it be so bad if the dominion of the church came to pass?

His state of dispassionate observance disappeared as Jason came back down to the solid granite he sat upon, and his own opinions took over. It was his guess that much of what happened in Dunkirk would drop under the radar. The Entity would declare a legal religious status when it was to its monetary advantage, and declare the opposite when it needed, say, state or federal funding. The true leaders would be unelected, even if elections for figureheads still took place. Much of the governance would occur behind closed doors, and many state and federal regulations would be selectively ignored. Dunkirk would become a fiefdom with willing serfs—collecting tithes and mixing these with other income sources into an untraceable and possibly corrupt stream of revenue and expenses. On the outside, all would appear gleaming and white, but on the inside, accountability would seep through hidden cracks. Schools and institutions would drop away from most governmental oversight. It would be the opposite of Camelot. Visible at all times, but enshrouded in mist once one entered the city gates. He was certain his own vision of that future would most closely match reality, should it come to pass.

Jason stood, stretched, and took a final look at downtown Dunkirk before packing up for the hike back down the steep hillside. In his mind's eye, he saw his son busy at work at a drafting table far below. He saw Art puttering in his kitchen, the Panhandle Authors' Group members busy at their day jobs, the musicians he played with in the symphony, Clearwater, and the Rag Tags going about their business. None of them would thrive in the future that he'd just imagined. Most would no longer want to stay or be welcome in the town. A feeling very like the one he had when Eric was being mistreated or misunderstood came over him, and he realized how much those people meant to him. Here was the place where friends and a sense of belonging had finally begun to fill the void that had been left by Miriam's disappearance from his life. And he knew that the town, as it was, needed protecting. He was surprised to feel an unaccustomed sense of duty arrive with that thought.

Unfortunately, the hike and his musings had only temporarily cleared his head from his more immediate problems, and as he descended, he found himself stewing about both Mr. Perkins and the *First Strike for Children Act*. He tripped on a tree root and luckily caught himself before tumbling down the trail. Realizing that he wasn't paying enough attention to where he was and where he was going, he stopped at the next level spot on the trail. Taking a breath, he heard two crows causing a racket in the treetops. They were diving at something, and he finally spotted the red-tailed hawk that hunkered at each one of their passes. The harassed hawk finally took off, followed by the squawking crows. Two Messerschmitts dive-bombing a beleaguered Ace Pilot Smithers in the smoky skies over embattled Dunkirk. He knew now that he, too, would need to enter the fray.

Officer Tennent

JASON HAD just driven back into town when he saw flashing lights in his rearview mirror. *Oh, shit,* he thought as he rechecked his speedometer, slowed, and pulled over to the side of the road. He rolled down his window and waited. He knew from past experience that this might not go well for him.

The patrol car sat for a minute before an officer emerged and walked up to the side of Jason's car.

"Hello, Mr. Deakins," said policeman Tennent. "Haven't seen you for a while."

"Officer Tennent," said Jason in recognition. "I wasn't speeding, was I?"

Jason knew Tennent from an incident that had occurred several years ago. Jason had stopped on a yellow light that had immediately turned red when he was rearended by a brand-new Volvo. Both drivers had gotten out of their cars, and the other driver had stormed up to him, yelling.

"What is the matter with you? Why didn't you keep going, you idiot?!"

When Jason had explained that the light was yellow, the man had said, "Yeah, that means step on it, you moron." And the exchange had become more heated after that. When the man had grabbed Jason's arm, the shock from that touch had caused him to become apoplectic. Jason had done his best to defend himself. Officer Tennent had arrived to find Jason holding the man down on the pavement with his entire body while the man was writhing and screaming at the top of his lungs.

Pulling Jason off of him had revealed to Officer Tennent the reason why the man was raging mad, and he had at first assumed that Jason was totally at fault for the accident. Jason with his bloody nose and banged up head spent half an hour in the back of the patrol car until things were sorted out. Witnesses and the other driver's own dashcam footage had shown Jason to be in the right, and Officer Tennent had apologized for jumping to conclusions, admitting that he was amazed at Jason's physical effect on others.

"Nope, I just wanted to warn you that one of your brake lights is out. The one on the left. You'd better get that taken care of. Just a warning this time."

"Oh, thank goodness. Thanks, officer. I'll get it changed as soon as I can."

Officer Tennent smiled at him. "You take care of yourself, Mr. Deakins."

Jason was relieved when he drove off. Not at getting away without a ticket, but at having someone who'd physically encountered him in the past actually smile and not harbor an irrational distrust of him.

Kenneth

ON MONDAY, Jason was approaching Art's house and his repair shop in the basement when he noticed a lone protester—something unusual for this early in the day. It had to be either someone who took exception to Art's ad or, Jason found himself thinking, one of the phantom stalkers who members of the authors' group were reporting about. Charlotte had called a few days after their previous meeting saying that someone—probably one of those standing outside of their meeting room—had followed her home by car and had sat outside her house with the motor running. She'd called the police, but the man had disappeared before they'd arrived. Dennis had confronted someone tailing him through the grocery store, but the person had denied that he'd been stalking him—he'd claimed that it was merely a coincidence that they'd followed the same route through the aisles.

The man in front of Art's house was walking slowly back and forth staring at the sidewalk near the shop's entrance. As Jason approached, he recognized Kenneth from the authors' group. He wouldn't have been surprised to learn that Kenneth was demonstrating against Art and his stand in the newspaper given how conservative he thought Kenneth was. But if Jason discovered that Kenneth was one of the stalkers, they would have to have words.

"Good morning, Kenneth," said Jason a little formally as the man looked up at his approach.

"Jason! I've been waiting for you," smiled Kenneth, which took Jason totally by surprise.

"You have? What for?" was all Jason could think to ask.

"I wanted to talk to you about something, and thought I'd catch you early. Is this a good time, or should I come back later?"

"Now's as good a time as any—I'm not too busy in the shop at the moment." He wondered if Kenneth was there to voice his objection to his business supporting Art, a misconception several others had.

"Great. Do you want to go get a coffee maybe? The Bitch's Brew is just a block from here. I'm buying."

"Sure, Kenneth. Let's get a coffee."

Kenneth Logan was a member of the Dunkirk Historical Society and had helped Luke Thompson, the author with a penchant for pornography, edit and publish his books on the history of logging in the area. Kenneth was active in a local church and was an avid fly fisherman. He had written two novels that were surprisingly dense allegories similar to the works of C. S. Lewis.

Jason was becoming curious about what Kenneth wanted to discuss. It didn't seem like it was going to be Art-related, so he began to suspect it had something to do with book banning and the authors' group. They chatted about the weather and general topics, entered the coffee shop, placed their orders, and then found a free table to sit at.

"You're probably wondering why I wanted to talk to you," began Kenneth, and with a nod from Jason, he continued. "It's about Robb and the book he wants to write."

"Kenneth, you know I have no control..."

"Oh, I know, I know," Kenneth cut in. "I can't stop him, and I'm not sure I want to."

Now Jason was confused and the arriving coffee orders helped him hide it.

Kenneth took a welcome sip of his foamed latte and then explained.

"It might surprise you that I'm not really against the anti-book banning idea. I write, too, and think we should all be free to write what we want, and others should be free to read it if they want to. Of course, I draw the line at pornography for children as anyone would. But I'm not against educational materials that are fairly explicit—like Maggie said—they have to be, don't they?"

"To me, they do," said Jason, and tasted some of his own drink.

"I'm getting old and don't think so quickly on my feet anymore. I got so frustrated at the last meeting I was at without really knowing why. And I lashed out. But now I realize I was really upset because I couldn't put together what I wanted to say in time." He took a minute, and Jason could see that he was still having trouble finding the right words.

"Let me back up. I'm a churchgoer, and our church does some really good things. We have an annual book drive for kids that I got started, we have our 'Eat with Friends Fridays,' we're progressive, I think, and our pastor writes about human rights issues in the paper. The church is a good thing, and it provides support to all of its members and even those who aren't members."

Kenneth took another sip of his latte, and Jason noticed for the first time how old he was looking. His once tall stature was becoming stooped, the lines in his face were deeper so that the razor no longer reached some of the crevices, and he had a slight shake in his hands now that Jason had never noticed before.

"All right, so, about Robb," he continued. "He's lashing out, too—and I can see why. He feels betrayed by his church, if you want to call Holy Grace that, and that bastard, the new elder, stole his wife and ruined his life. His reaction is completely understandable. But here's my problem with him and his book." He looked around the tabletop as if for the right words. "Actually, I don't know that the problem is fixable.

"You see, us older folks who have already chosen or not chosen a faith aren't likely to be impacted by a book like Robb's, but it burns my britches to have books that are anti-religious for kids."

"But atheists might love to have that kind of book available for their children, wouldn't they?" countered Jason.

Kenneth thought for a moment. "Yeah, sure. I guess if I was an atheist I might want that kind of book," leading Jason to realize that Kenneth took a much more nuanced view of religion than he'd expected.

"OK, here's the thing," said Kenneth, apparently finding what he wanted to say. "Our church is losing numbers, and it's the same for most of them around Dunkirk except for that... Entity, I guess people are calling it. Young people are less and less interested in checking us out unless their folks were involved in the church. And Robb is part of the problem. No, the Entity is part of the problem."

"I would say that the Entity is a problem, all right," said Jason.

"You see? You have strong feelings about them and you're not even a church goer. They say they want to take over the town, and people are rightly up in arms about it. I don't know much about them—I've heard that they aren't very welcoming to people attending their services who they haven't invited, and if you do attend, you're put under heavy scrutiny. So, instead of being 'live and let live,' they're antagonistic. They provoke strong reactions in people, and then the truths or rumors start flying around. If you're not a member, they make you distrust them. Now most of the town distrusts them. The young people distrust them.

"But the problem is that bleeds over to the other churches. The young people distrust religion now because of all of the things they've heard about the Entity. Oh, and the crooked tele-evangelists or other sect leaders, too, of course. So, here's this church that is taking over the town, wanting to convert people to their faith, and they're doing the exact opposite— driving people away from them and from the other churches in town."

Kenneth sat back with a sad expression.

"They're trying to grow, but they're killing us. They're killing belief in our town."

The pair were now nursing the bit of coffee left in the bottoms of their cups.

"So, I don't think I'll be able to come to any more meetings until Robb moves on to something else. I react, and I do so inappropriately. I have nothing against him as a person, but I feed off his strong feelings against the Entity."

"I'm sorry to hear that, Kenneth. We hate to lose you as a member. Is there anything I can do that will help?"

"Yes, there is, Jason. Let me know when Robb calms down, and I'll be back."

"Or I can try and talk to him and relay your thoughts."

"No. Maybe after a bit, I'll try and have this same discussion I'm having with you with him."

Seeing that the conversation was over, they both rose simultaneously. "Thanks for listening, Jason. That helped me a lot."

"Any time, Kenneth." As they were walking out the door, Jason said, "You know, we should have coffee together more often."

Kenneth smiled. "I agree, that would be great. See you, Jason."

As Jason walked back to his shop, he felt happy that he'd gotten to know Kenneth better and now had a completely different opinion about him. Adding to what he'd already heard from Robb and John Darcy, he also had an entirely different feeling about the growing aches and pains caused by the Entity—a creeping infection that was triggering a defensive immune reaction in the entire body of Dunkirk.

Jay

HIS PHONE rang while Jason was in the middle of spraying a final coat of lacquer on Kevin's French horn—one of the dwindling number of instruments in his shop. He checked his messages when he was finished and called his lawyer back.

"Hi Jason, thanks for returning my call," said Jay Fontaine. Jay had helped Jason and Ann with the intricacies of their divorce, and they were both happy with the results. "You were correct that Perkins was way out of line in breaking your contract."

This was good news to Jason. He had a written agreement and knew that it probably couldn't be terminated without good cause, but had no way of knowing how to effectively approach the school board about the issue. He'd tried to go through channels, but it was slow going, and the school system didn't see it as a priority nearing the end of the school year. So, instead of getting into a head-to-head confrontation, he'd decided it was time to lawyer up.

"That's a relief, Jay, so what do I need to do to straighten this out?"

"I already have it straightened out for you. I got in contact with both Mr. Perkins and the school board, and not only could they not provide a due cause, but after the school board conducted an internal investigation, they could find no substance to the claims that your business was in any way deleterious to the students or the school. They also contacted Art Parker, and verified that there was no connection between you and his posting in the newspaper. Mr. Perkins being pressured to discontinue contact with you based upon rumor and hearsay is obviously no reason for it to affect your business in the slightest. I think you will find Mr. Perkins conciliatory, and I've made sure that neither your personal nor professional relationships with him will be affected due to his own error in judgement."

"Great! So the whole problem is solved?"

"Yep. You should see business as usual."

"Thanks so much, Jay. You're a lifesaver."

"Only when you're on the winning side," laughed Jay as he said goodbye.

Jason let out a long breath. After being forced out of his space downtown, the call from Mr. Perkins had seemed like the beginning of the slow death of his music shop. He'd already begun wondering what he would do next, or if he should even remain in Dunkirk. Eric seemed to be doing fine on his own, and without Ann or a business to hold him here, Jason was finding few reasons to stay and several possible reasons to go. The politics of the state were becoming abhorrent with the domination of the extreme right wing of the Republican Party and their diminution of voting rights, women's rights, and human rights; and the encroachment of the Entity in the town was becoming oppressive to those not in the sect. Without his business, it would only have been his friends who kept him here, and while it was a good reason, it might not have been enough.

But now to his great relief it appeared that his business was no longer threatened, and he looked around the basement with a fresh eye into some improvements that would make the space more comfortable in the long run.

The TENs Unit

ERIC AND Abby came in and took off their coats while Jason was watching a soccer game on a cable channel.

"How was dinner?" he asked.

"It was good," said Eric. "Abby had some sautéed shrimp with linguini."

Jason knew that Eric had ordered either macaroni and cheese or mashed potatoes and pork chops unless he'd been adventurous.

"What did you have, then?" he asked his son.

"It was a new restaurant. I had the mac and cheese, just to be safe."

"Sounds good," said Jason. "The spot that just opened across the river?"

"Yeah, just east of the college," said Eric. "It's one of Dennis's designs. I did the drafting."

"The Lonely Oyster," said Abby. "A very inviting interior it is, too, Eric. It was really good food, but I don't know how long they'll survive with that name."

"At least it's catchy," chuckled Jason. "I'll have to try it out, especially since I now know it was one of Dennis's creations."

"Watching the game?" asked Abby, glancing at the TV. Eric had already plopped into a seat to take in the action on the screen. Like a sudden apparition, Grizzly lay curled up in his lap.

"Yep. It's British soccer. Arsenal vs. Manchester United."

"Oh," said Abby, taking the middle seat between Eric and Jason.

Jason turned down the volume on the set. "Eric's the one who got me hooked on soccer. I've never played, but he took a shine to it when he was in middle school, and we've been fans ever since."

"Yeah, he told me that soccer was the only sport that he liked." She glanced over, and Eric was absorbed in the game.

His eyes followed the action as he grinned and said, "I was the goalie, and it was a kick."

"So how did you two meet?" Jason asked Abby, after groaning at Eric's joke. "Eric mentioned that you often have lunch together."

"Oh, I've actually known Eric since middle school. I was a year ahead of him, and he was friends with my younger brother, Chad. Chad Williams?"

"Oh! Chad. You're his sister? I never put two and two together. I'm sorry—Eric mentioned your last name, and I never made the connection." Jason paused and then said, "We were so sorry about Chad."

Abby inclined her head. "Thanks. Yeah, his death hit us pretty hard, but it's been years now, and so life goes on."

Jason replied slowly. "You know, Chad helped Eric through some rough years when Annie and I were divorcing. He was quite the friend."

"Yeah, he was the best," said Eric.

"They were like two peas in a pod," said Abby, smiling at him. "Eric reminds me so much of my brother, funny and kind."

Just then Eric looked at his watch and said, "Eight o'clock. I'll be right back," and headed for the kitchen carrying the cat.

"He's getting ready for tomorrow," said Jason.

"I know," smiled Abby. "Anyway, I went away to college and training in Portland and just came back last year. I eat lunch in the nearby park every day when the weather's good and so does Eric. We remembered each other and have hit it off."

"That's great," enthused Jason. "And where is it you work?"

"I'm a physical therapist at the Dunkirk Rehabilitation Clinic."

Jason thought for a moment, and with Eric busy in the kitchen, decided that this was the right time to ask.

"So, Abby. You're aware that Eric is on the spectrum? That he is autistic? And that might mean quite a lot of baggage for you?"

Abby smiled reassuringly and was about to lay a hand on Jason's knee, but remembered the warning and held back. "Chad's autism was even more evident than Eric's. The whole family struggled at first, but in his last years we were all in group counselling which helped us see things from his perspective. I can't say that I know completely what I'm getting into with Eric, but I have a very good idea. I can tell that he loves me, and I love him, so we can make it work. Believe me, I've had two serious boyfriends who were neurotypical, and I can relate to Eric much better than I ever could with those two. He makes me feel comfortable, and I'm aware of the kind of emotional feedback that I may not get from him sometimes, but I know that his heart is golden, and that's what really matters to me. With the other two, I could never be sure."

"That's so good to hear, Abby. And remember I'm always here for support, too, if you should ever need it."

"Thank you, Jason. We should be OK, but I'm sure I will ask for advice from time to time. We're taking things at a slow pace, and we discuss everything in detail before and after it happens to make sure that we're both on the same page in the relationship. Eric is comfortable, and he has promised to let me know when he isn't, and I'm doing the same."

They watched the soccer ball fly across the field and then Abby asked, "Since we're sharing, can I ask you something?"

Jason turned to her. "Of course, what is it?"

"Can I touch you?"

Jason showed that he was unsure about this.

"I'm a physical therapist, and my life is touching people. I know that there is something going on with your body and I'm really curious about it. I won't judge, but do you mind?"

"All right," said Jason. "But be forewarned, you might not like it."

Abby stretched out her hand and slowly laid it on Jason's. She gave a brief hesitation when they came in contact, but held on much longer than Jason would have expected.

"Interesting," said Abby when she withdrew her hand, flexing her fingers as she did so. "Very interesting. It's like a TENs unit that we use at work to give electric stimulation to sore muscles, but you're the one providing the juice." She thought for a moment. "Say, you wouldn't like a job in the clinic, would you?"

They were both laughing when Eric rejoined them as Arsenal scored another goal.

Agreement

Later that evening, Eric had just finished brushing his teeth and was heading for bed when Jason said, "Hey, Eric? Do you have a minute?"

Eric turned toward the dining room table where Jason was seated and took a chair for himself beside his father. "Sure, Dad. What do you want?"

"It was nice to get to know Abby tonight. She seems like a very nice person."

Eric nodded. "Yeah, I like her."

"And you two are spending more and more time together it looks like."

"Yeah, I guess we are."

"Well, that got me thinking about the future," said Jason.

Eric looked over at him and met his eyes for a moment.

"It got me thinking that you and I might not be living together forever. I'm not saying that you're going to be running off with Abby, but something like that could happen. You're twenty-five, have a job, and have savings. Someday you will probably have a life of your own."

Eric took this in and nodded. "Yeah, I guess that could happen."

"Here's the thing. You and I are very comfortable together. We know each other's patterns and sometimes even what the other person is thinking. In fact, we're so comfortable that we hardly ever talk. You assume I had a good day, and I assume you had a good day, but we don't really know what the other did during the day. And we never ask."

"I guess that sounds right. We do our own things and don't need to talk about it."

"But we will. We will need to talk about it. If you're living somewhere else, I'll have no idea about how you are, or what you've been up to. If we don't talk, we can't know. And you never want to talk on your cell phone. So that can be a problem. I love you and want to be part of your life even if you live somewhere else. We need to work on communication for that to happen."

"Like I talk to Mom when she's gone in Cheney?"

"Actually, no. Not like you talk to Mom because you don't talk to Mom. She talks and you listen and barely say anything about anything. We will need to do more than that. You will need to really talk to me."

Eric thought about this. "But I'm not much of a talker, and I hate to use the phone."

"I know, son. It will take some work. It might take a lot of work, but to me it will be worth it. I hope it would be for you, too.

"I guess it would."

"So, I'm thinking that we need to start practicing talking more in the house. And using our cell phones. When we're on the phone, I'm going to start asking you for details if you don't tell me. I know you love details. You just need to express them. Is that OK? I know that you have a hard time with things that aren't scheduled, so we should set up some days and times where we will always call. Maybe you can set an alarm before hand so you'll be ready. Is that something that we can work toward?"

"Yeah, Dad. I know I don't like to talk on phones, but I will try. I love you."

They both stood, and Jason gave Eric a big hug. It had the same reaction as always. When Jason released him, Eric shivered and shook from head to foot, but with a grin on his face.

The Date

ALMOST LIKE a real date, Jason met Kris for an early dinner at Sambar, Dunkirk's only Indian restaurant. Kris had worked as a prep cook for an Indian food truck during college and had fallen in love with the food. Jason had rarely eaten it, but remembered the dishes he'd tried as being good, but a little spicy. He had no idea what to order and so Kris suggested the masala dosa. When he asked what it was, she said, "Kind of like a Mexican crepe," and he thought it sounded good.

"Have you ever been to India?" Jason asked.

"Nope, never even left the United States," said Kris. "I don't travel well."

Something about the way she said it caught his attention, but he let it pass. They were sitting at a table for two and sipping chai while waiting for their orders.

"So, is Kevin excited about graduating?" asked Jason. He was enjoying just being in the same room as Kris.

"He really is. This summer, he has a job lined up here with the Dunkirk Food Bank, but all he can talk about is what he's going to do this fall when he heads back to Indiana."

"Back to Indiana? He likes it there?"

"He's a Midwest boy at heart and just can't seem to get used to northern Idaho. He says he misses the lush deciduous trees and green crops and just feels hemmed in by the hills and mountains here."

This surprised Jason since he assumed that everyone loved the local scenery. "How about you, Kris?" asked Jason, a little fearful of what she might say.

"Oh, I kind of like the setting here. The air's much fresher, and I can't stand the humidity in the Indiana summers, myself."

Jason was heartened by this. "What's excited Kevin about going back this fall?"

"He's going to work for Public Health AmeriCorps, and hopefully find a part-time job, too. Ever since the pandemic he's been interested in public health and is thinking about going into medicine. He's got a good friend in Indianapolis who he can live with rent free, and Kevin wants to be with him and his other friends back there."

"So, will he come back next year?"

"Oh, I highly doubt it. He's applied to Indiana University in Indianapolis and to Purdue. We'll wait and see where he gets accepted. We can't afford it this fall, but with his jobs, and hopefully a scholarship, he thinks he'll have enough to start in the Spring semester."

"Then, you'll be an empty nester?"

"Yeah, and that'll be very weird. I'll miss him. To tell you the truth, I don't really have much of a social network here in Dunkirk. It takes a while to break into the local scene—and I've heard other newcomers say the same thing. I have some friends from a bird-watching club, and I've joined a book club that has stayed virtual since the pandemic, but that's about it."

"Sorry to hear that," said Jason. "You have a group of friends back in Indiana like Kevin?"

Kris thought for a moment. "No, not really. Now that I think about it, I've always been a little bit of a loner, or maybe more of an introvert. I'm not a hermit—I do like people, and that's why I love having my shop in the Mill. But I have to admit that I also like to get back home and have my alone time."

Their dosas arrived, and they mostly concentrated on the food and flavors when it did. Jason was surprised by the texture, especially, and really enjoyed the combination of spices.

Once they'd slowed down and satisfied their hunger, Kris said, "I don't know if I'll stay in Dunkirk after this summer though."

Jason's food suddenly lost all flavor. Around a bland bite of food, he managed to ask, "Oh! Why's that?"

"Well, like I say, I like it here, and Dunkirk is nice, but I'm thinking there might be better options for me out there. I'm going to take some road trips this summer and see what I think of Oregon or Washington."

"But - your business?"

"Oh, I can take that anywhere," said Kris, almost flippantly. She toyed with the remainder of her food. "It's not only the now-very-real possibility of the Redstar Mill closing. It just seems so oppressive in this state, and it's starting to get to me. More and more people packing guns so that it feels like a war zone. It makes them safe, but I'm scared as hell every time I see one. I'm past the age where I need to worry too much about women's health, but it's becoming nearly impossible to get an appointment lately and once you do get a doctor, there's no guarantee that they'll be there for your next visit. The turnover is incredible. You add in the oppressive laws about voting access, schools, and libraries. I mean, Idaho is getting to be like Afghanistan under the Taliban."

She tried to gauge Jason's reaction, but couldn't read him. "I hope that didn't offend you. I mean, I don't even know your political leanings or anything."

All Jason was thinking about was the possibility of her leaving after they'd just met. "Oh, no, I guess I feel pretty much the same way, but have been here so long I don't seem to notice it as much. My ex-wife, Annie, was the one who rooted us here, and most of my friends are from that period. The state's politics make me mad, but so far, we're a little isolated from them here in Dunkirk. Up in the northern counties though—I'd be outta there in a heartbeat."

He didn't know how to tell her not to move. It was her decision, and he hardly knew her. On top of the fact that a real connection was, of course, impossible.

This last thought received an official stamp when Kris said. "Luckily, a move wouldn't really be that hard for me. That's one thing I do like about never getting tangled in a relationship."

Jason was just going to ask what she meant when the waiter arrived. They both dropped their hands to their laps when he took their empty dishes.

Now Jason knew what had caught his attention earlier. *She's avoiding any kind of contact—just like me. And she says that she's a loner. I wonder if...*

The waiter asked if they wanted anything for dessert and both shook their heads. Jason asked for the bill.

The moment to follow up on what Kris had said seemed to have passed. He couldn't think of a way to ask her if she, as a near impossibility, was anything like him physically. That kind of question would become extremely awkward if she wasn't and he wasn't prepared to face that finality just yet. So, he said, "Thanks, Kris, that was really good dosa. Great suggestion," instead.

"Yeah, it was good. And it was nice to eat a meal with someone other than Kevin."

Jason paid, and they walked out to their cars. Jason had brought Kevin's French horn, and they took a minute to transfer it to Kris's trunk. He noticed her keeping her distance as they did so.

"We'll have to do it again sometime soon," smiled Kris as she got in her car. "My treat next time."

"Definitely!" said Jason as she grabbed her car door handle to pull it shut. "Oops! I mean definitely about doing it again!" he yelled in a rush.

"I know!" she said with a laugh and closed the door.

And what a nice laugh, he thought as he stood beside his car and watched her drive away. In his mind, though, she was a contentedly single woman in a fully packed car headed to Oregon.

PAG Meeting · June 2

ROBB HAD been working with Eric, and he passed around the table some of the pages they had in mind for their book, tentatively titled *The Ark: a LONG Voyage.* Jason had leafed through some of the pictures that Eric had drawn at home, but seeing them now placed on a page with Robb's descriptions, he thought they looked very engaging and would easily suit a young audience. Whereas he was skeptical about the book at first, he now saw that it had a real chance of success. Those feelings were echoed around the room.

"I also wanted to mention that both Eric and I received emails from Representative Bosworth's aide thanking us for responding to her questions," said Robb. "But the email also seemed to contain veiled warnings about continuing with the book, given that it was the type that would be unlikely to pass through the screening committee once, or if, that body is established under the proposed act. The email didn't come right out and say it directly, more like 'a book similar to the one we understand you are writing, etc.' Anyway, it's obvious to me that not only the Entity, but probably Bosworth and others know more details about our books than we might think."

No one else had received similar emails, and Morgan said, "It looks like your book is the one that has really struck a nerve somewhere, Robb. Any more threatening emails?"

"Not lately—they seemed to all come in a rush and then tapered off. I would expect a lot more once we get the book out the door, though."

Once that discussion had finished, Charlotte read from an opening chapter in her untitled draft about the *Palouse Kids*.

"'Keep up, Elizabeth, or we'll miss the train!' yelled Rebecca.

"Elizabeth stood at the entrance to the platform trying to take it all in. They had only been to the outskirts of Spokane once before when Papa let them come with him on a trip for supplies. They had seen larger buildings in the distance, but Papa had said that they had no time to explore the city. Today, the wagon ride through town to the train station had taken her breath away, and now she stood in front of a huge, smoking, steel machine. She was both exhilarated and very scared.

"Rebecca ran back and tugged her hand. 'Come on, silly, or you'll be left standing here forever.'

"Elizabeth finally allowed herself to be dragged from her spot and followed her older sister's lead. This was a good thing because she was so busy staring that she had a hard time paying attention to where her feet were going.

"They both tossed their bags up to Mama and first Rebecca and then Elizabeth pulled themselves up the high steps into the coach that seemed to float above the ground.

"Again, Elizabeth just stood. Gleaming brass railings, deep red velvet cushions, polished wood benches and racks made her think that she was in a palace. The sudden blast of the steam engine's whistle made her nearly jump out of her dress. She scurried to the seats they were all sitting in and chose to look backwards to where she had been as this part of their journey began.

"'So, ladies, are you all ready for your first train trip?' asked their mother.

"There were smiles and bobbing heads all around. They all began to chatter at once but were suddenly silent and grabbed each other's hands when the big locomotive jerked as it started off.

"Elizabeth was watching a man walk by on the platform, and all of a sudden it was as if he was standing still. Then he started moving backwards behind them, and she knew that they were on their way to Kamloops."

The group was familiar by now with the tone of the *Palouse Kids* series, and this one matched the other books perfectly. Unfortunately, it was the coming chapters about the boarding schools forced on native children that were of more interest to Jason, as he was sure they were to the others since there were only mild comments after her reading.

Morgan and Maggie both reported on the progress they were making on their books—his a modern-day primer illustrating the benefits of socialism and hers about young lesbian love—and at the end of the meeting, Dennis brought them up to speed on the anti-book banning demonstration.

"The Rag Tag Marching Band will herd us up Main St. to City Hall starting at 11:30 on Saturday, and then the mayor will give opening remarks at noon," he said. "We finally have all the necessary permits, and library and City staff are all on board. There is an added stipulation that the Peacekeepers be present—they're the local group trained to diffuse any disputes that break out during a public event. They'll be unarmed, as always, wearing orange vests, and will be especially watchful for any anti-church disputes. I don't know where the city got the idea that that might happen, but it won't. So, the Peacekeepers won't have anything to do, but they'll be there.

"The speeches will be in two segments. The first will be to ask for the repeal of the *Children's School and Library Protection Act* and request that the City of Dunkirk back this in a formal resolution. And the second part will be support for a new initiative that's being started by a groundswell movement to ban firearms in libraries.

"You all know that guns are permitted in all public buildings in Idaho, except for courthouses, detention facilities, etc. But there are several states that have banned guns in libraries. Vulnerable people feel threatened in a place that needs to feel safe. Lisa is all for this and is excited that the initiative is gaining traction."

"I hadn't heard about that second part," said Jason. "Who started it?"

"I guess it began down in Boise and is a very hot topic in Idaho Falls where all of the big censorship issues are happening. It's modeled on a law in Michigan which bans both open and concealed weapons in libraries. Many say it has no chance of success in this state and the Republican legislature is dead set against it, but I think it's worth the try to help get it onto a ballot," said Dennis.

He took down the names of those who wanted to speak at the event, and the meeting ended.

The Demonstration

IT WAS a sunny day, and the turnout was fairly good for the anti-book banning march up the street to City Hall. Jason always thought it was awkward that marches ending at the hall invariably went up Main St. which paralleled Riverside Road, yet the speeches afterwards were in the direction of the wide strip-park that ran at a right angle from Main, sloping gently down to Riverside Park. It was unfortunate that the narrow streets on either side of the strip-park weren't amenable for a parade, but at least the open expanse could hold a good crowd.

The Rag Tag Marching Band brought up the rear of the march, followed by stragglers who caught up at the last minute. Jason guessed that he could see at least 100 people ahead of him and there were plenty of supporters out on the sidewalks to watch them pass. Banners and placards, mainly featuring books, were popping up and down among the marchers to the tune of *We Shall not be Moved*. As they drew closer to City Hall, he began to notice an increasing number of men openly displaying their sidearms and rifles. He then remembered that this demonstration was also about a proposal to disallow firearms within public libraries.

The trombone player's truck was parked near City Hall and, as the parade ended, the band headed for it while the marchers continued around the corner of the building to the strip-park.

"Quite a good showing," said Art, a little winded from the trek up Main, puffing on his clarinet the whole way. He was pulling it apart and placing it carefully in its case while Jason wrestled himself from his sousaphone. Eric had already stashed his drum and gone off to find Abby.

"Yeah, but those guys standing over there are a bit of a surprise," said Jason, inclining his head to point across the street to an increasing number of armed men. None of them appeared to be from an organized group—they seemed to include bikers, men barely out of high school, guys fully decked out in camo gear, and a few men in business suits. He'd only picked out one or two women displaying guns, so far. "Thankfully, they're not from that militia."

Art eyed them from the side. "On the contrary, I'd say most of them are in a militia."

Jason then looked more closely. "That mishmash? I doubt it."

"Don't forget, we have one militia from right around these parts, and another just over in Plummer. Most of those guys are from those two. I wouldn't be surprised if there were more from Coeur d'Alene, too."

"Where are the uniforms then?" asked Jason.

"I tried to find out more about that group at the library rally, but no one seems to know where they came from. The press is guessing Spokane, and the police aren't saying. Local gossip has it that they are related to the Entity. The uniforms are apparently rare. These militias here are just guys who agree that they'll get together to," and he made air-quotes, "'defend their freedom.'"

"Well, I hope they don't cause trouble," said Jason paying attention again to packing up his sousaphone.

"Me, too, Jason. Me, too."

Jason walked with Art to the front of the hall and then parted with him and wandered down the opposite side of the park to the rear of the crowd where he'd arranged to meet Kris. She had said that she'd wanted to see him again, but also that she was becoming more interested in stopping book bans and was definitely against guns in the library.

"I missed the march," she said. "How was it?" as he joined her.

"Fine, and this is quite a turnout after all. I was worried a little by the number in the parade, but the park was already partially filled when we got here."

"Did you notice all of the guns, though?" asked Kris. "Should we be worried?"

"I don't think so. Look at all the police, and those people in orange vests are the Peacekeepers to help keep order, too. The saber-rattling is getting to be more and more common, but they've never overreacted."

When everyone from the march was assembled in the strip-park, Mayor Larson began his introductions and opening remarks. Apart from no choir interrupting him this time, and the switch in roles between him and Lisa, the first part of the proceedings was very similar to the earlier one in Library Park. Many of the same participants were there and many of the speakers said many of the same things.

But the situation changed when the topic turned to banning guns from libraries. The mayor had just introduced Sue Belkin who was the local representative for the 'Books Don't

Need Arms' initiative when many of the men with firearms coalesced into a large group near the front of the park. The rally speakers stood on the steps leading up to the City Hall entrance, and there was a paved area between the steps and the park. Sue was halfway through her speech when the armed mass to the side unfurled a large Second Amendment banner and held it up high along with an assortment of flags. Several of the Peacekeepers moved over to that corner of the park in reaction.

The motley militia was polite during the remainder of speeches, but as the mayor began his closing remarks, they marched their banner out in front of him and, a now swollen number of them, moved in to fill the space between the mayor and the front of the crowd, turning to face the rally audience as they did so. Where they all came from, Jason hadn't a clue, but he guessed that the rally had brought out protesters made up of nearly every type of gun owner in the area—and beyond—to protect their Second Amendment rights. Many of the Peacekeepers moved to place themselves between the militia and the rally crowd.

The interlopers were all chanting, 'Guns are basic rights,' and their sheer numbers began to force the rally crowd to move further back down the park. It was a peaceful but forceful counter-protest, although the presence of guns obviously made it seem more than that, and many at the front of the crowd were turning and weaving their way through the other rally folks to avoid them.

Jason was searching for Eric and Abby who had been toward the front of the crowd and finally picked them out, nearly face to face with the armed men. Mayor Larson was calling for order above the chanting, and Jason noticed Abby lifting up her phone to film him and then pan down the line of the militia and finally turn around to capture the rally scene. One of the militia had so many behind him that he had no choice but to try and create some space between him and the rally, and he gave Abby a gentle shove. Unfortunately, this threw her off balance and the phone jumped out of her hands as she tried to stay upright. Some other members of the crowd were being jostled by men in camo as well, and the front of the rally was retreating before them. Abby was bending over to retrieve her phone when Jason was amazed to see Eric say something and then push the man back. The man's pushing of Abby had obviously offended his son's sense of what was appropriate behavior. The next thing Jason knew, Eric was on the ground, having been forcibly shoved back by the man in camo and losing his footing. Jason was unsure what had happened to his son, but then, through gaps in the crowd, he saw Abby kneeling next to Eric and trying to help him up, glaring at the man the entire time.

The crowd had backed up several paces, except for two men and a nearby Peacekeeper who were helping Abby get Eric up when Jason began to make his way through the crowd to his son. Occasional contact by him made random crowd members twist their heads toward him in surprise or quickly step away.

Eric had a black and white sense of right and wrong, was stubborn, and subtleties had always escaped him. When he was young, he'd made a point of avoiding fights at any cost, but if he was dragged into one, he could never read any signs of contrition and went all in. This is what worried Jason at the moment. He hoped his son had moved past this.

He was very near them when Eric was able to stand, stepped up, and gave the man a hard push back. The militia man had a determined look on his face when those he was shoved into behind him pushed him back in Eric's direction. As he came forward, he positively decked Eric with a single punch. The chanting suddenly stopped.

Abby screamed, and Jason ran up and knelt by his son while the Peacekeeper stepped toward the man and started to engage him in a conversation to diffuse the situation.

"Eric, are you alright?"

Eric nodded and rubbed his jaw. "That man shoved Abby, and I was showing him what it felt like," said Eric, pointing directly at the man who was now looking a little confused. "I've never been hit before," he continued. "Not so that it knocked me down."

"Well, that punch was uncalled for, but you don't need to punch him back."

Then Jason's protective instincts took over. He stood and stepped toward the accused man and repeated what he'd just said to Eric. "That was absolutely uncalled for. This was a peaceful rally until you protestors showed up. You have no right to be here, and I think the police need to get involved," he said, waving his hand and trying to get the attention of the police who were already making their way over. The Peacekeeper was doing his best to try and keep some element of calm until other Peacekeepers along the line could reach him and help out. The militia had rallied behind their man, and several in the crowd were stepping forward to support Eric who moved up close behind his father.

Jason saw a few hands drop toward weapons and was thinking that the situation was not good. Not good at all. To stall for time until the police arrived, he raised his hands in a placating gesture and said, "Let's not have any trouble here. As I said, this is a peaceful rally, and there's no need for things to get out of control."

There were several shouts of "Yeah, move on," "Leave us be," "Assholes," and the like which Jason thought were not helpful in the slightest. The Peacekeeper had turned and, motioning with his hands, tried to get the shouters in the crowd to tone it down. The officers were just nearing them when the instigator took half a step forward. Eric then stepped forward in response, unfortunately knocking Jason into the man.

The air suddenly became electric between the two. Jason prayed that there would be no reaction, that maybe the camo gear was enough to shield the man from the shock that contact with Jason could cause. Instead, the opposite happened. The man's eyebrows momentarily flew up and then lowered into a fierce frown. His sidearm came out at the same moment and before anyone could blink there was a loud bang. Jason crumpled backwards onto the ground.

Several things happened then. Some of the militia scattered, but most remained and squared off with their weapons, immediately warned by shouts to drop them at once and by the drawn guns from the police officers. Many of the militia and the shooter instantly complied, but one, nearest the policemen, raised his weapon toward them and was immediately brought down by two shots. Meanwhile the crowd had panicked and had either flung themselves onto the grass or were running for their lives.

While several officers were using their weapons to cover the man on the ground and the defiant remainder of his militia, Officer Tennent was kneeling beside Jason, yelling into his microphone for an ambulance while feeling for a pulse at Jason's neck, pulling back, and then forcing himself to feel again. Eric was staring down at his father as if frozen, when Art ran up. "Oh my god..." he stammered.

Waking Up

JASON REMEMBERED snippets of several things before he could even open his eyes. Art saying, "Oh my god…;" Officer Tennent saying, "We still have a pulse;" and a stunned voice, "… right in the heart!" The odd thing to him later was that he couldn't remember anything about being shot. Only that Eric had been knocked down in an altercation, but not the events that followed.

He was in and out of consciousness for several days and was finally able to have a conversation with his doctor and retain what was being said to him on the third day.

"To tell you the truth, Mr. Deakins, we were incredulous at first. There was a hole in your chest just to the left of center, exactly where your heart should be, and we were still getting a pulse well after you'd been shot. You should have died long before, but your heart kept beating. You're only alive because you are one in every twelve thousand people that could have survived a shot like that. We opened you part way up to manage the bleeding and discovered that you have *dextrocardia situs inversus totalis*. Were you aware of this condition?"

"Dextro… what?" wheezed Jason, vaguely remembering having heard a similar word sometime before.

"*Dextrocardia situs inversus totalis*. It's a rare condition where every one of your organs is situated on the opposite side of where it should be, in other words, in a mirror image. In some related cases, only the heart, say is reversed, but in you, all your internal organs are on the opposite side from the norm. The bullet that should have pierced or nicked the heart just missed a major artery and went through lung tissue instead. You're one lucky son of a bitch, if you don't mind me saying so.

"You still have a lot of healing to do, and we're going to keep a close watch on you. We had to spread a few ribs to remove some bone fragments, and it may be several days yet before that left lung is reinflated. You should be with us for about ten days or so at a minimum," the doctor said.

He then studied Jason with his hand on his chin. "On a side note, I've been talking with your son, and he explained the strange reaction you seem to cause when people come into contact with you. Before we knew this, it took me and the surgical staff several minutes to get used to the strange sensations—like you were being subtly electrocuted while we were operating. We even stopped everything to make sure that no electrical equipment was shorting out in the operating theater. One nurse nearly had to leave her station, but she soldiered through." He reached out and touched Jason's arm as if to re-experience the effect and gave an odd smile. "Do you have any idea of the cause? Have you seen other doctors about this?"

Jason shook his head. "Nope," he whispered. "The few doctors I've seen have no idea why... I had a dear friend just like me... and we figured we were just wired differently." Jason gulped air. "One doctor tried to measure it... but couldn't detect anything... with an EEG." It took him a minute to catch his breath after this.

"It's all right, you don't need to speak, but there is something going on with you. We were curious and brought in a meter that measures galvanic skin response, or electrodermal activity, and your skin was off the charts, even for a baseline. In fact, it is so far off the charts that it might not even be related to electrodermal activity. I thought it might have something to do with your *dextrocardia situs inversus totalis*, but I have found nothing in the literature to indicate any connection. Nor can I find much if anything about EDA levels being as high as yours are. As you say, you're wired differently, and I have no idea how. If you allowed yourself to be studied, I'm sure a researcher would have a field day and love you for it."

Jason shook his head slightly. "I'll take a pass. Still... it's interesting to know ... that my effect is... measurable... and that it's a real thing."

"Oh, definitely real. I talked with the police, and the man who shot you has no idea why he reacted like he did. He said you bumped into him, and he suddenly felt so threatened that he wanted to kill you."

Jason found himself thinking that if he needed another reason to avoid crowds—this was it.

Visitors

ERIC AND Abby were constant fixtures in the ICU during the limited visiting hours. Abby was slowly getting past the shame she felt for bolting across the park the moment the gun was drawn and fired. Jason was never sure how Eric processed that emotion, but his son said that he had been picturing all of what could have happened within Jason's body and so was unable to respond. Jason reassured them both that it was impossible to know how one would react in any given situation, especially in such a sudden and dangerous one. He was very happy to have their support and was touched that the two appeared to be even closer now than they had been before the shooting.

More visitors began arriving when Jason was moved to the general care unit, with Eric and Abby assuming the role of gatekeepers, especially with the press. The police had been a frequent presence in the ICU, and the reporters showed up later when allowed. One reporter, John Darcy, whom he'd met with Robb before, was more interested in the exchange he'd had with Representative Bosworth's aide than with the details of the shooting. He also tried to engage Jason about the curious effect he had on people, but Jason had played the aching chest wound card to avoid it.

The militia man who'd been shot had spent three days in the same hospital and attracted most of the attention before being transferred to another facility in Spokane. Jason's shooter was being held in the local jail and garnered the remainder of the media's attention. The confrontation had made national news, but luckily the focus was on the militia and the police response to them during the event. Several arrests were made, and cries for both stronger gun control and for greater gun rights battled in the state and on social media.

Art Parker and many members of the Panhandle Authors' Group stopped by often, but Jason had two unexpected visitors as well. He was just waking from a nap when Kris Seever popped her head in. Jason was suddenly fully awake.

"Hi Jason, is this a good time?" she asked tentatively.

"Yeah, this is a great time," Jason wheezed. His collapsed lung and days of breathing tubes had caused a wispy rasp to his voice. "Come on in."

"Oh, good," she said and walked up to stand at the end of the bed.

"Have a seat," he croaked, trying to clear his throat again as he gestured to the chair next to the bed.

He tried to reach the water bottle and straw on the little table beside him, but it was just out of reach.

Kris could see that he needed the water and walked up to the bedside stand, but then hesitated. She finally picked up the bottle and reached forward to pass it to Jason.

Oh, shit, I can't let us touch, was his only thought as the bottle neared his hand. Luckily, Kris was holding the bottle at the bottom and Jason was able to grasp the top without any contact between the two. Then he remembered that she might have been having the same thought as he did when she passed the bottle.

He took a couple of big sips and then everything seemed easier.

"Ah, that's good," he said in a more normal voice. "It's great to see you. Thanks for coming by, Kris."

There was that beautiful smile, but her eyes betrayed her concern. "Yes, of course. I've been so worried about you," cheering Jason up immediately. "How are you doing?"

"Good. The doctors say I'm heading in the right direction. Some pain and trouble breathing, but otherwise good."

"I'm so glad to hear that, Jason. Do they know when you'll be able to get out?"

"They think maybe in a week or two, so not too long."

Kris looked down at the bed sheets. "I don't think I've ever been so shocked in my life. I saw the entire thing." She looked up and met his eyes. "When you fell down, I thought for sure he'd killed you..." she almost whispered.

Jason was a humbled that she seemed to care so much. They'd only met a few times, but he was glad to see that she'd felt the same attraction as he had.

"Lucky for me he was such a bad shot," joked Jason to break the mood and cheer her up. "And I'm OK."

"Yes," smiled Kris. "Yes, you are."

Jason could feel his healing begin at that moment. His euphoria dissipated soon after she left, however, when he remembered that a relationship between them was unlikely. *Unless she could tolerate me, like Ann did, at least for a while,* he wondered. *Would that be worth it? Or, maybe she wouldn't need to merely tolerate me. Maybe my hunch is right?*

A Lawyer

HIS OTHER unexpected visit was from his lawyer, Jay Fontaine. After pleasantries, Jay soon got down to business.

"Now, I don't have to be the one to represent you in this, Jason, but I was contacted by the District Attorney and by Justin Holt's lawyer and they both suggest that you might need an advocate. Holt is the man who shot you."

"Why would *I* need a lawyer?" asked Jason.

"Because Mr. Holt claims that he was acting in self-defense."

"What?" yelped Jason, sitting forward in spite of the pain he knew would come. If the monitors were still hooked up to him, alarms would have blared. "He shot me!"

"Calm down, now. I know. This is almost routine in a situation like this. The man has been charged with both assault and attempted murder and is casting about for anything that will save him."

Jason settled back into his bed with an aching chest as Jay continued. "His lawyer thinks his charge is valid because there is camera footage which shows you appearing to shove the man, and then he draws his gun in response." He immediately held out a hand to reassure Jason that this was apparently not a big concern. "Fortunately, there is another camera angle taken by someone recording the event for the library that shows Eric knocking into you and pushing you into the man. It was obviously an accident, and the reaction was beyond extreme for the situation. They of course need to review and verify the validity of the recordings, but that shouldn't be a problem.

"Unfortunately," he continued, "his claim means that this will go to hearing and may end up in court. There's no reasonable way that you would be found culpable, but you will need an attorney to represent you, nonetheless."

"Well," said Jason. "I guess you're hired then, Jay."

First Contact

JASON HAD suffered a setback due to a lung infection and was put in isolation for several days—and he slept through most of it. When back in the general care unit, he still had a bad cough which sometimes caused extreme pain in his chest.

The attention by the press had died down, but Eric and Abby still felt the need to be guardians and helped keep any visits short. Kris had come by frequently, and he'd slowly begun to know a little more about her and her son. She'd brought by a newspaper article with a picture of Kevin and his senior debate team winning the last high school event of the year. She always kept a respectful distance during her visits, and Jason now guessed that she was afraid of passing on some other respiratory infection to him, as she always wore a mask. Unfortunately, this also meant that there were no smiles to be to be enjoyed.

He was alone and reading Maggie's draft manuscript while he could manage to stay awake. It felt good to still have some contact with the authors' group. At his request to her, he was reviewing her young adult novel about the coming of age of a lesbian. He not only found her use of language very age appropriate, but the book was also a tender treatment of a delicate subject. He thought that if they banned this book in Idaho, it would certainly find a readership nationwide. He also realized that this joint effort to produce some books that would bring awareness to the censorship issue seemed to be challenging the authors to dig deeper than they normally might. And from what he could tell, some excellent prospects appeared to be on the horizon.

He'd finished a chapter when his eyes closed, the pages dropped to the bed covers, and he dozed off. He'd been in more pain than normal, and they'd given him some morphine to help ease it. Jason was dreaming that he was performing with a jazz band, but he couldn't find his music, and when he stepped up to the vibraphone, the tone bars had changed to sponges which made no sound at all when he struck them. Then, as happens in dreams, he was in the audience near the front watching the band commence playing, and the crowd started moving forward, beginning to press in on him. He'd started to panic when a hand reached down and pulled him back up on the stage which had morphed into a quiet, crowd-less room. The person who'd rescued him took form, and it was Miriam, holding his hand and smiling up at him.

He awoke with the same warm sensation radiating up his arm and the feeling that he really was holding someone's hand. He slowly opened his eyes, focused, and was startled to see Kris sitting in the chair next to the bed. When he realized that it was her hand he was holding, he reflexively jerked it away. Still waking and confused, he watched her reach out and gently retake his hand.

What the hell? was all he could think at the moment. But then he managed, "What's happened?" And then, hopefully, "Did my electric charge finally disappear?"

He noticed that Kris, now maskless, had been crying. She shook her head. "Nope it's still there. It's me. It's us."

Then he recalled his hopeful suspicion. "You mean we're the same?"

"Yeah, Jason." Then she positively beamed, "Amazingly—we are!"

He was still processing. "But how did you… you just happened to touch me?"

She was shaking her head again, and some more tears fell from eyes that did not look the least bit sad. "I came in to see you, and Eric was here. He said that he'd just popped in to check on you, but you were sleeping. I said that I'd stay for a while and headed over to this chair. That was when Eric told me, 'Be careful not to touch my dad, or you might be in for a bit of a shock.' I asked him what me meant, and he told me about your… condition. I was floored. I didn't dare tell him that I have the same thing going on with me. I was too afraid to try at first, but after he left, I took the chance to take your hand. And sure enough." Then she stared down at their two clasped hands.

Jason lifted them, still not daring to believe what he was seeing, but at the same time being flooded with a warmth that he'd experienced only with Miriam. He vaguely processed that what she said must be true—unless this was another part of his dream, and he hadn't really woken up yet.

Kris was crying and grinning at the same time. "I've never met a single person like you in my entire life," she choked. "I thought I was alone. I didn't dream it would be possible. But… But here you are!"

Jason tried to tell her about Miriam, but ended up coughing and wracked with pain. Kris intuitively reached out and held her hand on his chest which seemed to take his mind off the spasms, and he had the sensation of falling into warm water as he passed out again.

Together

Jason and Kris spent all the time possible with each other in the hospital and knew that they would likely do so for the rest of their lives. They shared their experiences—his with Miriam, the difficulties Kris and he had each faced, and the loneliness that they'd become so accustomed to. Initially, they clung to each other as if their lives depended on it—batteries being recharged after a lifetime of running on empty. But after the reality of having found one another had sunk in, they each felt that they could relax and be at peace with the world for the first time in a very long while.

When Jason moved home, their first intimacies were 'organic' as Jason later came to think of it. Compared to the jangled sex with Ann, being with Kris was sensual and utterly fulfilling, apart from the chest pain that Jason was still experiencing, but he knew that part would pass.

Naturally, they'd assumed that things would flow seamlessly after finding each other.

"But you were shot!" cried an anguished Kris. "This place just isn't safe anymore!"

Jason had been home for a week, and they were snuggled together on the couch as best they could to keep Jason comfortable. And he was comfortable—as long as she was with him. However, he was also realizing that fitting their lives together was not going to be as easy as they had first thought.

The guns and militias had Kris in a state. The community's reaction to the shooting had been a swift condemnation with calls to repeal the new law allowing the formation of militias and cries to adopt stronger gun laws.

The statewide backlash to these calls for reform had been even more adamant. Blaming what they saw as a riotous crowd compared to a well-organized, controlled response by the militia, several state senators were proposing bills that called for strict guidelines for any gatherings, and for the militia, local police, or the military to be authorized to step in and disperse any crowds that were deemed to be 'unruly.' Another legislator proposed no outdoor demonstrations and that only meetings in rooms with a capacity of 100 people or less could be authorized for assemblies. National groups like the NRA, the Freedom Caucus, and many white supremist organizations flooded the airwaves and the Idaho legislature with demands for further protection of the Second Amendment and calls to change laws regarding the right to assemble.

Dunkirk was shaken, and there were demonstrations for the abolition of militias countered by marches by gun owners and gun toters calling for a further strengthening of the Second Amendment. 'Militias—a God given, constitutional right' was the new catchphrase on banners and on talk radio.

The Holy Grace Church announced that it had created a militia 'to keep Christians safe in this time of great animosity towards them,' and the accompanying newspaper article contained a photograph of Cutler standing before a group of men dressed identically to the ones Jason had seen in front of the Goodwin building and at the library rally.

"I want to move away from here, Jason," said Kris now sounding deadly serious. "I'm suddenly realizing that with Kevin leaving soon, I have nothing keeping me in this frigging state. Except you, now, and I don't want to lose you. We need to get out of here."

"Kris, this is just a phase. I'm sure sanity will prevail," said Jason trying to hide the uncertainty he felt as he said it. He looked around the room. "We both have homes here, Eric is here, my music is here, and my business is in Dunkirk. Believe me, I've thought about moving before, but when it comes down to it, it won't be easy. Maybe even harder than it's worth. Besides, it would take time to find the right place to settle down. What if we end up moving to somewhere with even bigger problems?"

"Bigger problems?" asked an incredulous Kris, pulling her head back. "Bigger than armed men marching in the streets daily? Bigger than you being shot?"

Tears formed in her eyes, and she began to cry in frustration. He pulled her back into him and kissed her cheeks. "Don't worry..." and he knew this was the right time to add it, "Hon. Things will work out. We just need some time to adjust and to let the town settle down a little. Then we can see the best way to move forward. Don't you think?"

"No, I don't," she stared hard at him. "It's just not safe, and it's going to get worse. I expect someone to kick down our door at any moment." She thought for a second and said, "And in case you're wondering, no, I'm not going to be buying a gun to protect myself either."

"Well, Kris," Jason said reasonably. "Just look at me. I'm not going anywhere anytime soon. I'm not even supposed to carry any weight yet, let alone pack up a house. We have some time. Let's just see what we think after a few more weeks and after I've healed up."

She looked at him and then relented. "OK, a few more weeks." And then, "As long as we can live through it," in almost a whisper.

"We definitely can," he said. "I'm not against moving from Idaho in the slightest, but we'll just need to find the right place to land and be sure we can make a go of it there."

Kris seemed to relax somewhat.

Jason couldn't believe his luck in finding her, but the two initially had a hard time adjusting to the fact that they'd actually discovered someone who was completely compatible with them after entire lifetimes of virtual isolation and continually keeping others beyond arm's reach. Each time they got together in the week following Jason's hospital discharge had the air of a winning lottery ticket that could be swept from their hands by the wind at any moment. It took time for them to accept that they could be together as a couple forever. Given Jason's semi-detached relationship with Eric, the possibility of another person in his life was not a huge stretch. But for Kris, it caused unexpected stress and doubt. Kevin had been her sole companion since the day he was born, and she felt like she was being pulled in two directions. For a few days, Jason thought that this might harm their relationship, but Kevin had quickly stepped up. He'd convinced Kris that he couldn't be happier for her, and that he was heading off for college and a life of his own in any event. It had taken a visit with her therapist for Kris to come to terms with the fact that this was her life, and that a one in a million chance had just fallen into her lap. Now, the therapist was helping her with her newly acquired fear of firearms.

The Hearing

THE HEARING had been scheduled for as soon as Jason was able to attend, and he was driven to the courthouse by Jay Fontaine ten days after his release from the hospital. Justin Holt, Jason's shooter, was seated across the room and would stare steely eyed at Jason whenever Jason looked in his direction. Jason still couldn't understand how he could be on the defensive side of this case. Neither of the two principals in the matter were asked to testify. However, both the prosecutor and Jay were asked to lay a hand on Jason and describe their reactions to the judge. Jay had been accustomed to the sensation from Jason's divorce proceedings, but this was a new experience for the prosecutor, one which luckily for Jason was a mild reaction and discounted as a major contributing factor to the alleged assault.

After the first day when the prosecution had presented its evidence in videos recorded during the shooting, and had taken the testimony of several militia members, Jason began to worry that he really might be found guilty of assault. Jay didn't seem to be concerned and told him to wait and see what tomorrow would bring when they would be able to present their case.

Eric joined them on the trip to the courthouse the next day as one of the witnesses Jay was going to call. Eric answered all of the questions directly, and Jason was once again impressed with his maturity and professional demeanor, especially given that Holt seemed to be nonverbally taunting him the entire time. The video which clearly showed the actual sequence of events was played multiple times in slow motion with much dissection by both sides. Two video experts gave testimony, each verifying the authenticity of the recordings.

By the end of the hearing, it was clear to all present that Jason was faultless, and the accusation that he had started the confrontation was found by the judge to be without merit. The next scheduled hearing targeted Holt for assault and illegal discharge of a firearm, but neither Jason nor Eric was required to be present. After asking their preference, Jay took them both out to Eric's favorite restaurant to celebrate.

Advice

Jason wasn't yet able to work on instruments, but he was taking walks to rebuild his strength and stamina. He stopped by Art's house to check on the shop and to visit with his friend.

"Glad that you can get out and about now, Jason," smiled Art as he opened the door and invited him inside. "I've got some coffee—and a coffee cake I baked—all hot and waiting. Come on in."

The pair sat at the small kitchen table, and Art poured some coffee after slicing them each a piece of the cake. He patted his belly. "I made this cake for you, and maybe you should take it home when you leave. After all, it's you who needs to regain your strength, and some weight. Not me."

They each tried the cake. "Hey, this is good," said Jason.

"Why so surprised?" asked Art. "You're looking so much better, Jason. You can't believe what everyone went through when we thought you were, well, dead."

"Oh, yeah, I'm much better compared to that!" laughed Jason and immediately regretted it as he caught his breath sharply from the pain.

"Ouch," said Art. "Sorry about that. But thank your lucky stars you're alive and able to laugh about it." He took another bite of cake and a sip of coffee. "So, how are things otherwise?"

"Good," replied Jason. "Actually, so much better than good. I know you ran into her at the hospital, but do you know much about Kris?"

"No, not much. Only that you met someone who can actually stand you," grinned Art. "So, tell me more."

Jason filled him in about her and told him the story of Miriam that he had never related before.

Art had learned about his reversed internal organs during a hospital visit. "Incredible," said Art. "I knew you had that… that, electric-type thing going on with you, but I never thought that there might be others with the same—thing." He considered for a moment. "So, you say that Miriam had a mirror image heart, and so do you. Does that mean that Kris has the same condition? Her organs are in backwards, too?"

"That was one of the first things we wondered. It had never occurred to her to ask before, so she discussed it with her doctor and found out from some scans she'd had taken that everything seems to be fine with her, internally. She'd also had some arrythmia, and they'd done an echocardiogram of her heart and found nothing irregular other than her heartbeat. And that it had been difficult to find a technician who could stand to give her the test!"

Art laughed. "Now I know what the doctor meant when he told me that your operation had met with some unexpected difficulties. Anyway, I thought that your organ reversal would be the answer for your 'effect,'" making air quotes.

"Us, too," said Jason. Then he suddenly broke out into a huge smile. "Us," he said again. "I don't care what the cause is anymore, just as long as I have her. I'd never have thought it possible."

"To that!" said Art, and they clinked coffee cups.

Surprising Art, Jason suddenly turned serious.

"Art, would you ever leave Idaho? Would you ever move to escape the aggressive and, to me, ignorant conservatism it's embracing?"

Art stared at Jason in silence for several heartbeats.

"That's a very good question, Jason. A very good question, indeed. In fact, it's one I ask myself nearly every day lately. Why? Are you thinking of moving?"

"Sometimes, but it's really Kris who wants to get out of Dodge. The shooting was so shocking, so personal, and the aftermath looks like things are only going to get worse. She wants to go, but so far, I want to stay."

Art looked up toward the ceiling for a moment. "I've wondered how many times in history people have faced the same dilemma. Stand and fight, or flee to live another day? Sometimes it was obvious—in hindsight, and there would have been no choice. You know, like if you knew in advance that it would be run or die. Here come the Huns, here come the conquistadors and their smallpox, here comes the plague, here comes Vesuvius. But other situations are more nuanced. Here comes the Third Reich. But could we have won the war without the Resistance? Here comes McCarthyism. But could we have fought that back without those who held fast to basic principles of democracy? What if people hadn't stood up during the civil rights movement in the South?

"You have to wonder in a state like Idaho, don't you? It is so overwhelmingly Republican and is bringing in people attracted to white supremacy and Christian nationalism. Dunkirk, Moscow, and parts of Boise have been bastions of the liberals, but at the statewide level, does it even matter? We get a few Democrats into the legislature—does it make a difference? It used to. We used to have a Democratic governor once in a while and Democratic Senators and Representatives. That will hardly be possible now. The state is so far right that even the local seats in the State House are tough to get into by the minority party.

"Plus, here in Dunkirk, in other towns in Idaho—and in growing areas of the country—there is the Entity, or versions of it, stealthily trying to change things into a whites-only Christian government. The rich and powerful will love it because they'll become even richer and more powerful. Who can say what luck they'll have in bending everyone else to their will?

"So, should I stay, or should I go? That's an epic question. Leaving has a chance of making it worse for everyone else, and staying means the possibility of making it worse for you. And there is always the chance of staying and having it become too late to leave. We could be in the Warsaw ghetto and not even know it. When do camo shirts become brown shirts? How do we know if we're passing the point of no return? Are we overreacting? Who knows? No one does—either this is more like a fad, or it's already too late."

"Um, thanks, I think. It's really hard for me to see any advice in this, Art."

Art stared at him and then grinned. "Oh, didn't you know? I suck at giving advice."

"Ah," said Jason and then smiled. "That's why you never write letters to the editor."

"You haven't seen nothin' yet. The editor has just agreed to let me be a columnist. You'll be reading my sage words every week or two."

Jason was concerned by this. "But Art—people were practically camped on your doorstep after that ad you posted. Aren't you worried that they'll turn into an army?"

"Nope, not in the slightest. I figure that I'll be hitting them from so many sides, they won't know where I'm coming from." He finished his coffee. "Really, I decided that it's time I stepped up and offered my humble opinions to try and keep the other side honest. Besides, I asked around and none of the other bi-weekly contributors have ever had any confrontations at their homes. It seems that when you have a more official status, those who disagree tend to leave you alone—except in letters to the editor."

"I sure hope you're right," Jason said as he stood. "Thanks for the coffee cake—and the advice."

"Anytime," said Art. "Oh, and thanks to you, I have a new fishing partner."

"Good, maybe he can teach you how to catch, too," grinned Jason. "Who is he?"

"Kenneth Nelson, from your author's group. Quite the nice guy, and interesting to talk with. We met at the hospital when you were recovering and found out that we both flyfish. I'd never run into him before because he fishes up above the old bridge. You're right, he's already taught me a thing or two, and I now have trout in the freezer. I'll have you and Kris over for some fresh fish soon."

On his way home, Jason found himself thinking about how different those two were and wishing he could listen in on the conversations Kenneth and Art must have while they casted their lines.

PAG Meeting - August 2

I**T HAD** been nearly two months since Jason had been able to attend a meeting of the Panhandle Authors' Group, and he received a warm welcome back. At their request, he recounted his healing process and assured them that he was doing well.

During the meetings held in his absence, there had been much discussion of whether the book banning project, as it was now called, should be shelved for the time being. Some had argued that it should be dropped immediately, seeing that people's lives could be at stake, and others insisted that they should hold fast and that recent events meant that there was an even greater reason to publicize how extreme the censorship issue had become. Dennis recapped the main points for Jason's benefit and said that no decision had been made by the group as a whole.

"I'm of the opinion that there was no connection between the censorship issue and the militia being at the demonstration," said Dennis. "I think they were there solely because of the initiative to ban guns from libraries. Really two separate issues."

"And several of the others and I keep saying that the whole project was ill-conceived in the first place," said Sharon. "The two were definitely linked because in today's political climate, it doesn't matter what the issue is on the surface. Anything that speaks of being 'woke' will draw opposition, and it could turn violent at any time. I don't know why you keep wanting to antagonize those who want to keep conservative values alive. They'll just hit you back. Just look at Jason."

And everyone did. Jason couldn't think of anything to say about the argument, so he merely shrugged. "How are the books coming along, though?" he asked.

"I'm happy with the new direction I'm taking in my *Palouse Kids* book," said Charlotte. "I've found that the probable cause for the deaths of so many of the indigenous children at the boarding school in Kamloops was likely tuberculosis and so I've added that to the storyline. I think it adds another dimension to the book."

"Actually, very well for me, too," said Dennis. "I'm making good progress on my political thriller set in the South and have drafts out to several here for review. For me, it's been fun. I've been so dedicated to my Seattle series that it's nice to break away from that and come up with completely new characters set in the '50's in the South. I grew up there anyway, making it easy for me to picture, and now I'm wondering if I can keep the same momentum in the Seattle series after this. We'll see." He then looked toward Maggie. "And Maggie is as good as done with hers."

"Yeah, Jason, I've sent out query letters about the book to literary agents and have already received two requests for copies of my manuscript from them," she said.

"Two requests?" asked a stunned Jason. He knew that to even hear back from one agent was nearly impossible, but from two was unheard of by anyone in the group. "Wow, I knew the book was good when I read a draft, but that is fantastic news! I'll bet you'll be published in no time."

Maggie shrugged, a little embarrassed. "I have a huge advantage in that I'm writing in one of the most popular areas in publishing right now—LGBTQ+. It could be, though, that the agents are eager for more, but highly selective after they get copies from authors. Still, I'm hopeful." She paused. "The only thing is that I doubt the book would ever get banned. I've been researching, and so far, no books similar to mine have been on the lists of books being pulled from the shelves. It would just be how it's received in, say Idaho or Texas, that will tell. We'll see. If I get published, that is."

Eric had shown Jason a draft copy of *The Ark: a LONG Voyage,* and Robb now held up a more finished version.

"I think you've seen this, Jason, and in my opinion, it's coming along nicely," flipping through some random pages for everyone to see them from a distance. "I'll pass this around, and any comments would be welcome. Eric has done a fantastic job with the illustrations, and it's nearly ready for submission."

He handed the copy to Morgan, sitting next to him, and then said, "You saw the letter to the editor that Ed Cutler wrote before the rally."

Jason and the others said they had.

"This book is sure to get a huge reaction from the Entity if it comes out," continued Robb. "And, you know that Bosworth and the legislature are gunning for books like this, too. They're going to attack me, but I'm used to that, especially when coming from the church. But it's this authors' group that I'm worried about. There's a chance that they'll come after all of us—like the stalking, threatening phone calls, and public accusations."

He looked around the table. "So, I've been thinking that I probably shouldn't move forward without your consent, since this might impact us all."

With Kenneth no longer attending meetings and Charlotte now fully committed to opposing censorship, the only two strong voices against Robb moving forward were Sharon's and Tamra's. Emily was quiet during most meetings and initially against the idea; she now seemed to agree with the majority.

"I won't stand with you if things get bad," said Sharon. "And I hate to say it, but this may be my last meeting. I'll have to think about it."

"That goes for me, too," said Tamra.

"Fair enough," said Morgan. "But consider this. We're all authors, and we write where the whims take us. It could be that without the goal of writing a banned book, one of us would have come up with one of the books we're writing anyway. And then later, another of us might have, too. There's always been the chance that an 'objectional book' would have popped up in the group at any time. Given our nature from previous books, I don't think it would have rattled any of us. We would have said, 'Hey, it's your choice—write what you want, but it will likely bomb.' Now, many of us have decided to write those bombs at the same time, so it's really no different. We've just shared a common inspiration and are going with it." He thought for a moment. "It's like Indian food. A little garam masala and curry in a dish add a bit of dash. A lot of garam masala and curry make it a full-blown Indian mouthful. It's when it all happens at once that it makes you sit up and take notice, which is the whole point of this exercise."

Sharon, in her normal scowling manner said, "Like I said, I'll think about it."

Then Tamra piped up. "I don't think Robb should publish that book." She had been so quiet at meetings lately that her voice seemed to stand out.

She looked embarrassed for a moment and then blurted, "It goes against God, and it's just another example of Christian bashing. You're all against poor Pastor Cutler and my church all the time. You're all part of negative world—you people never stop."

It was now clear to everyone that Tamra was a member of the Holy Grace Church.

"Wait a minute, none of us are bashing Christianity here," retorted Morgan.

"Yes, you are. You just can't see it," said Tamra, "because you don't experience our persecution—and it happens on a daily basis."

"You're right, I don't experience it. In fact, I don't think that your persecution really exists," said Morgan.

Tamra took umbrage. "Doesn't exist?" she said with raised eyebrows. "There is anti-Christian bias everywhere you look. We're under continual attack."

"Under attack?" asked Morgan. "You're the ones who keep pushing your beliefs on others. We only react when you go too far. It's live and let live, as far as I'm concerned, but your church keeps pushing the boundaries of common courtesy."

"If bias doesn't exist, then why are we not allowed to show our devotion outside of the confines of our church or homes without ridicule? If this is a free country, why can't we sing our hymnals outside when and wherever we want? Why can't we pray when and where we want? Why can't our kids have the moments they choose during the day when they can pray in school?"

The two paused and seemed to choose this time to take a breather. In his mind, Jason saw a muddy, smoking battlefield in Dunkirk with two lone soldiers facing each other. Each holding a weapon, but unsure if either theirs or their opponent's rifle was out of ammunition.

"Look," said Tamra with a sigh. "A non-Christian life really is a threat to us. Not only do we believe that you are all doomed if you don't embrace Jesus Christ as your savior, but you threaten us and our youth. There is so much immorality with the flaunting of homosexuality, adultery, and the emasculation of men in our society. And then the schools teach things that go completely against the Bible. Science has its place, but so much is just theory being promoted as fact."

Morgan was about to reply, but Tamra held up her hand that she wasn't yet finished with her thought.

"It is a matter of our children's souls. If they should be tempted away from the church and should begin to doubt the word of God and the Bible, then they will be lost forever. Would you want to watch your own child slip away and be doomed to an eternity in the fires of hell? Honestly?"

Morgan took a moment. "That is so hard to answer since I don't believe that hell exists in the first place. So, to me it's just an imaginary fear."

"Imaginary!?" Tamra stared disbelievingly at him, and he returned a wan smile.

"This is how I see it," he continued. "We all have the same basic fears and worries. Will I have a warm, safe place to live? Enough to eat? Where will my next paycheck come from? Is this sickness serious?

"And we also have the non-physical worries. Am I being a good enough person? Have I done enough to help my fellow man? Enough to help society, the poor, the less fortunate?

"But, there are many of us who live with manufactured fears on top of those—and the manipulators are the cause of this. Oh, no! Foreigners are coming! Vaccinations will make you sicker than the disease! A shadow government is really in control! And I'm sure that some of my own fears are being manufactured just like this, too.

"I hate to say it, but my view is that religion can offer comfort, but it also manufactures all sorts of fear as well. You live with so many fears that I'll never know. It's like an extra layer of sorrow has been laid over you."

Tamra had been shaking her head vehemently. "Oh, but that's not true. I, we, have the light of Christ shining on us. We're not fearful at all for ourselves—He has saved us. We're only fearful for the fates of others."

Morgan raised his eyebrows. "Honestly? You don't need to worry about us, we're just fine. In fact, we'd be worse if we had to live under the shadow of Christian dictates."

"And we're perishing" replied Tamra, "in this now-immoral country that was created by God for us in the first place. Robb's book and others like it only make it harder for this country to find its way back to the light."

She turned to Robb as she stood up. "Don't publish it Robb," and she strode out of the room.

Everyone was silent, and Jason noticed that no one stood up to ask Tamra to stay.

Then Dennis said, "Well, at least now we know who told Cutler and Bosworth about the goings on here."

"Spies and moles," said Morgan, peering dramatically around the room. "Anyone else want to fess up?" which immediately lightened the mood for everyone but Sharon. She avoided eye contact, but gave no indication of wanting to leave.

"Looks like I picked the right meeting to come back to," said Jason. "I wonder if this will put the brakes on Bosworth and his crazy proposal."

"With this legislature?" asked Dennis. "I highly doubt it."

The remainder of the meeting was taken up with the group members talking about and confessing their own fears, both real and imagined.

The Picnic

THE WEATHER was pleasant, and they were sitting around the picnic table set up on Jason and Eric's small back deck. The chicken and a pork chop had just come off the grill, and the mashed potatoes, slaw, and corn were being passed around the table. This was Kevin's last day in Dunkirk. Jason had finally had a chance to spend time with him and enjoyed his energy and his excitement at moving back to Indianapolis. The Public Health AmeriCorps program Kevin was going to join in the fall suddenly had an opening available, and so he was off to Indiana a month earlier than planned. Kris and Abby had become close during their hospital visits and were chatting about weaving which had become Abby's new passion. Eric focused on petting Grizzly in his lap, but was also interested in hearing about Indiana, since his out-of-state travel experience consisted solely of Washington.

Once they'd all finished eating, Abby clunked on a plastic glass to get everyone's attention. "Ahem," she said, grinning and tossing back her long hair. "Eric and I have an announcement." Jason quickly glanced at Eric. As usual his face was difficult to read, but the subdued smile on it revealed much. "You know that we've been spending more time together, and that my apartment is way too small for a couple. So," and she looked around theatrically, "we've decided to buy a house together!"

This came as a shock to Jason since Eric had never mentioned a thing about it, but at the same time, he found that he wasn't really surprised. Eric had been spending more and more time over at Abby's, and the pair had obviously become true partners. "That's fantastic!" he said. "Are you looking, or have you picked one out?"

"As a matter of fact, that's why I wanted to announce it. We found a nice little place on Fir St. which isn't too far away. It will be just perfect for us, and even has a decent, fenced-in back yard that Grizzly will like or in case we ever decide to get a dog."

"That's great, Abby!" said Kris. "Have you made an offer?" When Abby nodded excitedly, she asked, "Can we see it?"

"Well, of course!" said Abby.

Jason wanted to ask if they could afford it, but knew that they could. Eric was a squirrel and had stashed away all of his earnings the entire time he'd lived with his father.

"Now, you're not going to miss me too much are you, Dad?" asked Eric. "You know we'll be just down the street."

Jason smiled. "Of course, I'll miss having you around but, luckily, I think I've found someone to help fill the gap."

Both Eric and Kris grinned at this. As Eric had been spending more time with Abby, Kris had been doing the same with Jason.

"And," continued Jason, "we're going to keep up the good communication channel. Right, Son?"

Eric nodded. Jason waited and then Eric remembered, met his eyes, and said warmly. "Yes, we are, Dad."

"So," asked Kevin, looking at Kris and Jason. "My big question is, what are the two of you going to do with two big empty houses?"

The pair had been holding hands, and Jason felt Kris give his a gentle squeeze. He gazed at her and then around the table. "We're still not sure which house we'll be living in, but we did agree that we're staying in Dunkirk, at least for the foreseeable future. We've talked a lot about it, and it's so tempting to take this opportunity to pick up stakes and move for a fresh start somewhere more... sane. That's what Kris really wanted to do, especially after the shooting, but she agrees that it's better to stay put for now. We want to help keep Dunkirk the kind of town we'd like to live in."

As the conversation moved on, Jason patted Kris and stood up. "Anyone need anything else?" he asked. Seeing headshakes, he walked across the wooden decking and opened the sliding door.

He washed his hands in the kitchen and then rested his forearms on the side of the sink, staring out the window at the deck, immediately forgetting why he'd come into the kitchen in the first place.

He found himself wondering if they would all look back on this lunch thrown in Kevin's honor and come to see it as a goodbye party. He thought about the choices that Eric and Abby would face and hoped that Abby, or someone like her, would always be there to help Eric 'read the room.' He was curious about where Kevin would end up. He also wondered if he would be staying in this house where he and Ann had raised Eric or whether they'd move to the house where Kris and Kevin had lived. Or maybe they'd sell both of these and find someplace new. Somewhere they could both run their businesses out of?

Kris, rising from the table to see what had become of him, brought him back to the present, and he walked out with the conflicting emotions of the happiness in seeing her, the melancholy of the past, and a little anxiety for the future.

Dishes

JASON AND Abby were washing up after the meal. Kris and Kevin had gone back to her place to let Kevin finish packing. Eric had offered to help with the cleanup, but Jason and Abby had both told him that they could handle the dishes. Jason was washing and rinsing and passing the plates and silverware to Abby while she was drying and telling about some of her more interesting patients—without naming names.

"So, do you have many patients from the Holy Grace Church?" asked Jason out of curiosity.

"Oh, yeah, a few are from the church," said Abby. "They won't come out and say it, but after a while I can tell."

"How do you know? How are they as patients?"

"Just like everyone else, really. I don't know how to describe it, exactly. The women especially don't seem to be up on local events or politics, and both the men and women seem to avoid talking about religion and politics in general. They'll say stuff if I should bring it up, which I rarely do anyway, but they never raise the subject. It's all about the weather, their kids, and for the men, sports. Oh, I lied. When we talk about healing, most will say that God will be the one to do it—not the PT's or routines."

"So, except for that, not so different from anyone else, really. They never try to convert you?"

"Oh, heck no. At least not yet." Abby thought as she stacked the plates and put them in the cupboard. "Actually, one-on-one, they are very nice people. I have two neighbors who are friendly and have helped me out a few times. Once I had a broken pipe in the bathroom, and the neighbor in the house across the street who is a church man came right away with a box of tools, and had the water turned off in no time. Very helpful.

"But as a group, I don't get them. They stay by themselves in church and such, don't join in civic events, but every once in a while, they'll do these provocative things—like that singing during the library demonstration. I mean, what was that for? If they wanted to take over the town like they say they want to, they could do it by just being stealthy. You know, buy up property, move in, buy up more, and eventually they'd own everything—as a big surprise to the town. Instead, they rile people up against them, grab the spotlight. You know, I think their leader just thrives on the attention. And I've thought about this. Being persecuted is part of early Christianity, and I think that it's ingrained in them now. They create situations so that they will feel or say that they are being persecuted, just to keep with tradition."

Jason was done washing, let the water drain, and watched Abby as she put the silverware into the proper trays. *There's so much about this woman that I love, he thought. I'm glad we're getting to know one another. I'm glad that she's family.*

John Darcy

Jason HAD driven home from his first gig with Clearwater since the shooting and felt good that he was able to literally get back in the groove playing with them. His breathing stamina was still not up to par for the saxophone, but luckily, they had performed at a Panhandle College venue and the School of Music had been kind enough to let him use their vibraphone. He felt energized by the performance and, rather than reading before bed, he decided that he wanted to work on editing his book about Miriam. Kris had set up a spare loom in their extra room and was happily working on a new project with some folk music playing in the background. He fired up his laptop and first checked his email.

At the top of his inbox was a message from Dennis.

"Darcy has posted his report on the *First Strike for Children Act,* and it's a stunner! Read below," his short message said. John Darcy, the reporter who had briefly interviewed Jason in the hospital and had spent time with various members of the authors' group, had published the first in a series of reports to go with his podcast, and it confirmed much of what many had suspected. Jason read through the attachment.

The posts in the barbed wire fence that existed between Church and State in Idaho have rotted and disappeared into the range, and the rusted wire has been rolled up and tossed aside. The cattle are lost in the trees, and the wolves are roaming close to homes. This is the story of a spontaneous gesture that has uncovered yet another example laying bare the extent to which the church has infiltrated our houses of government.

The Panhandle Authors' Group, an informal collection of writers in Dunkirk, Idaho wanted to make a statement about the Children's School and Library Protection Act *which they viewed as an unnecessary level of censorship by our state government. They spontaneously decided to try and write books that could be banned under the act in order to bring attention to this censorship and display unity with local librarians. Simple enough. If the books were published and disallowed from local libraries, this would raise more attention to the measure. One of the group's members, Dennis Harris, joked at the beginning that they may also be able to sell more books with the publicity.*

But then a local pastor, Ed Cutler, the well-known leader of the Holy Grace Church, caught wind of their plan—before a single book was even written. How did he discover their attempt at protest, and why did he care? This is where it gets both personal and public.

Among the books proposed by the authors' group was one being written by Robb Fenton and illustrated by Eric Deakins, a children's book which brings into question the survivability of the animals on Noah's Ark. Fenton apparently had two strikes against him in the eyes of Cutler. First, he had been excommunicated from the church and was shunned by its members and, second, his book went against a strictly literal interpretation of Noah's voyage. Cutler wanted to stop this book in its tracks and wrote an open letter to the editor of the Dunkirk Gazette in which he called the authors sinners for even thinking about writing what they had proposed. This strange and abrupt letter caught my eye.

Soon afterwards, the framework for a bill, the First Strike for Children Act *was introduced to a State House committee by Representative Peter Bosworth. This proposed language not only wants to allow only those books that pass screening by a committee to be available to libraries, but it also wants to screen any manuscripts written by state authors—pre-publication. Was the timing of this a coincidence?*

This made me curious enough to drive up to Dunkirk and interview some of the members of the Panhandle Authors' Group and to learn more about Ed Cutler and the Holy Grace Church. Along the way I came to know several podcasters who had also been interested in Cutler and his advocacy for Christian Nationalism and the Quiverfull movement.

Through email exchanges available in the public record, some sent to me anonymously, overheard conversations in the halls of the capitol, and interviews with members of the Panhandle Authors' Group as well as members of the Holy Grace Church including Ed Cutler himself, it is easy to verifiably document the influence of the Holy Grace Church on the crafting of laws in our state. There is no wall to climb over, the doors are wide open.

On the personal level, Ed Cutler was heard on several occasions disparaging Fenton and in one instance said, "I want that book of his buried." In a sermon, he stated that science was one thing, but directly attacking the Bible was an attack on all of the members of the church, specifically mentioning Fenton and his book. When questioned, Cutler chalked all of this up to fallout from a simple dustup between himself and

Fenton. How Cutler learned of Fenton's book in the first place is still unclear, but a few days later his letter to the editor appeared in the Dunkirk Gazette.

On the public side, two aides of Cutler met with Bosworth, as is documented in his schedule. This meeting was conducted behind closed doors, and no notes are available. However, that same afternoon, Bosworth met with two of his own aides, and the three pounded out the draft of the First Strike for Children Act which became very public. I was forwarded an email exchange between Cutler and Bosworth that finessed the wording of the Act.

This is but one flagrant example of The Holy Grace Church and our legislature marching in lockstep across Idaho. Next in my series I will look into other apparent Church-prompted bills: The school vouchers that were implemented to benefit private schools, with the hidden motive to weaken public education and to funnel money into religious schools; the move to eliminate DEI from our universities; and a bill to eliminate same-sex marriage.

Of course, the language of many of these initiatives is spun so that the Children's School and Library Protection Act and the First Strike for Children Act are couched as ways to protect our libraries and make life easier for our librarians; the Idaho Parental Choice Tax Credit is worded so that it appears to be a benefit to public schools; and the anti-DEI move is worded so as to appear to promote equity, where in reality all of these do the exact opposite. The anti-same-sex marriage bill needs no explanation.

Thanks to information provided by another podcaster, I have also learned of the influence the Holy Grace Church had *on the legislation that allows private militias to be formed in our State. Ed Cutler has just announced that the church now has its own private little army.*

Stay tuned.

Jason was alarmed by what he read. He wasn't sure that this report and the other podcasts addressing similar issues would do much to restore the separation between church and state, but he reasoned that at this point, every bit helped.

Opposition

JASON WAS having an odd sense of *déjà vu* without the rock in his shoe—he was walking Kris to the weekly Dunkirk City Council meeting where she was going to present a non-agenda item. She had wanted to become more involved in local issues and to speak up about the sale of the Redstar Mill, but was concerned about crowds. Jason had told her that his solution was to speak on the record the week before the issue became an agenda item, and it would still count. She was nervous about speaking in public, and he'd assured her that this council meeting would be lightly attended.

It was a simple thing, but he loved being able to stroll along the sidewalk holding someone's hand. This route was so familiar to him, but he realized that he may soon be taking a different one into or through town. He and Kris had found a building that was zoned commercial and had a very nice living area above a space that could easily accommodate two shops. It was along Riverside Road and seemed perfect. They'd made an offer through a different realtor than Dunkirk Realty, but it was contingent on the sale of both of their homes at a reasonable price. Someone was interested in Kris's house, but so far there were no bites on his.

They entered Dunkirk City Hall and climbed the stairs to the chambers. At the top, Kris was suddenly hesitant. "Um, I need a sec, Jason. I'm not sure about this."

"You don't have to if you don't want to, but I can tell you that once your testimony's over, you'll see that it's not really that big of a deal. I can stay with you if that would help."

"I'm not so much afraid of the people—well, OK, maybe I am. But I'm more worried that my voice will shake so much, they won't understand me."

"You've practiced enough that I don't think that will be a problem. Remember, it's only three minutes, max."

She looked down the hall to the chamber doors and took a deep breath. "OK. You're right. I can do this. Easy as pie."

He started to walk down the hall with her, but she squeezed and then let go of his hand. "That's OK, Jason. You need to get to your meeting, and I can do this."

He looked at her, trying to keep his face neutral.

"Really," and she smiled. "See you at home."

He gave her a hug and was about to turn back for the stairs and his meeting when he asked, "But you don't mind if I stay, do you?"

She grinned, grabbed his hand, and led him into the council chambers.

Jason was proud to see that Kris hid her nervousness well as she stepped up to the mike to give her testimony.

She quickly studied the paper she'd brought and then began. "Thank you, Mister Mayor, and Council members. My name is Kris Seever, a resident of Dunkirk, and I'm here to testify about the proposed planning and zoning changes for the anticipated sale of the Redstar Mill coming up at your next meeting. I want to state on the record that I hope that sale won't be allowed as proposed.

"My store, Kris Weaves, is located on the third floor of the Mill, and I could not have hoped for a better location in all of Dunkirk. The sales, of course, are very good in that spot, but that is not the reason I consider the location to be so outstanding. The collection of artists there forms a hive of creativity and inspiration. I can't describe the level of artistic enthusiasm that you can find when you spend some time in the Mill. I know that I've created some of my best weavings in the shop simply from being in the midst of so much imagination and encouragement.

"You may not also be aware that that three-story tall gray tower is like a beacon to shoppers and artists throughout the Northwest and beyond. Just the other day, I had a customer from Maine stop in my shop who had made a special trip from visiting relatives in Spokane just because she'd heard so much about the fantastic art coming out of the Mill. All the way from Maine!

"If the Mill is sold, it will be a huge economic blow to the community, and also a social blow. It is coming to the point where this very city council will need to decide up front whether they want the town to become a church town or not. If this sale goes ahead as the Holy Grace Church would like, the fate of the community will have been determined. By you. I believe we're on a razor's edge, and it's up to you to prove me wrong. I'm asking you to please specifically and publicly address this matter of church-held real estate in your upcoming meeting. Otherwise, you are giving tacit consent for the change of Dunkirk back to its origins—a closed-shop town—ironically, like it was when the town was owned by the Redstar Mill.

"Thank you for your consideration."

There were no questions from the council members, and Jason suspected that her last words had struck too close to home for the two new members and they didn't want to draw attention to what she'd just said. The mayor assured her that her concerns would be addressed at the next meeting, although Jason harbored serious doubts about this.

Kris and Jason slipped out as the formal agenda started, and Jason wrapped his arms around her the minute they were outside.

"You did such a great job, Kris! What were you so worried about?"

"I don't know. As soon as I stood up, it was like I did that kind of thing every day."

"Well, you might have to if this sale keeps moving ahead," Jason lamented.

Kris seemed unphased. "The co-op is starting to rally around the cause, and I'm going to be there with them to help the community be involved in any way I can." She looked at her watch. "Oops, Jason, you better get going yourself."

He gave her a long kiss and then headed to Gandalf's. On the way, he reflected that it seemed he was learning something new and unexpected about people every day. Kenneth, Robb, Abby, and now the hidden talents of this wonderful person, too.

Final Chapters

THE AUTHORS' group was gathered in Gandalf's and, as usual, there were busy conversations while everyone was getting settled. Jason was in his normal seat off to the side, opening and booting up his laptop. While he waited, he looked around the table and the strangest sensation came over him. He took in all of these, his friends, and suddenly felt the exact same warmth that he felt whenever Miriam or Kris held his hand. He was overcome for a moment and was glad that the meeting hadn't yet started.

Perhaps it was because he'd found Kris, that Eric had found Abby, and that some of these authors now had brilliant new creations that might make a difference, that he felt an unaccustomed sense of contentment at this meeting. Not only contentment, but more assurance that things could work out. There was a groundswell effort mounting to save the Mill. The Entity might gain in strength, but in the end could not ultimately subsume the town if they stayed aware and vigilant. The draconian legislation they were enduring would surely find push-back, or be legally challenged, and eventually revert to more equitable laws. Jason had decided that, given his recent experience, he could be a good advocate against the legislation allowing civilian militias. It would take effort, but hopefully he, Kris, and many others were going to help make a difference in Dunkirk.

As the meeting started, Dennis brought some order by saying, "Hi everybody, how about if we have our readings first tonight so that we don't eat up all of our time discussing John Darcy's excellent report on the separation of church and state. Jason has a section of his book he'd like to read, so how about if he goes first, and then I believe Emily has an outline she'd like to go over for a new novel she has in mind."

Emily was just saying that she did have an outline and was excited about it when Dennis quickly interjected. "Sorry, Emily. Two quick things I just remembered first though. The good news is that the *First Strike for Children Act* has been confined to committee for further review and refinement. And the bad news is that the new Christian Action Center in the Goodwin Building has contacted me and wants to learn more about our authors' concerns and, as they stated it, our 'problems.' Coincidentally, I've declined several calls from Representative Bosworth in the last few days. My guess is that they are working together to try and find out more information to bolster Bosworth's bill. I'm not sure why I'm suddenly the contact person for this, but after the presentations we can talk about who here wants to join me, what responses we should make, and whether or not we should meet with them.

"Sorry, Emily. You were saying?"

"Just that I do have an outline ready to share and would love some feedback, after we hear Jason's piece."

On a cue from Dennis, Jason looked down at his laptop, but paused before reading. He took a moment to make the mental shift from the current topic to the time and place in his biography.

"Miriam was on the city bus and had decided that it was pouring so heavily outside, and the ride was so short, that she wouldn't even bother to take off her plastic rain bonnet until she got home. The bus stopped near Seattle's Pioneer Square, and more drenched people got on. A young man carrying an instrument case headed down the aisle, chose the seat in front of her, and slid up against the window. Another man in a raincoat followed and sat down beside him. They settled in, and the second man took down his hood in relief to be out of the rain.

"She tried to look out the window, but the downpour was so heavy that not much could be seen outside. Besides that, it hurt her neck to not be facing straight ahead, so instead she watched her fellow passengers. The bus pulled into traffic and within a stop or two she could see that the man who'd pulled down his hood was becoming extremely agitated with the man next to him—jerking aside and creating distance between them to the point that when the bus reached the next stoplight, he jumped up and moved to another seat, giving the man with the instrument case a funny look as he did so.

"*Oh, my God*, thought Miriam. *I don't believe it!* She reached out her small hand and placed it gently on the shoulder of a complete stranger, just to be sure."

Jason, finally feeling at ease with his story, his place in it, and in Dunkirk, continued reading aloud to his friends.

ACKNOWLEDGEMENTS

I want to thank my wife, Lynn Ate, for her suggestions and the laborious time she spent in editing multiple drafts. My wonderful assessment editor, Jessica Hatch of Hatch Editorial Services, gave direction and depth to this story. Brianna Ackley, Joann Muneta, and Todd Broadman provided valuable feedback, and the beta readers at Entrada Publishing provided most welcome comments about the very rough first draft.

ABOUT THE AUTHOR

David Ackley grew up in Fairbanks, Alaska and raised a family in Juneau. His professional career in Alaska included both fisheries biometrics and management positions with the state and federal governments. He has earned Master's degrees in Chinese Language and Literature (Wisconsin), and in Fisheries Science (Alaska). David is now retired and living in northern Idaho. Please visit the Rain and Breeze Books website, www. rainandbreeze.com, for more information about David and his books.

www.ingramcontent.com/pod-product-compliance
Lightning Source LLC
Chambersburg PA
CBHW060646190726
48289CB00002B/295